A ROSE POINT HOLIDAY

HER INSTRUMENTS: BOOK FOUR

A ROSE POINT HOLIDAY

M.C.A. HOGARTH

Studio MCAH
PMB 109
4522 West Village Dr.
Tampa, FL 33624
mcahogarth.org

CONTENTS

AUTHOR'S NOTE

This short novel takes place during the first and second scenes of the epilogue of Her Instruments Book 3, *Laisrathera*. The author recommends reading the full series first, starting with Book 1, *Earthrise*. And for the curious, the cover art is by Ilse Gort. Thank you, Cara!

Blessed is the season which engages the whole world in a conspiracy of love!

HAMILTON WRIGHT MABIE

Three phrases that sum up Christmas are: Peace on Earth, Goodwill to Men, and Batteries not Included.

AUTHOR UNKNOWN

ACT 1
THE VIGIL

CHAPTER 1

"The holidays are almost here, milady. How would you like to prepare?"

Reese looked up from the maps spread on her desk, wondering if she looked as flabbergasted as she felt. She was trying to work on the whole 'facial self-control' thing, since it seemed a useful management tool for Liolesa. "The what?"

"Holidays," Kis'eh't said from the corner where she was reviewing equipment lists on her data tablet. "Typically religious observances or celebrations of milestones considered significant by society."

Reese covered her face as Irine snickered. "Ignore her, Felith. Tell me what I apparently don't know about these holidays that need preparation while we're in the middle of a million other things that also need preparation, not the least of which is my wedding."

Felith folded her hands behind her back. Unlike Reese, she had a face of masklike smoothness, so the only way anyone could tell she was amused was the twinkling in her eyes. "The end of the year, milady. Our holiday season begins at Solstice and lasts until the New Year Feast. I assume Lord Hirianthial hasn't mentioned it?"

"Nor anyone else on this close-mouthed planet, no," Reese said. "So tell me what we're in for."

"Are there are presents?" Irine asked, ears perking. "Please say there are presents."

"It *is* the giving season," Felith said. "And there are three major events. Are you otherwise engaged? Shall I come back later or...?"

"No, please," Irine said. "Interrupt us. We're trying to carve out bits of land for immigrants without running afoul of inheritance laws and it involves math and Reese hates it."

"I told her I could write a formula," Kis'eh't said absently, still reading her data tablet.

"I want to understand it myself. I did our account books, I can do this."

"We were always in debt," Irine muttered.

Reese eyed her, then reached over and ruffled the Harat-Shar's hair until the tigraine started laughing and pushing her away. "There," Reese said. "Now that I've dealt with that, please, Felith, interrupt us."

Felith perched on one of the seats scattered in the room Reese had appropriated for her study; her future study, anyway. Right now all it had was a desk and a few chairs, and one moth-eaten rug pulled out of storage... or rat-eaten, or whatever it was that occupied the vermin niche in the local ecology. Eventually Reese hoped to have lots of filled bookcases, both with Alliance-made books she could afford to lend out and some of the beautiful handmade Eldritch versions. And more furniture. Matching furniture.

At least there were heated floors. The wind off the sea kept it from getting as cold as it did inland, but even she thought it was brisk out.

"There are three major events during the holidays," Felith said. "The Solstice Vigil is the first. You know what the solstice is?"

"Shortest day of the year," Kis'eh't said, still reading.

Felith glanced at the Glaseah. "Yes, this. We also call it Longest Night, and when we first landed it was the most dangerous night of the year. Our predators liked to hunt at night, and we were ill-equipped to fight them. It became custom for men to stay out to guard our homes."

"I can't imagine that ended well," Kis'eh't said, finally setting aside her tablet. "A castle this size? How many men did you deploy in this exercise?"

Reese said, "I don't imagine most of the houses were this size back then... were they?"

"Ah... not typically. But great houses like this one would send out their guard as well as their nobles. And their male servants as well. But it was dangerous, then," Felith said. "As the years passed and we culled the creatures, and as we fortified our buildings, it became less so. The Vigil became symbolic. Men now gather in the chapel to keep the Vigil until midnight; then they return to the house to wait out the remainder of the night with their families, who greet them with food and warm drink."

"Warm drink, like... what, wine?" Reese asked, thinking of the hot drinks they'd been served before.

"No, no. The men mull their own spirits in the chapel," Felith said. "They call that gentleman's punch... it's not fit for a woman to drink."

"Sounds interesting!" Irine exclaimed. "What's in it?"

"Probably hard liquor," Kis'eh't said. "Though how that will keep them awake, I don't know."

"The punch gives them courage for the fight," Felith said. "And makes wounds hurt less when they fall."

Reese shuddered. "Right. Back to the food and drink part that's not disturbing. So the rest of us women are inside... doing what for several hours? I hope something other than waiting?"

"In the past, women used to bide at the windows with candles, or if there were enough individuals, they would sing," Felith said. "These days, we play board games in the sitting room, and have a little mulled cider and eat pastries."

"Angels, can you imagine those first Eldritch women?" Irine asked, wide-eyed. "Sitting in their houses all night, hoping their men are going to come back?"

"They were the ones who needed the punch," Kis'eh't agreed.

"I guess that's why they drink now," Irine said. "Making up for all the years their ancestresses were stuck inside, singing and waving torches around, hoping to glimpse their spouses and brothers for the last time before they got torn apart."

Felith was striving not to cover her eyes. Reese didn't blame her. "So! Back to food and drink."

"Yes," the Eldritch said, recovering. "There is a tea we make... a stimulant, so that it's easier to see the dawn. When the men return from their vigil, we eat, drink, and exchange gifts. That's an intimate gathering, milady. You are expected to invite only family. All the families will have their own gatherings while they wait for their menfolk to return."

"Right," Reese said. "So far, not so bad. What's next?"

"A week after the Vigil we have the Lady's Day," Felith continued. "On Lady's Day, the lady of the House goes to her province's largest town—the one associated with the manor, that usually is—and distributes gifts to her people. Then she celebrates mass in the town church: that's the Ladymass, which gives thanks for the gifts of the Goddess."

Irine was already scraping maps off Reese's desk until they found the one encompassing the entirety of the province Rose Point oversaw, Firilith. "I don't think we have more than one town."

"I'm not even sure we have one town," Kis'eh't said. "Ignore those, they're probably centuries out of date. Let's see what the satellite maps pull down."

"The what?" Felith said, baffled.

"Here," Kis'eh't said, and set the tablet to project over the desk. The four of them studied it, Felith with a blank expression and the remainder of them more intently.

"I'm... not seeing anything," Irine said, reluctant. Looking down at her paper map, she pointed. "There are supposed to be settlements here... and here..." She let her finger drift up to skim the projected map. "Those look like they've been overgrown or covered in sand."

"There are people living in Firilith," Felith said. "But I think they are concentrated in Rose Point's castle town, milady. Down the road from us."

"That one still has roofs, at least," Kis'eh't said. "That will make our job easier, then, if we need to give gifts to everyone. How does that work? Do we have a census? Does the lady bring individual gifts?"

"No! Goddess and Lord." Felith stared at them. "The lady gives a handful of symbolic gifts. The people who wish to have a chance at receiving them travel to the town where she is celebrating mass, you understand."

"That's not going to cause resentment or anything," Irine said.

Reese scowled. "No, I get it. If you have six or seven hundred..."

"Minions?" Irine offered.

"Serfs," Kis'eh't said, mouth quirking.

Reese cleared her throat and said, firmly, "Six or seven hundred *tenants*, then handing out individual gifts is impossible. What do ladies usually give, Felith?"

"Candy to children, thrown from their carriage," Felith said. "And a little money to those charged with managing the town, the guard, so on. Then there are a handful of gifts given to the attendees. Most ladies give a log as a promise that they won't let their people be cold, and a fruit of some kind as a symbol that they won't let their people go hungry... a seed to symbolize fertility... the gifts are sometimes specific to the House. So, for instance, Jisiensire gives a horseshoe that denotes wealth in the coming year."

"Reese in a carriage! I'd like to see that," Irine exclaimed.

"I am not riding a carriage. I'm either riding that horse if we need me to look like an Eldritch lady, or I'll have someone drive me in a real vehicle. No carriages."

"Aww—"

"No carriages," Reese repeated, eyeing Irine. "Anyway. I think I have an idea what I want to do for Lady's Day. Go on, Felith. What's last?"

"The New Year's Feast," Felith said. "It is hosted here, at the castle. A celebration for all the people of the province, who can attend if they wish. They eat from your table, milady. And they bring you gifts. Also usually symbolic."

"Don't start," Irine said to Kis'eh't.

"But I wanted to guess at the symbols used to represent submission to oppression and indentured servitude!"

"They're tenants," Reese said firmly. "Tenants, Kis'eh't."

"Ours are tenants," Kis'eh't said. "And perhaps the Queen's."

"And Lady Araelis's," Irine offered.

"But I wouldn't guess at anyone else's," Kis'eh't finished.

"You're going to offend our native," Reese said.

Felith's cheeks colored. "I fear Kis'eh't is correct. But you are also right, milady. Your people will never be like the serfs that suffered under the hands of the Queen's worst enemies."

Surprised, Reese said, "Thank you."

"Truth, milady, and I am glad to offer it. If I may speak so boldly."

"We like bold speech here," Kis'eh't said. "You fit in just fine, Felith-arii."

Felith beamed, and even on her schooled face that shone.

"So," Irine said. "The Vigil, Lady's Day, and the New Year's Feast. That's everything, right?"

"We light a daily candle as well, starting at Vigil and ending at New Year's," Felith said. "But otherwise, yes... that is the whole of it." She paused, then added, "The solstice is next week."

"Of course it is," Reese said, covering her face. "Okay. Irine, you are now the party planner. Go to it."

"Whee!" Irine leaped from her seat. "I'm gone! And you really should let Kis'eh't write you the formula. You'll be less crabby, and you absolutely need to be less crabby with two weeks of parties coming!"

"As if a wedding's not enough," Reese said with a sigh to Kis'eh't after the Harat-Shar had departed with Felith.

"You did say you wanted to stay..."

Reese thought of Hirianthial, smiled. "I did, didn't I." She rolled up the map and tossed it to the Glaseah. "Go ahead and do your coding magic. But explain it to me when you're done."

"My gift comes early!" Kis'eh't exclaimed. "Goddess be praised!" As she gathered her data tablet with the map, she said, "Dare I ask why the change of heart?"

"I apparently have presents to arrange and less than a week to do it," Reese said. "We'll just say I now have more urgent things to do."

———

The decorating commenced immediately. By the following morning, enormous swags of fabric and evergreen boughs were being carried into the castle, the resinous scent wafting in on the shoulders of the men pressed into service to haul them... because they were large, and they were going everywhere: on mantels, hung from window sills and doors, lining entire rooms where floors met walls. The clutches of berries Reese had assumed to be real were in fact painted glass beads—the fir cones, though, were genuine, and scented with something enough like cinnamon that the faint hint of cardamom that cut through the sweetness surprised her. Also glass were the stars hung everywhere light could catch them.

The broad golden bowl that appeared in the middle of the great hall, though, mystified her. Particularly since it was large enough for her to sit in.

"Should I even ask?" she said to Irine.

"That is the firebowl," Irine said. "Apparently Felith neglected to mention that the candles we're supposed to light every day have to be lit from a fire in this bowl. Everyone's in the household comes from here, and the central fire has to be kept lit from Solstice until the New Year. That's when we let it go out."

Reese eyed it warily. "That sounds dangerous. What do they do, fill it with coals? Wood? Why here, and not a fireplace that's properly vented?"

"I don't know," Irine admitted. "Kis'eh't said she'd come up with something for us. Felith wasn't sure whether she should be scandalized by the suggestion, but she decided since this was a new sort of house, new ways of doing things seemed called for."

Reese chuckled. "Good for her."

"She's more than three-quarters converted to modern thinking," Irine agreed, satisfied, surveying the hall with her hands on her hips. "Apparently we should have colored rugs and wreaths and a lot of other things that we don't have because we aren't Eldritch, but now that I know about them I can have them made for next year. Which is when—fair warning now—Kis'eh't is going to insist we align the Order of the Universe to coincide with the local end-of-year holiday so the Pelted immigrants can have their celebrations. She said we could skip this year because we're so busy."

The idea of juggling two holidays, one of them foreign and the other an excuse to celebrate every holiday the Pelted and their alien allies observed within a single week....

"That *face*," Irine said, staring at her with sagging ears.

Reese rubbed it, hoping that would wipe the expression off. "Sorry. There's just so much to do. I'm spending money as fast as the Queen lends it to me. Or gives it to me, I can't tell and I'm afraid to ask. And everything's broken or ancient. You know."

Irine hugged her, which shouldn't have come as a surprise but did. It was a welcome surprise, which was also new. But nice. Reese leaned into the tigraine with a sigh that ruffled the fur on Irine's neck. "Sorry. I just want to get it right."

"Of course you do. But you're stressing too much about things, arii. You should go get Allacazam and take a nap."

"Later, maybe. I need to talk to Belinor and Val first, see if I can get them to go into town."

"Ooh?" Irine glanced at her, brows arched. "Are they going to scout for you?"

"Hopefully," Reese said. "Well, that and they really do need to see if there's a church there that can handle a Ladymass. Since Val's High Priest now, he's got a good reason to be nosing around." She studied the hall. The fireplace in it was worthy of the name, longer than she was tall by twice her height, and it was completely bedecked with greenery and stars. The boughs were pretty: they reminded her of postcards of Terra in winter, with snow-dusted firs and glowing hearths. Her family hadn't celebrated Christmas, which had seen a revival after the Rapprochement with the Pelted had brought the Christian Hinichi back into contact with the Church that had inspired their religion... but she'd always found the winter imagery moving, and envied, just a little, the heroines of her romances who could curl up beside a fire with hot cocoa and toasty slippers. "This is looking really pretty, arii."

Irine bounced on the balls of her feet. "And this is just the great hall! The part I really want to work on is the sitting room where we'll be having the Vigil party. Since the boys are going to be freezing their tails off in the chapel for half the night, I want them to have someplace warm to come back to. And nice."

"The chapel is nice!"

"The chapel is beautiful," Irine said. "I love how you refinished it. And the roses are glorious. But you decided to leave the roof half off and it's *cold* out there, Reese."

"They can light a fire," Reese said. Then paused. "Can't they? Or is that against the rules because it might cause basilisks to come eat them?"

"No idea," Irine said. "Don't really want to know either. Brr." She shivered. "Anyway. I must go discuss pie with the girls!"

"Pie sounds very good about now," Reese said wistfully.

"There will be pie," Irine said. "That's one thing Felith and Kis'eh't both wholeheartedly agree on." She gave Reese another quick hug. "Remember the nap!"

"Later," Reese promised. She drew in a deep breath after the tigraine had gone, tasting the pine-and-cinnamon-and-sea-brine smell of the hall and watching the firelight glitter in the stars. She'd never really had a winter holiday that meant anything to her, but something about this one was already seeping into her heart. This year it was definitely going to be a bit thrown together, but by next year? With the castle in order, and hopefully the town too, and more tenants, and her Pelted residents...

She'd be married by then. What a strange—and wonderful—thought. Of course, she'd have to survive all the preparations... she smiled to herself and turned, and found her fiancé at the door, as if summoned by her thoughts, and... who knew? Maybe he'd sensed what was going on here and been drawn back. The Queen was keeping him so busy she rarely saw him, but that was all right, because it made the sight of him standing so still, staring at the hall, so much more vivid and precious.

And that stillness was shock. But a good one, from the warmth in his eyes. She'd made him happy, and when he found her amid the bustle in the hall, he let her see it. Advancing to her and taking her hands in his, he said, "Theresa! I had no idea we would be observing the holiday."

Were her fingers tingling? Her fingers were tingling. Was it abstinence that made him just holding her hands so intense? "Felith told us about it, and... well, we are a part-Eldritch House. It seemed the right thing to do."

"It's wonderful," he said. "But do not tell me you have time for the entire season?"

"The whole kit and caboodle," Reese said, knowing in that moment that she was going to do it, and do it right. "The Longest Night Vigil, Lady's Day, and the New Year's Feast."

"But with so little notice...."

"We've done crazier things." Reese grinned at him and was delighted when he grinned back.

"So we have. But this... this is special." He looked up at the swags of blue velvet lining the walls. "A House is not a home until it has celebrated the Vigil season."

All the more reason to do it. "Just make sure Liolesa gives you the day off!"

He laughed. "I'll make sure of it." He kissed her fingers. "I am here accompanying Valthial, if you will believe. He said you asked for him? He's been waylaid by someone who'd like a decision or three on the chapter-house, but he is here."

"Poor Val," Reese said. "I should rescue him. Can you stay?"

"I was planning it. I have been too long away from my betrothed and hoped she might have time for a ride before we return to our respective duties...?"

Riding with Hirianthial? Blood, yes. Especially if it meant a stolen kiss or two. Wasn't there some Terran Pagan custom about kisses and greenery? She'd have to get Kis'eh't to look it up. "I think my appointments can wait a few hours while I discuss Laisrathera's future with its co-leader."

He smiled over her fingers and kissed them again, breath on skin. "Then go you to Valthial, and tell him I asked him not to delay you."

Cheeks warm, Reese said, "I won't give him a choice."

CHAPTER 2

The situation with the Queen's Tams was more complicated than Reese had realized when she first met Malia and Taylor. She'd assumed that all the Tam-illee hanging around the Eldritch planet were members of the Tams: that part was true, initially at least. But then Lesandurel Meriaen Jisiensire had arrived with his flotilla of foxes and she'd discovered that only the Tam-illee directly employed by Liolesa were considered members of the Queen's Tams, and while all of the Tams were members of Lesandurel's extended, adopted family, not all his adoptees were Tams. The ones who'd been cleared to run the courier ships to and from the Eldritch homeworld actually constituted a very small number of the percentage that Lesandurel had put to work in all the enterprises he'd accidentally accrued while keeping himself busy over the centuries offworld.

"Because," Taylor had said when explaining why she was free to take a contract with Reese, "he's not the sort of man to be idle."

So while a large number of those Tam-illee remained fiercely loyal to Lesandurel and were planning to go wherever he went, some of them had been attracted to the challenge of building a modern settlement on a pristine planet and shown up on Reese's doorstep asking for work. A lot of them wanted to become residents, because it was exciting to design and build infrastructure, and maintaining it once it was in place was far more satisfying than dealing with someone else's work. And really, given how much there was to do, Reese didn't think they'd run out of new things to build anytime soon.

That was how Taylor came to be permanently detached to Laisrathera. She'd resigned from the Queen's Tams to take on the work in Firilith, and her extended clan—all previously in Lesandurel's employ, but not in Liolesa's—had come with her. Since they were enthusiastic, intelligent, hardworking people, Reese welcomed them with open arms and land grants, once she was sure she could give land grants, and since then Taylor had taken up residence in Rose Point in the new Office of Development. It was a rare day they weren't in one another's offices at least twice.

This time, Reese was heading to find her, and passing through the great hall she found the firebowl was working. That was the only word she had for it, because as she drew nearer she could see that there was a fire in it, could feel the heat of it drying her skin, but she had no idea *how* it was on fire. From all appearances, it was full of liquid. That had a skin of flame on it, pure and clear and strangely silent.

She had no idea how long she'd been staring at it, but it had mesmerized her completely because when Kis'eh't said, "Do you like it?" she jumped.

"I do," Reese said. "But... what... how does it work?"

Surveying it with satisfaction, Kis'eh't said, "Science."

Reese eyed her. When nothing else was forthcoming, she said, "All right, fine. Just as long as science doesn't set the castle on fire or blow something up."

The Glaseah chuckled. "It won't."

"Good. Because if it does explode, it's coming out of your paycheck."

Folding her arms, Kis'eh't said, "What paycheck?"

"The one you're going to get when we're making enough money to pay people."

"This sounds familiar," the Glaseah said, shaking her head.

Reese managed a wan grin. "I am almost completely sure this time is different."

"You mean there's some doubt?" Kis'eh't eyed her, thoughtful.

"There's a lot going on," Reese said. "Starting a town from scratch... it's... expensive. The Queen's helping, but I can't help this itch between my shoulders, you know? I want us to turn a profit as soon as we can."

"Mmm," Kis'eh't said, frowning. "Well. Better to be too worried about that than to end up in debt again."

"Particularly since I think I've used up all the queens who might bail me out. That I know of, anyway."

Kis'eh't laughed. "Well, don't worry about the firebowl detonating. It's good science. I would know. Where are you off to?"

"Taylor's, to talk about the town renovations."

"Town renovations! Sounds interesting. I'll come. I had to talk to her anyway about prioritization of the gem grid supply." At Reese's fierce look, the Glaseah lifted her hands. "You get to go first, I promise!"

"Good," Reese said. "Then you can come."

Kis'eh't nodded. And added, "Reese? You're not moving."

Shaking herself, Reese said ruefully, "The fire is really pretty."

"It is, isn't it?" Kis'eh't said, pleased. "Science!"

———

"So how many people are we talking about?" Taylor asked as Kis'eh't studied the solidigraphic model of the entire province of Firilith with interest.

"I don't know. That's what I sent Val and Belinor to find out." Reese tapped her fingers nervously on the table near the edge of the model. "It can't be too many or we'd have noticed from the satellite imagery."

"And you want to... do what, exactly?"

"I want my town," Reese said, trying not to find the words 'my town' absurd, "to be a real town, Taylor. Eventually a town to rival anything you'd find on a Core planet."

Taylor looked up at her, eyes wide.

"I said that out loud, didn't I," Reese muttered.

"You did. Did you mean it?"

Did she? She hadn't even considered it before it had come out of her mouth. But having said it, the thought of Laisrathera becoming a hub for commerce and culture and... Blood, should she even suggest tourism? She had no idea how closed Liolesa wanted the world to stay, so there would probably be a throttle on some of that. And it was probably insolent to want her town to be nicer than the capital...! But the capital was already built out, and someone had designed it for horses and stone buildings and lamps that had to be lit by hand. The crumbling remains of the little settlement that crouched near Rose Point could be renovated and expanded a lot more easily than the capital. So why not?

"Let's start with the basics," Reese said finally. "Which is that they

15

should eventually have working showers and heaters, when they're ready to ask for them."

"One thing at a time," Taylor said with a nod, but there was a light in her eyes that boded well for the future. "So you want some of this done next week?"

"I want a plan for the necessary infrastructure, anyway. We can't go in there swinging until we get a feel for what the people there want and need." Reese stopped as the door to Taylor's office filled with fur and robes. "And here are the people who can tell you the size of the project. Some of them, at least. Irine, Sascha, what are you doing here?"

"Don't look at me," Irine said. "I'm just following Sascha because I haven't seen him in far too long."

"You saw him this morning," Kis'eh't said dryly from her corner.

"Like I said!"

Sascha grinned. "I ran into Val and Belinor at the stables..."

"Where, mind you, he was planning to leave," Val said. "Following your betrothed, Lady Eddings, who was on his way back to Ontine."

"But I heard what they were up to," Sascha finished, "and asked Hirianthial if he minded me staying and maybe running a quick aerial survey. Something a little closer than a satellite could get."

"Did they see you?" Reese asked, appalled. She could only imagine what the natives would think if their first encounter with their new foreign lady was a sparrow flashing by overhead, flaunting its offworld tech with flashing wings and the hum of its engines.

Sascha snorted. "What do you take me for, Boss? Of course they didn't."

"But you did get pictures?" Taylor asked. "I could use pictures."

"I did, yeah. It's... interesting."

"Oh, I don't like that word." Reese sighed. "All right, hit me."

"You have twenty-eight residents, Lady," Belinor said, serious as always. "God and Lady be praised. One is a youth still in a boy's coif, which is a true blessing. You have a fertile populace."

"Twenty... eight?" Reese repeated.

Taylor glanced at her, then cleared her throat and said heartily, "So the good news is that we can renovate houses for twenty-eight people pretty quickly!"

"Oh, they don't live in separate houses!" Belinor said. "Those twenty-eight people belong to four families."

"So three houses," Val said. "Because the priestess lives in the church with her family."

"The church is in excellent condition," Belinor added. "You will be able to take your mass there quite comfortably, Lady."

"Did you say twenty-eight people?" Irine asked, one ear sagging.

"Twenty-eight is more than I was expecting," Kis'eh't said. "I'm impressed."

"Three houses and... whatever it is that's attached to the church," Reese said to Taylor. "Actually, just count the whole church, I'm sure we don't want to sit in there without climate control, come summer. What can you work up in a week?"

Taylor grinned. "What can't I do in a week!"

"That sounds like I can leave you to it, then," Reese said.

"Excellent," Val said. "Because if that can be done without your oversight, I'd like to have a word with you. If I may have your ear, Lady Eddings?"

"Sure," Reese said. "Fuzzies, help Taylor if she needs it. You too, Kis'eh't."

Puzzled, Belinor murmured, "Why is Kis'eh't not also considered a fuzzy? That refers to fur, yes? She has fur?"

"We're fuzzier than Kis'eh't," Irine said.

"They're softer in the head," Kis'eh't said, placid.

Reese grinned and left them to explain that colloquialism to the young priest. She wasn't entirely happy about the size of her settlement, but Kis'eh't was right... it could have been much worse. And overhauling four houses was a far more tractable project than overhauling forty. Assuming she could start on that renovation immediately. Either way, she was confident she could leave that in Taylor's hands while she researched presents for the Vigil.

But first, she had to deal with whatever new bomb Val was planning to drop on her head. As the priest joined her outside Taylor's office, she leaned against the wall, one hand on her hip. "'If you may have my ear'? Don't tell me you're getting contaminated with proper Eldritch formalities."

"I've been in too many meetings and it's all your fault. Lady."

Reese snorted, amused. "I doubt it. You got yourself elected High Priest all on your own."

"Woe! I'll have to go back to blaming myself for it, since you won't conveniently shoulder the blame for me." He grinned, which was good... if he could be teased, he hadn't changed too much. She couldn't help worrying that they would lose the irreverent young firebrand who'd been through so much with them. But even though he'd let Liolesa put the Lord's red stole over his shoulders, he still insisted on wearing pants instead of a robe, had committed to his short hair by trimming it up at his chin, and was apparently still willing to banter with aliens.

Usually. His eyes had turned serious.

"What is it, then?"

"I hear you've decided to celebrate the holiday? Did anyone explain the Longest Night Vigil to you?"

"Felith told us what's expected," Reese said, hesitant. "You... are about to tell me that she left things out."

"Unavoidably, as she's a woman." Val smiled crookedly. "It's nothing to be wary of, I promise. But there's a cultural context you might appreciate understanding. She's told you that a week after is Lady's Day, I'm sure?" At Reese's nod, he continued, "That's because the Longest Night is considered the Lord's rite. And while Lady's Day is a celebration of gifts and blessings, it's understood that those gifts and blessings are available because of the sacrifice made by the Lord."

"Oh," Reese said, quieter. "Because of the basilisks the men used to kill on that night."

"Exactly. The Vigil is sacred to us, as men, and as priests. You won't see any priest until the following day, because we keep the entire vigil, from sundown to sun-up. Don't be surprised when Hirianthial returns but Belinor and Urise and I don't."

"Right," Reese said. "I'm guessing you do something closer to the original rites in private."

"We honor the bloodshed that has kept the planet safe since we landed," Val said, sober, and evoked with that image a reciprocal of Mars's blood-stained soil. She understood, instantly, and knew he saw it in her eyes. "Having said that," he finished, "there's a ritual the Lady of the House may enact on the Longest Night if a man has died in service to her people during the year."

And a lot of people had died, making Laisrathera possible, and Liolesa's plans. Something in her settled: this was another thing she and the Eldritch shared, this understanding that sacrifices needed to be honored. "Tell me what I need to do."

CHAPTER 3

R eese had never had money for gifts before. She'd done her best to observe the holidays and natal days particular to her crewmembers by giving them bonuses, but that hardly counted when her bonuses amounted to either coffee money or promises of future money because she didn't have any to hand out. She guessed they'd gotten used to it; they'd been united in their poverty, and gradually they'd stopped keeping track of any gift-giving occasions at all. Or maybe the crew had given each other presents and she didn't know about it, and they'd been too nice to mention it for fear that it would make her surly? That wouldn't surprise her, given how things used to be.

But now... now things were different. So different the possibilities were dizzying. She was operating on loans and gifts, certainly, but they were serious loans and gifts, and carving out even the tiniest sliver of that budget for presents resulted in an enormous fund. The only word she could describe when contemplating what to do was *glee*. After all these years, she finally understood why people enjoyed giving presents: it was a whole different experience when gift-giving was a pleasure, not an obligation that shamed her because she couldn't perform to expectation.

So she shopped and planned and researched—not just cultural background, like with Bryer, because what did you give a Phoenix anyway?—but also mundane things like how to wrap presents, because when had she ever learned? And she somehow kept on top of her mound of duties, and consulted with Taylor about what she was planning for the town, and pondered her invitations. Longest Night was a family affair, which meant, for her, all the people she'd come to care about. Val and Belinor and Urise couldn't come, since they'd be involved with their priestly duties. Felith, surprisingly, begged off when invited, and at first Reese wondered if she'd upset the woman, or maybe transgressed against some stupid Eldritch custom about mixing aristocrats with servants... but Felith had family of her own, certainly. And maybe, Felith had a man she wanted to wait for? Reese eyed her speculatively and wondered who she could assign to figuring that out so she could encourage it. Maybe all happily affianced people turned into matchmakers; if it was as fun as being able to shop for presents, she could understand why.

Taylor and Malia were celebrating with Lesandurel, and were visibly excited at the prospect. Reese guessed the Tams on assignment didn't see their Eldritch very often, or the rest of their families.

There was only one invitation she waffled over sending, because it seemed impertinent. But Liolesa was Hirianthial's cousin and they loved one another, and Hirianthial had been gone for fifty or sixty years and almost died in the bargain. So Reese squared her shoulders and hit 'send' on that particular request, and started wondering what on the bleeding soil she was going to get a queen for the holiday.

It was almost funny that she could be paralyzed by how many choices she could make now that she had more than two fin to rub together. In the end, she read an article that concluded that "the best gifts make a person feel seen," and that had stuck with her. It was good to be seen. And rare, she thought. Maybe her gifts this year wouldn't be as good as they could be, but if paying attention to people made for good presents, then she could get better with practice.

She looked forward to it.

———

For the women's vigil, Irine chose a chamber on the third floor in a corner of Reese's wing of Rose Point. It overlooked the courtyard and was tucked directly over a second floor room that opened onto the castle's wall walk. The height and corner placement gave it a pleasant feeling of being high above the fray, and it was a small enough room to be cozy once the Harat-Shar was done decorating: a rocking chair, a bench, several more chairs grouped around the fireplace on a soft rug; the evergreen boughs, several mysterious handbells, and the hanging glass stars. Reese started leaving her presents in the inglenooks as she finished wrapping them, and soon everyone else was too.

Hirianthial, Sascha, Val, and Belinor arrived from Ontine early on Solstice day and joined Urise in whatever preparations were proper for the men of the household. They took dinner with everyone and then left, and Reese watched them walk across the courtyard in their cloaks and coats, their breath puffing white and their bodies casting diffuse blue shadows as the sun sank below the sea. When she returned to their corner room, someone had laid out the Vigil food on a trestle table against the back wall: pastries and cheeses, hot coffee and tea and chocolate, brandied fruits and candied nuts. The room smelled like pine and cinnamon and coffee and it was wonderful.

"I probably don't need to tell you this," she said as Irine arrived with Allacazam in her arms. "But you did an amazing job."

Irine blushed at the ears, but grinned, too. "I didn't do it alone! Felith was hugely helpful. And Kis'eh't too. Did you know Felith's got a sweetheart?"

"I wondered! Do you know who?"

"I'm guessing he's in the Swords," Irine said.

"Not Olthemiel!"

"No... but maybe Beronaeth." Irine chuckled at Reese's speculative look. "Yes, me too! I think they'd work really well together. Plus, it can't hurt to link our people with the Queen's more closely."

Reese eyed her. "Don't tell me you're thinking politically as well as amorously now."

Irine sniffed. "Arii, I grew up with a lot of siblings. If you think there's no politics with that many brothers and sisters and mothers and fathers, you have a lot to learn."

"Don't I though," Reese said ruefully.

Behind them, Kis'eh't said, "Are you going to step into the room or stand at the door blocking the way all night?"

"We're going in!" Reese said. "At least, I'm planning to. But I'm waiting to see if the Queen will come."

"She will," Kis'eh't said. "It's not night yet. Irine, it's beautiful!"

"Thank you," Irine said again, glowing now. "I can't wait to eat your pie."

"I can't wait to eat my pie either." Kis'eh't padded into the room and dropped to her haunches on the rug. "The fire is nice, when you don't need it to stay warm."

"Just us girls!" Irine exclaimed, looking around. "And none of our new friends either. It feels strange, doesn't it?"

"A little." Reese touched the rocking chair, tried giving it a nudge. It creaked against the floor where one of the rockers left the rug. "But it's not the same, even if it's just us. Things have changed."

"We've changed," Irine said. When Reese glanced at her, the tigraine nodded. "Yes, me too. All of us."

"We've helped shape a world," Kis'eh't said. "What else, then, when the breath of the Goddess has moved through us?"

That didn't seem to need commentary, so Reese sat on the rocking chair, leaned back, and inhaled. Safe, warm, fed... she understood, in the most ancient way, the truth of this holiday. Out there, people she loved were making it possible for her to be here, and her job was to wait for them and welcome them home. Two parts of a circuit, and both necessary: the gratitude as well as the service. All her life, she'd been reading stories about those things, and all her life she'd thought the gratitude somehow less everything. Less important, less needful, less exciting, less heroic. How little she'd understood. How unsurprising, too, when she'd always tried so hard not to close those connections with other people.

She was very glad to have decided it was time to stop fearing those connections so much.

The mood must have been contagious, because Irine's voice was low when she finally spoke. "This is good."

"Very good," Kis'eh't agreed.

Quiet for a while. Then, Irine said, "Um... should Allacazam be here?"

Reese choked on her laugh. "I think Allacazam's technically an it. I just never felt right using 'it' as a pronoun for him."

"Right."

A tingling silence, then they all burst out laughing.

"Pie!" Irine crowed.

"Yes, cut the pie," Kis'eh't said. "The Queen will be here soon."

"The Queen is here!" said a voice at the door, merry and clear. "And she has brought candles lit at your astonishing firebowl. I hope you haven't set out any of the window candles yet!"

"No, we haven't," Reese said, rising as Liolesa entered. And behind her came... "Lady Araelis!"

She hadn't seen much of Hirianthial's House cousin, but what little she'd seen had worried and saddened her. Araelis had lost her entire House to Surela's machinations, and while the aftermath of the civil war had kept her busy—no doubt because Liolesa was giving her work for that purpose—the fierce and talkative extrovert Reese had met at Ontine had vanished beneath the widow's mask. It was anyone's guess if she would return, even for the sake of the child she was still carrying.

"Alet," Araelis said, with a little smile, and Reese was grateful for even that small try at a normal expression. "Liolesa said I should come because you'd like hearing the Solstice custom of the Stranger."

"Something to do with granting shelter, I guess?" Kis'eh't said. "Because of the monsters."

"Just so." Liolesa offered her candle to Reese, who took it hastily. "It is required of us to offer shelter to women and children on the Longest Night if they request it, even if they aren't of our family. The Stranger does not need to receive gifts, but she does have the first food and drink of the night."

"I'm glad we didn't touch the pie," Kis'eh't told Irine.

"So am I, but we can cut it now!"

"Yes," Reese said. "Please, Lady. Sit." To Liolesa, she added, "Ah... I'm guessing I don't bow?"

Liolesa snorted. "Don't be ridiculous, Theresa." She drew the strap of her bag over her shoulder and brought it to the inglenook where the presents overflowed in a river of gold and silver paper and ribbon... and there began setting her own offerings. Reese couldn't remember ever seeing her in a dress so simple, much less one short enough to reveal her boots. In fact, she wouldn't have bet Liolesa had any outfit so ordinary in her wardrobe. The only thing that gave her away was the ruthless confidence with which she carried herself. She wasn't dressed like a queen, but Reese doubted she could ever stop radiating the assurance that had ruled a world, and now ruled an empire. It made the enthusiastic light in her eyes charming, because how often did anyone see her that pleased about something as mundane as arranging presents?

Apparently it wasn't a new thing either, because Araelis said, "You and gifts, Liolesa."

"My favorite part of the holiday," Liolesa said, surveying her work with satisfaction. "Far more fun than Lady's Day and the mass and all the rest of it."

"I would have thought you would like those things?" Reese asked. "Aren't you the High Priestess of the Church?"

"That is exactly why I don't like them," Liolesa said. "They're work." She stepped back. "Perfect! And such a lovely room here, Theresa. I sense the hand of your pard. Am I right?"

"Oh!" Irine exclaimed, and touched her furiously blushing ears. "Are they on fire?"

"Not as long as you don't dip them in the candles," Kis'eh't said, amused. "You should place them, Reese, if they're supposed to be seen. At the windows, I take it, alet?"

"Just so."

Reese found no candleholders on the window sills, but they were made of very solid stone and the pillars the Eldritch had brought were fat enough that she didn't worry they'd fall over. She looked outside toward the chapel, but saw no lights there... were the men sitting in the dark? Had they found the glass she'd left there, in keeping with Val's instructions? She hoped so.

Kis'eh't was cutting the pie; Irine had already pressed a slice on the bemused Araelis, who'd probably taken the first bite for courtesy's sake and was now eating with more gusto. Liolesa was watching her, standing a little behind and to one side of the chair. Noticing Reese's surreptitious study, the Queen smiled, a quirk of her mouth that conveyed concern and satisfaction both. It also looked so much like one of Hirianthial's smiles that Reese found herself flushing and didn't know why. Probably something to do with planning to marry a man related closely enough to an empress to share mannerisms with her.

"Have pie!" Irine said, giving a plate to the Queen. "Other things too. But pie first, because Kis'eh't bakes like her goddess."

Kis'eh't snorted but didn't pause in her cutting to disagree, which was good because that meant Reese could claim the next slice.

"I am acquainted with Kis'eh't's pies and admit I was hoping to see one make its appearance." Liolesa put spoon to pastry. "And you have coffee as well, which I predict will become a staple at all the Solstice Vigils from now on."

"I don't know how you stay awake all night without it," Reese said.

"We play games," Araelis said over her plate. "Board games. Charades. Some card games, though not many."

"And sing, betimes."

"Oh!" Irine said. "I forgot that part. Felith said she would give me sheet music for some of the songs for the end of the year but she never got to it and I forgot to remind her. I could have run that through the computer, had it generate some music for us."

"Most of the Vigil songs need a full choir," Araelis said. "At least ten women."

"I have never had so many." Did Liolesa sound wistful?

"It's rare," Araelis agreed.

"Yet another thing that makes no sense," Kis'eh't said, sitting back down by the fire with her plate and a cup of coffee. "Your population's always been small, and no doubt your family gatherings reflected that. So why have songs that only groups can sing? You'd think those would have become less popular, and songs that could be sung by two or three people would be more prevalent."

"There are some," Araelis said. "Duets and solos. But rare."

"And melancholic," Liolesa added. "We should play games instead."

"We could do adjective-noun-verb?" Irine said. "All you need for that is a data tablet to draw on and keep time. It's like charades, but with pictures. You get the computer to pick a random adjective, noun, and verb, and then you have to draw it and other people have a minute to guess what it is."

"That's a good game!" Kis'eh't said. "I'm horrible at drawing, which makes it fun. I can start?"

"Yes," Araelis said. "I think I'd like to see the horrible drawing of a Glaseah."

None of them were good at drawing, it turned out. Or guessing. Even Araelis laughed at some of the more ridiculous suggestions. After that, they moved on to an Eldritch card game that Araelis offered to teach them and Liolesa declined to play, saying only that she preferred to watch games of chance. Reese wondered if she hated gambling because she had to do it with the fate of a world too often... or if she'd gotten so good at it that she didn't want to ruin everyone's fun? But the card game was fascinating, and they all enjoyed trying their hands at its intricacies. They ate the brandied fruit and washed it down with more coffee and then Reese introduced hot chocolate with marshmallows to the Eldritch, who hadn't ever floated marshmallows in hot chocolate before and found it bizarre— "Do we wait for them to melt before drinking? Or are you supposed to use a spoon? But then it's lumpy when you try to sip it..."

By midnight, it all felt so natural that Reese could almost imagine how it would be in a decade, in two decades: they'd be here in a room just like this, but bigger. There would be children—girls and boys, because the boys weren't allowed to go to the Vigil until they left their nurse's care—

and it would be perfect. Whose children would come first, she wondered? Irine's? Hers? (She tried not to get distracted by the anxiety and anticipation that thought generated.) Would Kis'eh't ever have kits of her own? What about Bryer? She tried to picture a female Phoenix waiting through the Vigil with them and hid her smile against the lip of her coffee mug. This time she was the one who noticed Liolesa's gaze, and she lifted her brows a little, just enough to say 'I get it. This is what we work for.'

Liolesa smiled back—just her eyes—and returned her attention to the others, who with Araelis's intrigued permission were attempting to discover if Allacazam could communicate with the unborn child yet.

They heard the men before they saw them, their voices echoing in the stone stairwell: Sascha's laughter, Bryer's low murmurs, Hirianthial's replies deeper still. Then the three were on the threshold, and Reese and the others stood to receive them... because that's what they were doing, wasn't it? This was the welcome back from the cold, and unlike some, they really had been in the cold, with Rose Point's chapel open to the elements. Sascha went immediately into his sister's arms, and Hirianthial came next, wearing a long fur-lined cloak in burgundy that accented the color the wind had chapped to his cheeks and the brightness in his wine-colored eyes when he beheld: "Lia! You came!"

"Of course I did," she said, warm. "Your betrothed would have not forgiven me had I turned down her invitation."

"And rightly so." Hirianthial came to her and kissed her cheek, putting those so-similar faces in close proximity so Reese could see just how similar they were. Her heart give a great double-pulse, watching Liolesa turn her face up to receive the greeting. When had she ever seen Eldritch so liberal with their affections? And what a compliment, to be trusted with the sight. There was real joy in both their eyes, and even their faces, for once. That was what centuries of friendship looked like, and it was wonderful.

Turning to Araelis, Hirianthial said, delighted, "Araelis... how glad I am to see you here!"

"Where you did not expect?" Araelis said. "You may blame your cousin, Hirianthial. She is a most managing female. Nigh unto interfering, dare I say."

"We would not want her any other way," Hirianthial said. "I am so pleased you've come."

Araelis glanced past him at Reese and smiled, and unlike the first smile she'd offered when she arrived, there was real pleasure in it. "I am, also."

That left... "Theresa."

Reese sucked in a breath as he came to her and took her hands, and she could tell he was holding them in a completely different way from how he had before they'd announced their engagement. Maybe it was the thumb gently tracing a circle on her palm, where no one could see it? She cleared her throat before she trusted it with his name. "Hirianthial."

For a moment, that was all, and it was as if no one else was there. His eyes, full of joy and promises. Hers, full of... well, probably adoration.

Then his eyes grew somber, and he dropped her hands to turn toward Bryer, who'd remained by the door. The Phoenix was carrying the glass she'd left in the chapel, and he passed it to Hirianthial, who received it with both hands. The wine in it was darker than blood, but it reminded her of it all the same. Offering her the cup, Hirianthial said, quiet, "My Lady. One glass was poured, but never claimed."

The room had become so silent she could hear her own heart racing in her ears. This was it, then, and she was determined not to ruin it. Reese swallowed and carefully set one hand on the bell of the glass, then slid the other under the foot, praying she didn't twitch it out of their joined hands. Deep breath. She closed her eyes and remembered what this was about and let it steady her, and when she was ready she opened them and spoke the words Val had taught her. "We grieve for the fallen and commend their spirits to the ranks of the Lord and God. In the name of Goddess and Lady, we give thanks for the sacrifice."

Araelis and Liolesa murmured something low in their tongue in unison, heads bowed.

Hirianthial released the glass into her hands—her care—and Reese brought it to the fire, set it on the hearth. Though her hands were shaking the glass got there in one piece and the wine stayed in it. She bowed to it, since she wasn't wearing skirts, held it for several seconds. Then she exhaled. Turning to face the room, she said, "I... got that right, I hope."

Did she need any proof that it had been a good idea? Araelis's eyes were glittering with unshed tears. Liolesa was studying her with approval and that too-clear sight that suggested she was taking notes. And Hirianthial... she was used to his loving looks. This raw one, that thanked her and thanked God and Goddess for unexpected graces... she looked away to keep her composure.

"That was most beautiful," Araelis said, voice clear despite her wet lashes. "Thank you, Theresa."

"And appropriate," Liolesa said. "Well done, Lady."

Hirianthial reached for her hand and curled her fingers into his, resting his other hand over hers. She relaxed completely. "So... is it time for food or presents?"

"Now we have both," Liolesa said, satisfied.

"Good, 'cause I'm hungry!" Sascha exclaimed. "I hope you left pie for us!"

"There are other things, too—" Reese began.

"Pie," Bryer interrupted. "Only pie."

Kis'eh't preened. "It's a good thing I made two."

CHAPTER 4

I t had not occurred to Reese while indulging herself in her first real shopping spree that what she was doing implied reciprocity until the presents in front of her chair started accumulating. Of course other people had gotten her things. Everyone was getting everyone things. But this evidence that people cared about her and wanted to demonstrate it was overwhelming. She stared at Irine and Araelis, who'd been pressed into service distributing the hoard, and tried not to visibly shake despite the racing of her heart.

The light touch on her wrist distracted her. When she found the courage to look up, she found Hirianthial's calm gaze on hers. Very soft, he murmured, "It's well, my lady."

After that, it was still frightening, but she could handle it. Especially since he left his hand on her wrist, petting, just the faintest of movements against her skin.

"One for Kis'eh't, one for the Queen—wow, that's a big one—what else?"

"A strange custom, putting the gifts in front of the person they're intended for," Araelis said, looking with puzzlement at the silver bag. "Almost as strange as each of them being wrapped in different colors."

"Oh? How do you do it?" Irine asked, curious.

"We don't put all the gifts together this way," Araelis said. "They stay with the person who gives them, and the giver hand them out one at a time, to be opened." She glanced at the bag before setting it in front of Bryer. "And all our gifts are wrapped in the same color. One color per person."

"Who assigns the colors?" Kis'eh't asked. "How do you know who has which color? Do you agree beforehand? What about new people?"

"I... I don't know," Araelis admitted. "I never wondered. But here we have the last of them and...." She trailed off and frowned. "Liolesa. I am the Stranger!"

"You are no stranger to me," Liolesa said. "And I knew you would be coming, so I couldn't resist. As you yourself said..."

Araelis sighed. "You and gifts, yes. But you will make your new outworld family feel guilt for not having anything to give me."

"They have given you their hospitality," Liolesa said. "I have given you nothing but exasperation for several weeks. Indulge me, if you will."

"I suppose I must. But I refuse to open this first. I want to see what presents one gives a Harat-Shar."

"That's our cue," Irine said to Sascha, who chuckled and reached for the nearest box.

The answer to Araelis's question revealed a lot more about the gift-givers than about Harat-Shar. But Reese was relieved that the present she'd picked for them caused them both to lean closer to the box, studying its contents with furrowed brows... and then to break into peals of laughter.

"What is it?" Kis'eh't asked, mantling her wings.

"You bought us a heated blanket!" Sascha exclaimed between whoops.

"I'm not planning to keep the castle any warmer than I did the ship," Reese said. "Especially given how high the ceilings are. And, you know. The one place you want to keep warm is probably the bed. For a lot of reasons."

"For a lot of reasons!" Irine said with a giggle.

"Being about to get married has been good for you, Boss," Sascha said, grinning. "Once you're actually married, you might give up blushing completely."

"I doubt it," Reese muttered, but she was smiling too.

Bryer gave them feathers, which Reese's reading had revealed to be a significant offering; only good friends received feathers, particularly those long enough to be used to decorate one's aerie, rather than one's person. They were beautiful to boot, and the twins weren't the only one who exclaimed over their metallic sheen and the rainbow colors that seemed to

30

refract near the rachis. Kis'eh't's gift of cinnamon oil, she had declined to explain, but the twins grinned at one another and then waggled their brows at her, which the Glaseah suffered with amusement and a benign expression.

Hirianthial's gift to Irine came wrapped in burgundy paper, and Reese bent closer to watch her bring forth a cloisonné jewelry box. "This is beautiful!" Irine said, golden eyes wide. "But... I don't wear much jewelry."

"Yet," Liolesa observed. At the tigraine's startled look, the Queen said, "Oh, but you are Laisrathera's second most prominent woman, Irine-alet. Did you not realize? A minor noblewoman, we would say. And a noblewoman has gemstones. They are a symbol of her wealth and authority."

"I don't have any wealth," Irine protested.

"Yet," Liolesa said.

Irine's face was reflecting the same sort of shock, panic, and confusion that Reese imagined her face often did when confronted with the way the Eldritch kept changing her life. She could sympathize. She also was just a little bit glad she wasn't the only one dealing with it anymore. Maybe she could offer the practical advice this time? Reese hid a grin. That would be the day!

Sascha shook his head. "Guess we'll see what comes to us," he said. "Here's mine from Hirianthial, and I'm guessing it's not a jewelry box." He unwrapped the gift carefully—unlike his twin, he was one of those people who didn't tear wrapping paper, and the Eldritch custom of securing the paper with intricate folds rather than tape or glue lent itself to his more deliberate approach. That revealed a wooden box. "Or maybe I'm wrong?"

Reese couldn't see what was in the box when he opened it, but she could see his shoulders tense, his ears sag, and his eyes widen. He was so still she wondered if he'd picked up some of Hirianthial's body language... or maybe that was all his, because there was more reverence in it than shock.

Raising golden eyes, Sascha said, "This is what I think it is."

Quietly, Hirianthial said, "It is, yes."

Sascha bit his lower lip. "Then..." He looked up at Reese, let out a huffed breath and shook his head. "Then I'm glad as all hells the two of you figured things out, because I wouldn't want to have to choose. And I won't have to." He lifted a dagger in a sheath of leather and ivory from the box and Bryer hissed approval. Glancing at him, Sascha said, "Yeah? You think I'm ready."

"Know you are," Bryer said.

31

"What is this?" Kis'eh't asked, curious. "Some invitation to a fealty ceremony, I'm guessing?"

Irine rested her hand on her brother's shoulder, her own face resigned. "You want to be Hirianthial's bodyguard."

"He doesn't need a bodyguard," Sascha said. "He can take care of himself in a fight pretty damned well."

"But the Lord of War does need an aide," Hirianthial said, "And a shield-brother who has proven himself in combat would make a very good one."

"I like it," Reese said, before Sascha could dither about it. "He needs a Harat-Shar of his own and I've got Irine."

Sascha laughed at that. "If you're sure, Boss."

"What's there to be sure about?" Reese said, holding his eyes so he could see her sincerity. "As you said, we really have worked things out. There's no either-or here, arii. You work for him, you're still part of my team."

"Team Earthrise," Irine said, pleased.

"It's what Laisrathera means," Reese said with a nod.

"Then, with all that settled..." Sascha lifted his chin, his hands tight on the dagger as he met Hirianthial's gaze across the rug. "I'm your man, arii. And I'm honored you'll have me."

That was good. Very good. Reese didn't think anyone could top that present, especially since the only one left was an envelope on the floor. Irine picked it up, glancing at the outside. "This one's from the Queen." She grinned at Liolesa. "Probably something crazy, right?" She pulled the flap up and slid the paper out of it, and Sascha leaned over her to read. They glanced at one another, then both jerked their heads up to stare at Liolesa with nearly identical expressions of skepticism tempered with awe.

"How do you *know*?" Irine exclaimed.

"How do you know *everything*?" Sascha finished.

Liolesa folded her fingers together over her ribcage, the picture of studied innocence. "I am very good at guessing."

As the twins started laughing, Kis'eh't said, "Oh, put us out of our misery already! What is it?"

Reese plucked the paper from Irine's hand and skimmed it. "It's... a notification from Fleet that they're detaching Soly's hold here for a term of 'at least one year', possibly more if the situation warrants...." She trailed off, squinted at the twins, then glanced at Hirianthial.

Said he only, eyes warm with merriment, "Narain."

"Oh!" Reese said. Then more speculative: "Oh? Really?"

"I like him," Sascha said.

"He really likes him," Irine said with a last gasping giggle. "I do too."

"Fleet's good people."

"Steady income." Irine looked up at the ceiling. "Stable personalities. Good marriage material."

"Good in bed," Sascha muttered.

"Harat-Shar?" Kis'eh't offered, deadpan.

"Okay, true, comes with the package."

More laughter. Even Araelis smiled.

Reese shook her head as the twins scraped up all the discarded paper and tidied up the rug, setting a bow on Allacazam. To Liolesa, she said, "Your gifts are scary."

"I prefer to think of them as... carefully targeted."

Reese choked on her laugh. Liolesa's smile had a decidedly mischievous air.

"Who's next?" Irine asked. "I am voting for Kis'eh't."

"I should have more pie!" Sascha said. "Speaking of. Anyone want anything? Refills? Go, Kis'eh't, let's see what everyone got you."

Kis'eh't looked at the stack in front of her and wiggled the toes of her forepaws. "At the rate we're eating, these had better be seeds for apple cultivars."

Like the twins, Kis'eh't had received a feather from Bryer. Irine gave her a jar that puzzled the Glaseah even after the explanation that it was claw conditioner: "Why do claws need conditioning?" But Irine was adamant ("Because yours are getting brittle. And yes, I look!"). Sascha had inspired her to laugh by giving her a geode. "A book-end for your office. When you finally stop being everywhere at once and choose one."

"I have been busy," Kis'eh't demurred, and opened the tin that contained Hirianthial's offering. Peering into it with an expression even more baffled than the one she'd used on the claw conditioner, she said, "These are beautiful." For the gathering, she held up a little ceramic crow, then displayed the tin where three others nestled in cushioned slots. Each was painted to resemble a unique bird: sparrow, bluebird, robin, cardinal. "But... what are they for? There are a lot of them. Are they for a game?"

"I'm afraid it's something of a jest," Hirianthial said. "They're pie birds. For venting steam from the filling."

Kis'eh't's ears fanned out. "Trust the Eldritch to come up with an ornate and handmade solution to something that could be solved by a fork and a few poked holes." She considered the crow, then smiled and shook her head. "These are almost too pretty to bake with. But a tool made for a purpose should never be relegated to decoration when it can fulfill that purpose, so. I will use it." She sighed, chuckled a little. "A little link to the past, in more ways than one."

"We ate a lot of good desserts on the ship," Reese said, quiet.

"Good memories," Sascha agreed.

"We also love your pie because it's good, though!" Irine assured the Glaseah hastily.

Kis'eh't laughed. "Well, I like feeding you all. It's a Goddess thing."

"Food comes from the Lady," Araelis said, and it had the weight of ritual. When they all looked toward the Eldritch, Liolesa nodded, a tip of her chin.

"I can't disagree," Kis'eh't said, after a pause. She tucked the birds back into their cushioned tin and took up Reese's box. "All right, Reese. Should I be worried?"

"Maybe?" Reese said, sheepish.

Kis'eh't chuckled and plucked the ribbon loose. "And what is this...? Ah!" She laughed. "An apron to go with the birds!"

"An apron?" Irine asked, and giggled when the Glaseah turned it to show off the legend on the breast: 'Kitchen Goddess.'

"Very appropriate," Kis'eh't said. "But what's this in the pocket? Did you leave the washing instructions in it?" She pulled out the envelope that Reese had vacillated so long over including, and as the Glaseah opened it, Reese found she was biting her lip. When Kis'eh't didn't say anything immediately, she said, "You really haven't picked out an office...."

"This isn't an office," Kis'eh't said, low. "This is an invoice for a fully-outfitted laboratory."

"I... got it right? I hope?" Reese asked. "I asked for a lot of people's help. Between Taylor and Hirianthial and a couple of the Fleet people, we figured out the sort of stuff someone who does inorganic chemistry needs."

Kis'eh't's eyes flicked up to hers. "You remembered."

How could she forget? The Glaseah's distress and frustration at the tiny chemical analyzer on the *Earthrise*, complaining that organic chemistry wasn't her specialty while they struggled to discover the reason the drug barons had sent them to harvest the crystal people. "I try to pay attention."

Kis'eh't's thumb chafed the back of the invoice. "Maybe you should open your gift to me now."

"Out of order?" Irine said.

But Reese was already digging through her stack until she found the flat package marked with Kis'eh't's name. Were her hands trembling? Something about how serious the Glaseah was... no, not just serious. There was something in Kis'eh't's face she'd never seen before. Like someone standing at a precipice. Peeling the paper back, Reese found herself with a folder, and in the folder... very official copies of... "Patents?" She paged through them, and now she really was shaking. "Kis'eh't... these... these are...."

"Patents, yes," Kis'eh't said. She had folded her hands in her lap, forepaws pressed against one another until the clawtips shone against the fur. "You said Laisrathera needed money, and I have a little to give."

"A little!" Reese exclaimed, stunned at the final sheet listing the bidders requesting the rights to develop those patents. "Kis'eh't... Blood and freedom... this is... you're rich!"

Kis'eh't grimaced. "No, Reese. I earn a modest income off the royalties of my old articles. But I'm only rich if I do something with those patents, and doing something with them requires... a lab, with people in it. Along with a lot of other things. Travel. Administration and overhead. Accountants. I never bothered because I didn't have the expertise to set up those things, and I wasn't willing to go back to academia."

"That means it is now time for my gift," Liolesa said. "Please, alet. Open your final present."

The Glaseah glanced at her, then looked at the envelope. Reese could understand her trepidation, given how similar it looked to the envelope that had stunned the twins. But she desperately wanted to know what was in it, because it would give her something to focus on that wasn't the fact that one of her crewmembers had just handed her the rights to several apparently very valuable pieces of intellectual property.

Liolesa's gift gave her ample opportunity to focus on something else, because reading it made Kis'eh't's shoulders crumple. As they all stared, startled, their most practical, unflappable crewmember pressed her face into her hands... and started crying.

The only reason Irine got to the Glaseah first was that the Harat-Shar didn't have to vault a tower of presents to reach her.

"What is it!" Irine exclaimed, fretful, tucking some of Kis'eh't's forelock back from her brow. "Is it bad?"

"No!" Kis'eh't said, mopping at her streaming eyes. "But Goddess... alet..."

"Are you going to ask me how I knew?" Liolesa said. "You of all people?"

"No." That pulled a watery chuckle out of Kis'eh't. "You did research. Of course. And if you do the research, it's all there to be seen."

"So are you gonna tell us what's going on?" Sascha asked, tail twitching.

"It seems so petty now, thinking about it," Kis'eh't said, almost to herself. She sighed and straightened, but didn't seem to mind Irine's arms around her waist and Reese's around her shoulder, so both of them stayed. "I would have had a very good career in materials research, but the grant that was going to propel me to that point was conditional on my foremost research assistant being fired. Because he was human, and the grant-giving entity didn't want any humans involved in or benefiting from the research."

"That happens offworld?" Araelis asked, surprised. "I thought xeno-phobia was the province of Eldritch. Or perhaps humans?"

"Oh, no. We Pelted do it too." Kis'eh't sighed. "They fired Abraham, without so much as giving me a warning... and demanded that I strip his name from my research papers. I refused. I left."

"She does not say," Liolesa added, quiet, "that she was courted by mili-tary, university, and corporation alike. There are discussions of her work that involve words like 'genius.'"

Kis'eh't shrugged her shoulders once, dismissing the accolade. "I won't work for bigots. The evidence of the Goddess's mind is Her gift to us. It belongs to all of us, not just a select few."

All this time she'd been employing a genius? Who had just now given her all her patents... Reese started to feel lightheaded, and was grateful when Kis'eh't slipped an arm around her waist and squeezed.

"So what's the Queen's gift?" Sascha asked.

"I wrote to her research assistant and asked if he was interested in working for her," Liolesa said.

"And he said yes. Except that he's not a research assistant anymore. He's a respected professor with a research team of his own. And they're willing to come. Which would make me...."

"The administrator of your own foundation, I should think," Liolesa said. "That would be the best way to structure it. Laisrathera receives your patents and endows the foundation, and elects you the chair of the foundation, charged with their development. You could employ your friend to do the field work, if field work is necessary, in concert with any partners you might wish to accept in the endeavor. It would be yours to administrate. You would choose." Liolesa's mouth quirked. "No bigots."

"No field work, though," Sascha observed. "So I guess less science and more paperwork."

"That's always how it happens," Kis'eh't said. "The more significant the discoveries and the more of them you make, the more responsibility you accrue." She breathed in. "Abraham... we kept in touch at first but we both got busy... he was... he was a friend. The chance to work with him again... he was brilliant. Working with him was like prayer." She stared at the paper—a letter, from what Reese could see from this angle—and shivered once, like an animal twitching off water. "This would make the world a major center for materials research."

"And you the woman in charge?" Irine said. "Sounds good to me. Aren't you already Royal Advisor to the Queen because you're good at science?"

"Those would make great credentials for some kind of cabinet position," Sascha agreed, leaning back with an arm on the seat of the empty chair behind him. "Minister of Science and Technology?"

Bryer fluffed his feathers. "Best sense. Would say 'If Goddess opens path, do not be stupid, walk it', yes?"

Kis'eh't stared at him, then blurted a laugh. The Phoenix gaped an avian grin at her.

"I would not much mind becoming a center for materials research," Liolesa said. "Indeed, contemplating the apoplexy that development would inspire in my enemies gives me *great* pleasure."

The Glaseah rested her head against Reese's. "It's the only thing I've missed since I left," she confessed, and there was a hint there of a yearning that Reese had never heard in her voice.

"Then you need miss it no longer," Hirianthial said. When Kis'eh't lifted her head, he finished, "Yes?"

Kis'eh't folded the paper, squeezed Irine and said, firmly, "Yes. To you all. But you have no idea what you're getting into...!"

"When have we ever?" Irine complained.

"This opportunity..." Kis'eh't trailed off. "Reese. Liolesa-alet. Thank you. This is not a gift. This is... this is my life back."

"You return to it with better perspective," Bryer said. "Some things are aligned by the universe."

"Yes," Kis'eh't said. She sighed and wiped her eyes again, chuckling. "All right. You go now, Bryer."

Returning to her chair, Reese thought that she was the one who'd gotten a gift—above and beyond the staggering one of the patents—in the form of that glimpse into Kis'eh't's hidden heart. How many of them had known that story about why she'd left? The only thing she'd told Reese when applying for a job was that she'd left academia due to 'differences of opinion.' Reese was willing to bet no one realized just what that had entailed, and what Kis'eh't had given up. The happiness that eased her shoulders and haunches now...

She'd done all right with that gift, when she'd feared she was presuming too much. Reese felt the relief so powerfully that she sought Hirianthial's gaze, hoping he felt it too... and he caught her eye and gave her one of those infinitesimal Eldritch nods, and the tiniest twitch of a smile. Such gentleness in his gaze... she knew he not only agreed with her, but that she'd managed to get another thing right by treating his ability to 'hear' her as something normal.

No wonder Liolesa worked so hard at this gift-giving thing.

Shopping for a Phoenix was hard. Reese could have figured that out before she started reading all the cultural information she could find on them; having done so, she concluded that it was never going to be as easy to give gifts to Bryer was it was to everyone else. The Phoenix life philosophy shunned attachment: "pass through the world and leave only shadows" was a line she picked up from an overview about it. But being a pragmatic as well as spiritual people, they regarded some attachment as inevitable, and had strict rules about how those bonds were to be chosen and maintained. Reese hadn't realized how astonishing it was that Bryer not only stayed with the crew, but that he had obviously chosen them as some of those attachments, and for a Phoenix he was positively effusive compared to many of his species.

But enough Phoenixae—that was the proper plural, though it sounded funny to her because so few people seemed to use it—lived among offworlders that there were a plethora of articles about how to shop for them. That was probably the source of the gifts she watched the twins and Kis'eh't giving him. "Focus on consumables or on items that make maintenance of the Phoenix's physical body or exercise of the Phoenix's duties easier," was the common advice. Kis'eh't gave him fertilizer for the Rose Point gardens, since Reese had told him to do as he willed with them. Irine had teamed up with the Glaseah and found a number of seeds that

Felith had reported would grow well this far north: vegetables, fruits, flowers, trees that bore nuts and trees that offered shade. Sascha had picked out a harness that flying Phoenix could use for tools and pouches, which Bryer tugged on and examined with evident approval.

Hirianthial's gift came in a box similar to the one that had held Sascha's dagger, but it contained what looked like a pumice stone. Reese squinted at it, wondering what it was.

Bryer knew, though. His crest arched once, fluffed and then settled. He cocked his head and said to Hirianthial, "Reminder?"

"Promise," Hirianthial said. "I have not forgotten our shared duty, and would have you at your best."

"What is it?" Kis'eh't asked.

"That's for your talons, isn't it." Irine flipped her ears back. "As if they need to be any sharper!"

"Any blade grows dull when used," Hirianthial said.

Bryer's hissing chuckle surprised them all. "Eldritch aphorism. Works as well for Phoenix. Is an appropriate gift. I accept both promise and utility."

That left hers and the Queen's, and he picked up the envelope first. "Will see what the Queen gives. Maybe I will need apron afterward."

That startled them all into laughing as Bryer unfolded his paper. "A map?" He looked at her, crest spreading in puzzlement.

"A cliff," the Queen said. "There are birds there always. Circling and skating on winds that seem to contradict one another. If I could fly, I would want to test myself on those winds."

Bryer's pupils dilated. He looked at the map again, then folded it and slid it back into the envelope. "Gift is cliff? Or revelation?"

Liolesa's smile was wry. "Oh, alet. I doubt anyone is surprised by that revelation about me."

Which, Reese though privately, was true...and not true, like everything about the Eldritch. She didn't doubt that everyone knew Liolesa's courage and thirst for challenge. It was that she had thought of what it was like to be winged, and let it be heard in her voice, just a little, that she would have liked it, that was the revelation.

"Now, captain's gift," Bryer said.

"Not an apron," Reese assured him.

"Very good. I do not cook well." The Phoenix pulled the tissue out of his bag and peered into it. With delicate claws, he lifted one of the long filmy banners, the silk whispering as it slipped over the bag's edge.

Holding it up, he said nothing, then set a hand on the calligraphy the computer had generated for her, and which she hoped was right.

"Battle at Surapinet's complex," the Phoenix said, looking at her.

"Yes."

He peered in the bag and drew another out, this one sky blue to the first's bright red. Reading the dates: "Fight at palace, fleeing."

Reese nodded.

The third was the yellow of buttercups, with silver paint. "Fight at palace, second time." He frowned at the fourth scarf. This one was white and reading the date, his feathers sagged in confusion. "Now... date of hire?"

"That was a fight too. Your longest fight," Reese said. "Your advice was the weapon, and you were battling my tendency toward self-destruction and stupid choices. You sometimes confused me, but talking to you always helped. And in the end..." She waved a hand at the room. "We won, didn't we?"

Bryer hesitated, then gaped a grin. "Clever gift. Very thoughtful."

"But what is it?" Araelis asked, curious. "Other than beautiful?"

"Eye-trained Phoenix—that is, the ones who learn how to fight— they're allowed to fly banners at their aeries when they win battles," Reese said. "But they have to be given the banners by someone whose life was saved at them."

Bryer added, "Need five before can request mate."

"Oh!" Irine exclaimed, then darted a look at Reese. "You are sneaky!"

"You have no idea," Sascha said, eyeing Reese. "Because having given the gift like this in public, where everyone could hear it explained... that means in a few days Hirianthial's probably going to give Bryer one for the fight on the battlecruiser." He glanced at the Eldritch. "Am I right?"

"He did save my life there," Hirianthial said, studying the ceiling with rather too much nonchalance.

"Hooray!" Irine exclaimed. "Then we can have baby Phoenixes!"

Bryer chuffed a laugh. "Harat-Shar." And then, as he rolled the scarves and put them back in the bag, "Have work. Have an aerie. Now, have proof of worth. Yes. We can have baby Phoenixae." He pressed his palms together and bowed his head to Reese, the long neck arcing and the feathers shivering. "Best gift is gift of continuity through generations. Now I may participate. Thank you."

"You're welcome," Reese said. And added, shy, "I can't wait to see baby Phoenixae too."

"We're down to three now," Sascha said. "Who's next, Boss? You or Hirianthial?"

"Or the Queen!" Irine exclaimed. "We should do her next."

"She's been ambushing us with crazy gifts all night," Sascha said, eyeing Liolesa. "She is due for it."

Liolesa hadn't moved from her chair where she was as relaxed as Reese suspected she ever got, with her hands folded on her ribcage and her feet in front of her, neatly aligned but at least stretched out. Even leaning back she had a perfectly straight back. But her eyes were merry. "I suppose I am in for my portion now, am I."

"Don't worry," Kis'eh't said, amused. "We don't have a planetary bank to back up our gifts yet."

"Yet!" Liolesa laughed as she sat up and rested her hands on her knees. "The sweet sound of ambition. I approve. What first, then?"

What do you get a queen was apparently a question that required a great deal of brainstorming, because the twins, Kis'eh't and Bryer had all gotten together on their presents for her, and they were...

"Toys?" Liolesa said, reading the packaging on the first gift.

"That's a good one," Sascha said. "It's a ball of goo and no matter how hard you throw it, smash it, or tear it, it always bounces back to the same shape."

"For those frustrating moments," Kis'eh't said.

Liolesa stared at it, then smothered a sound that was almost—Reese swore—almost a cackle. "Oh, that will be very useful, yes. And this... a... sliding puzzle?" She toyed with it with a furrowed brow, much to everyone's delight, but set it aside unsolved to look at the others, which included a bead that projected a starfield, a pocket-sized board that could be used to play four different games, and a palm-sized palomino horse plush. Watching her bent over all of the toys with her crew gathered close, demonstrating or pointing out features, Reese grinned. Toys seemed a crazy thing to give a woman who had everything, but it made sense in context. Liolesa had been heir since birth, Hirianthial had told her once, and been driven by her internal sense of duty and prophecy all her life. When had she ever had time to play? When had anyone ever invited her to?

Hirianthial caught her eyes and murmured, "Never."

She liked the tenderness in his eyes, and the indulgent amusement when he watched the tableau. And it was funny, in a sweet way. Also funny in a funny way, because she imagined the next time Liolesa had one of those infuriating meetings with the remaining recalcitrant nobles, that gob of goo was going to get a pounding.

"So, here is Theresa's gift to me, and it is large!" Liolesa ran her hands over the lumpy package. "I am consumed with curiosity."

"It's not a little paper envelope so you should be good," Sascha quipped.

Liolesa laughed. "Thank the Lady for less earth-shattering presents, yes?" She opened it with surgical precision and a mass of pastel rainbow-colored cords spilled out, satiny and soft, with a matching blanket of pale yellow fabric and soft pillows in white and cloud blue. Startled, Liolesa caught the linens before they could fall out of her lap and said, "Good-ness, Theresa. You have given me..."

"A pouch hammock," Reese said firmly. "Much as I like your beds—and I admit beds do have their uses, and no, Irine, don't start—there's nothing like a hammock for catching a nap." As Liolesa spread the cords out to find the loops, Reese finished, "You carry everyone all the time, my lady. I thought, once in a while, someone, or something at least, should carry you."

Liolesa looked up sharply. For one instant, so fleeting Reese almost missed it... she saw the woman instead of the ruler: not someone who wished for an easier life, because there didn't seem to be anything in Liolesa to wish for that, but someone who could be caught off guard. Reese held her breath, because the one thing she didn't want to do was reveal that she'd seen it, so that everyone else could notice and make much of something she knew, instinctively, Liolesa would have hated to have discussed.

"It is delightful," Liolesa said. "I shall have someone hang it in my favorite garden, so I might try this... napping you speak of."

"Which you've heard of but never indulged in," Araelis said dryly, almost like her old self.

"I've been told sleep is useful," the Queen said. "I shall have to discover for myself!" She wrapped the hammock into a tidy bundle using the blanket. "Thank you, Theresa. I look forward to using this gift."

"So long as you do," Hirianthial said.

"We can detail some of the Swords to cordon off the area," Sascha said. "That way we'll know she can't get out before she's tried it."

"And you call me managing," Liolesa said to Araelis. "And now, Hiri-anthial." She lifted the small package, tilting it. "Shall I shake it?"

"You do that here too?" Sascha asked, amused.

"Only when we are very young," Araelis said. "And lacking in comportment."

"Oh, well, then certainly I must not shake it." Liolesa paused, then gave it a little jiggle. "No noise, alas!"

As everyone laughed, Hirianthial said, "I'll remember this propensity for cheating next year."

"Oh will you!" Liolesa slit the paper open and withdrew a book, and seeing it Reese inhaled. It was exactly the kind of book she would have read about in stories on her data tablet, wishing she could see it with her own eyes: small, with a leather cover scrolled with gold leaf and set with precious gems. The pages were leafed in gold, and when Liolesa opened it, she glimpsed the glossy darkness of real ink, applied by someone's hand.

"This is glorious," Liolesa murmured, thumbing through it.

"A Book of Hours, I assume?" Araelis asked.

Liolesa had reached the front page and stopped on it. Her mouth pressed into a firm line, and she let her head drop. The shaking of her shoulders... Reese wondered wildly who could comfort a queen who wasn't supposed to be touched if she started crying? And then she realized Liolesa was laughing. Helplessly, until she had to wipe her eyes.

"Hiran Jisiensire!" she gasped. "A Book of Hours from Saint Wilthelmissa!"

"You spent so much time there in meditation," Hirianthial said. "I thought you should have a souvenir."

"You are a terrible man," Liolesa said, shaking her head as she examined the book. "And it is an exquisite gift."

Reese wondered if there was some Eldritch custom that explained why a prayer book was funny... but no, Araelis looked just as bemused. A private joke between friends, then. And a very good one, too, because Hirianthial was looking almost smug, which was an expression she didn't think she'd ever seen on him. He cocked a brow at her and she grinned. Maybe in ten years, or twenty, he'd be giving her things that no one would understand but her, and wouldn't that be fun? Especially if she did the same...

"Now it's Hirianthial's turn," Irine said.

"Yes, let us see to the man who has given pie birds and prayer books," Liolesa said, setting her plush palomino on her lap so she could pet it.

Prayer books made Reese think of Val, so while Hirianthial was sorting through his pile, she said, "The priests aren't here... if you want to give them gifts, when do you do it?"

Liolesa glanced at Araelis with arched brows. Araelis looked away; unlike the Queen, her face was more mobile, and there was exasperation there, and pain. "I see I am being deferred to. Because you like to make us examine our own wounds, don't you, my Queen."

"You are best qualified to answer," Liolesa said. "This was more lately your duty than mine."

Araelis waved that off, a little twitch of her hand. "It cannot be argued, and even if it could it would be a useless exercise. I take your education into my hands, then, Theresa. Priests are not permitted to receive personal gifts during this holiday."

"The entire holiday, or just the Vigil?" Sascha asked.

"The season entire," Araelis said. "It is considered...."

"Gauche," Hirianthial supplied.

"Yes. One does not single out any member of the Lord or God's clergy for special treatment...or the Lady and Goddess's, at that, though I suppose the High Priestess is an exception." Araelis eyed Liolesa.

"Better to beg forgiveness than ask permission?" Sascha offered.

Liolesa said, "The proscription is intended to prevent the cultivation of specific priests and priestesses by their lieges. I, however, am difficult to bribe, so I would not worry overmuch about me."

Hirianthial shook his head. "More to the point, one ordinarily cannot take vows to the Divine Mysteries and keep one's worldly position. The Queen is the only Eldritch who has a dual identity: she is both the secular head of state and the religious head of the Church. She is truly an exception."

"And everyone wants to curry favor with her anyway," Kis'eh't said.

"That also," Hirianthial said.

"Except when they don't," Liolesa said, with a dark look.

Araelis cleared her throat. "As I was saying. The lady's role during the season is to fund her churches. You, Theresa, are obligated to send each of your local churches food and alms, including your personal chapel and clergy here at Rose Point, and also to send a tithe to the capital for the Church at large."

"So you get your bribe either way," Sascha observed.

Liolesa dandled her plush horse on her knee. "It is good to be the Queen?"

"Except when it's not, I'm betting," Reese said. "So... no gifts at all? That seems harsh."

"One gives personal gifts to one's priests on their natal days," Araelis said. "But they should be modest. The vows require chastity, poverty, obedience, and humility."

"So we shop for Val like we shop for Bryer," Sascha said. "We can do that."

"I'll figure out his birthday. And Belinor's, and Urise's," Irine said. She grinned. "I already know what I want to get Val and Belinor!"

"I'm afraid to ask," Reese said. "It's probably meant to give them ideas, isn't it."

Irine purred. "They can't do anything until they have ideas!"

"I can guess, but I don't want to know," Kis'eh't murmured.

"Good plan," Sascha said. "Hirianthial, you're on!"

Reese expected these presents to be good: after all, they'd had 'their' Eldritch for long enough to know him, at least insofar as anyone could know an Eldritch given the Veil. She wasn't disappointed, either. Irine's gift was a mysterious steel clip which Hirianthial examined with evident confusion until she said, "It's for your dangle. Now that it's too long for your hair, I thought you'd want to loop it so that it wouldn't be exposed."

"Ah!" he said. "Yes." He offered it to her on his (bare!) palm. "If you would?"

"Wouldn't I!" Irine exclaimed. "Another present for me!" But she plucked it up with pinched fingers, careful not to brush his skin, and padded up behind him to consider his shortened hair. Reese missed the extravagant length of it, and wagered he felt naked without it. Plus, she'd noticed the male Eldritch she saw seemed to wear the length according to their station, and as blood cousin to the Queen, Reese didn't think you could get higher without marrying her. But there was something endearing about the bob, which at shoulder-length was longer than Val's defiant chin-length style. It made him look younger, and she liked how it emphasized the length of his neck because that made the flare of his shoulders much more evident.

She…was getting distracted. With his head bent for Irine's touch, Hirianthial glanced at her with one of those new, simmering looks she still hadn't gotten used to, and she blushed at him.

"Here," Irine said, not noticing—thank Freedom for small mercies—as she took the dangle up and tucked it under his hair. "I can hang the end of it in front of the ear? Behind?"

"Behind," Liolesa said. "The before-ear style is more typical of young, single men."

"A display?" Kis'eh't asked. "Hoping to attract mates?"

45

"But women have the wealth here, right?" Irine said, absently as she worked. "That's why I have a jewelry box."

"That's right," Araelis said. "Men wear jewels there as... advertisement? I hope I can use the word that way. 'Look how good I look wearing jewels. Would you not like to see yours here instead?'"

"Ha!" Sascha said.

"But then they... hide it behind their ears when they marry?" Kis'eh't said, confused.

"Naturally," Araelis said. "One wouldn't want other women to covet one's goods, after all."

"There!" Irine said, stepping back.

"Very modest," Araelis said.

"And no longer hanging down my back," Hirianthial said. "Which, while a pleasing reminder, is a technical violation of the dress code for a man at war."

"They are not supposed to have strands longer than their hair," Liolesa said before someone could ask. "It invites an enemy to yank."

Hirianthial shook his head once, testing the clip, and the prayer bell chimed softly. "Perfect. Thank you, Irine."

"She even hid it properly," Liolesa said.

"Well, if women here go around poaching other people's men, and sharing's not allowed," Irine said, "I don't want anyone getting ideas about Reese's."

Reese covered her face.

"Just keep your face in your hands, Boss," Sascha said. "You'll want it there when he opens mine."

"This should be good! Do open that one next," Liolesa said.

"A book," Hirianthial guessed, unfolding the paper. Reese watched—if she was going to blush, she should at least know what she was blushing about. Was it her imagination, or was Sascha a little tense, waiting for Hirianthial's reaction? What on the soil had he given him?

The Eldritch merely looked at it for a long moment. "I will accept this gift on one condition."

"What's that?" Sascha said, hesitant.

Hirianthial looked up, eyes sparkling. "That we wager that there isn't anything in it I don't already know."

A heartbeat pause, and then Sascha erupted into laughter. "There's no way!" he exclaimed.

"I've lived six hundred years, Sascha...."

"I bet you spent three hundred of them as a virgin!"

"Oh God," Reese said, and really did cover her face. "Don't tell me. It's a picture book written by Harat-Shar."

"It is a marital aid," Hirianthial offered, setting Sascha off again.

Peering at the spine, Irine added, "It's a good one too! We had lots of fun with it!"

Kis'eh't waved a hand. "Enough about the book... what are the terms of the wager?"

"And how will you discern if he's telling the truth?" Liolesa wondered.

"Lia! You are supposed to be on my side, do you recall."

"It's a valid question," Kis'eh't said. "But I'm pretty sure there's no way to prove it, so we'll just have to go on his word."

"We shall have to bet something substantive," Hirianthial said. "What shall you give me if you lose, Sascha?"

"A week of abstinence?" Kis'eh't mused.

"Hey!" Irine exclaimed. "Don't punish me and Narain! We had nothing to do with this!"

"I don't know!" Sascha said. "What do you want?" Seeing the look in Hirianthial's eye, "Oh, hells, what did I just do."

"Then if it is my choice...you will learn to ride a horse."

"I already can ride a horse!"

"You can sit on a horse," Hirianthial said, mouth twitching. "That is not riding."

"Can it be a solidigraphic horse at least? No? Battlehells." Sascha pressed his palm to his forehead. "Fine. If I lose, I'll learn to ride a real horse. What if you lose?"

"It's got to be good," Kis'eh't said. "Since learning a new skill is a serious commitment. Particularly a useless one."

"I beg your pardon!" Hirianthial said, laughing. "Riding is a very useful skill here!"

"Not for much longer, once we get the Pads down and real shuttles," the Glaseah answered.

"Kis'eh't is in the right," Liolesa said. "You must make a sacrifice for this one, Hiran. It's only fair, given the gift."

"Very well," Hirianthial said. "Then, with my lady's permission, if you win, you and Irine may bathe me."

He looked very pleased with himself, as well he should, given that even Bryer joined the laughter for that one. It was the look on the twins' faces: half avarice, half shock, like someone holding a winning lottery

47

ticket. And then Sascha's face fell and he scowled. "This means you're completely sure you're going to win, doesn't it."

"Six hundred *years*, Sascha."

"Almost seven hundred," Araelis said.

"But half the pictures in that book are kinky! Or involve tails!" Irine exclaimed.

Hirianthial had his hand spread over his mouth and chin and an impish look in his eyes. "Medical school rotations. Acute care."

"Oh hells." Sascha sighed. "And the saddest part is that those poor bastards probably did them all wrong."

"If they wound up in the hospital, yes!" Irine folded her arms.

"Now you know why it's dangerous to assume things," Kis'eh't said. "Never bet on a hypothesis when you can bet on a theory."

"Oh, look at their ears," Liolesa said. "You must give him a consolation prize, cousin. Why not show him an Eldritch version of their book?"

"You have pornography?" Irine squeaked.

"We do reproduce," Araelis said, folding her arms over her belly.

"Yes, but... I figured... you would just... pick a position, sanctify it, and then tell everyone who's doing anything else they're wrong?"

Liolesa threw the plush at her. As Irine ducked with a squeak, the Queen said, "These toys are quite useful! I feel better already! Shall I get the goo?"

"No, no!" Irine giggled. "No, I'll never get any of it out of my fur!"

Ignoring them with what Reese thought was saintly patience, Hirianthial had gone back to unwrapping. "Here I have another book, from Kis'eh't?" He paged through it, intrigued. "This is... a book of stories?"

"The Glaseah also have mind-mages, which we call dva'htiht," Kis'eh't said. "Among us, they are considered saints and legends, and their gifts are reminders of the Goddess's infinite power and generosity. That book is about the first cohort of dva'htiht; there were six among the first generation of natural-born Glaseah, and they had many adventures which have been much embroidered in the years since their birth."

"Glaseah have mind-mages?" Araelis said, astonished.

"Glaseah revere mind-mages," Kis'eh't said. "And tell stories about them to children, and write musicals about them, and most of all, train them and give them the tools they need to thrive, which includes support from their society."

"Ouch!" Sascha said. "Not sure if this is a gift to Hirianthial or a smack on the hind end for the natives, arii."

"No," Hirianthial said. "Perspective is always a welcome gift. This is treasure, Kis'eh't. I thank you."

Bryer's gift was addressed to both Hirianthial and Reese, but she let him open it because it was fun to watch him. He shared Liolesa's precision with the paper, but Liolesa went through her gifts' seams like a surgeon with a scalpel while Hirianthial was a little less... well, ruthless was the word that came to mind, and it made her grin. But the gift itself stole her breath away, because it was a long parchment stretched between two rods, inscribed with a single piece of calligraphy, and she recognized it after hours of reading about the Phoenix. Reaching for the bottommost rod, she said, "Oh, Bryer!"

"That's beautiful," Irine said, eyes wide. "What is it?"

"Gift for leaders of a flight," Bryer said. "To be displayed. Indicates this is a safe haven place." He eyed Reese. "Must be lived up to, but think that will not be a problem."

"No," Hirianthial said. "I think Lady Eddings was living up to that even when she was Captain Eddings." He rolled it closed. "But we will hang it in the great hall, so that all who come may see it."

"Now we're down to Reese's gift and Liolesa's," Irine said. "This should be good!"

"Mine first," Reese said. "Because Freedom knows what your cousin's gotten you."

"Yours first, then."

As he took the small box, Liolesa said, "Shake it, cousin!"

"Liolesa!" Araelis said, exasperated.

"I shall not," Hirianthial said. "As I suspect it is small and will rattle."

"It's small, at least," Reese agreed.

He unfolded it to bring out the box, which was, in fact, a gift box for jewelry. But she hadn't put a gem in it, but....

"Oh...," Hirianthial said, reverent. "My Courage."

Blushing, Reese said, "You're still using the generic one it came with. Soly told me they're supposed to be switched out for a personal one, so..."

Hirianthial held out the disc-shaped pommel for the rest of the gathering to see. Reese had gotten the design specifications for it from Solysyrril, then sent away for the design: on one side, Laisrathera's new star on peach, and on the other, the Royal House's unicorn on blue. Because he belonged to them both... the Eldritch Lord of War, and Laisrathera's future sword-bearer.

"That really is perfect," Sascha said, satisfied.

"As long as it fits?" Kis'eh't said.

Hirianthial had already taken the hilt from his scabbard and was twisting off the plain ball on the end of the sword Fleet had found him on the battlecruiser. The new one did fit, perfectly.

"Oh, that is well done," Araelis said.

"You see," Liolesa said to Irine, "We do share, sometimes."

"Since I'm pretty sure any enemy of Reese's is going to flatten her on the way to you, I don't think that counts as sharing," Irine said. "That's more of a mutual defense pact."

"She's stealing your lines," Kis'eh't observed to Sascha.

"She's my twin. Everything I have is hers anyway."

Irine rested her cheek on her brother's shoulder. "The Queen's gift is left?"

"Another small box," Hirianthial said. "But not an envelope, so perhaps I have been saved."

"The envelopes are far more dangerous, I admit," Liolesa said.

Araelis looked at her only gift, which was another of those envelopes. "I tremble in my chair."

"You probably should," Hirianthial said, and opened the last box to reveal a red loop—string? Wire? She couldn't tell from where she was sitting, but the sight of it brought the stillness back into her fiancé's shoulders.

"It was not ready in time." Liolesa sounded apologetic. "But you needed one of your own." She smiled. "You can't have mine, after all. I rarely play, but I must at least maintain the pretense of having some domestic accomplishments."

"A guitar string?" Sascha guessed.

"Too long," Bryer said. "Harp, maybe."

"A pedal harp, yes," Hirianthial said, tucking the string back in the box. "Thank you, cousin. I will be glad to have one again."

"You play harp!" Irine said, wide-eyed.

"And lute," Araelis said.

"Though never as well." Hirianthial smiled. "A home should have a musical instrument. I look forward to it."

"As do I," Liolesa said. "And now we come to our hostess. Go on, Theresa. You have certainly earned your furbelows this year."

"My what?" Reese said.

"Ruffles," Araelis said. "Frills. Things you add to clothes to make them pretty?"

"And more expensive," Liolesa added, amused.

Reese shook her head and went to her stack. Even lightened by Bryer's joint gift of the calligraphy scroll and Kis'eh't's of the patents, she still felt like she had a pile of treasure, probably because one of the boxes was almost as long as she was. But there was an envelope, and as she eyed it warily, Irine said, "That one's from us."

"Does that mean it's safe?" Liolesa asked.

Thinking of the flat package Kis'eh't's patents had come in, Reese said, "I'm not too sure about that." But she lifted it onto her lap anyway and opened it to the creamy tint of parchment paper. Before she could pull it out, Sascha leaned over and rested a hand on her wrist.

"Before you look, maybe we should explain," he said, golden eyes serious. "You know you haven't been paying us a steady salary, right?"

"Right," Reese said, rueful. Figuring out payroll had been on her list of things to do, but admittedly it had fallen by the wayside, and no one had reminded her. Why would they? They had food, clothes, a place to sleep, and dozens of Tam-illee and Fleet people running around with their power plants, tool boxes, and genies synthesizing or building whatever anyone asked for. There was no doubt the crew would need money of their own, eventually, but there was no pressing need yet. And since being in a position not to worry about the basics had been rare on the ship, well... maybe they'd all forgotten about it? Or maybe she had, and her crew had been humoring her... again...

"No, no, stop that with your face." Sascha shook her wrist. "It's not a problem right now."

"Except we knew what we wanted to get you, and it did cost more fin than we had saved up," Irine said. "So we borrowed it! An advance against our future salaries."

"From...."

"Your other half," Sascha said, dryly.

Reese eyed Hirianthial, who was far too good at those innocent looks. Had he learned them from Liolesa, or had the Queen learned them from him? Maybe they'd inherited them from a mutual relative.

"It was a good cause," he said, unperturbed by her scrutiny.

"Right," Sascha said. "So we bought this, fair and square, and now it's yours."

This was not an explanation guaranteed to settle the flutters in Reese's stomach, but what could fluster her anymore? She'd had a castle dropped on her by a queen! Reese pulled out the parchment and looked at the certificate with its embossed seal and all its real ink signatures... and almost dropped it. "You didn't!"

"We did," Irine said smugly. "And it's in the middle of your hometown, too."

They had bought her a Founders' Stone. The certificate of authenticity came with a photograph of her new tile on the Liberty Wall, one she recognized even though her visits to what was charitably known as 'downtown' had been rare. The custom of selling such tiles to fund the maintenance and rebuilding of Mars's habitats and ports was as old as its colonization, but even though the Eddings family had been eligible to claim one of the coveted Founders' Stones, they never had; having proof of continuous residency since the emancipation wasn't enough if you didn't have the considerable sum required to pay into the pot. As far as Reese knew, no one in her family had ever seriously considered it. The only times it had come up, the idea had been dismissed: better things to do with money than get your name stamped on some piece of rock where everyone could see it. Reese had never thought of it because using the *Earthrise* to create a continuous source of wealth had turned out to be so much more difficult than she'd dreamed. It hadn't taken her long to understand the most strategic investment she'd be making was what bulk foods could be used to stretch the value of her last bent coin.

She knew the twins were thinking it justice that her name should endure in the place where she'd been disinherited. Reese was mostly thinking that some of her windfall had come back to the place she'd been born, which needed it so badly, and so long after she'd given up hope that she'd be able to help. Her eyes watered. "This is... this is wonderful." She wiped her eye with the side of her palm and added, "And completely worth the money you stole from me to buy it."

"It wasn't stealing!" Irine objected.

"It was creatively misappropriating!" Sascha agreed. "And with help, too."

She reached over and took a furry hand in each of hers and squeezed them. "It's perfect. Thank you."

"There's another thing I got you, but it's up in your room," Irine added. "You can look at it later."

"Oh, blood—"

"It's not anything as racy as you're thinking!" Irine exclaimed. "It's just clothes! But... you know. Personal. Just replacing things that are getting a little old. You know."

"Right," Reese said, sure she was blushing now. "I'll definitely open that one by myself then."

"Big box next!" Irine said.

"The smaller one's less intimidating," Reese said.

"That's why you should do the big one next!"

Hirianthial laughed. "That one is from me, you will find."

"Do that one next definitely," Sascha said. "Angels know what the Queen's gotten you."

"I feel my reputation is taking an undeserved thrashing!" Liolesa complained. "Not all my presents are heart-rending or earth-shattering!"

"Some are merely astronomically expensive," Kis'eh't said dryly.

"Hirianthial's box," Irine said again.

"Right." Reese had to perch at the edge of her chair to get it to fit lengthwise on her lap, and it was heavy. Was she nervous? She was nervous. She glanced at her fiancé, who lifted his brows just a touch, and there was encouragement there, and tenderness. So she undid the thick satin ribbon and lifted off the cover and gaped at the coat lying on the puffed satin interior. And the jewelry. No, she stared at the coat first because the jewelry was intimidating.

As she lifted it from the bed of tissue, Hirianthial said, "I thought you would need something to wear on Lady's Day, and you were not likely to go in a gown."

"Not if I have to ride a horse," Reese agreed as even Araelis exclaimed over it. Not a coat, now that she was looking at it more closely... something like a cloak, but with a fitted layer beneath it that could be buttoned over her chest, and slits for her arms, and a hood. And all of it was velvet in pale peach that deepened to a warm coral color at the bottom hem. And lined in cream-colored satin and fur...! She ran her fingers over the fur, astonished by the texture of it, the glossy hairs on top and the soft plush layer just beneath.

"I recall you liking the cloak you borrowed at the townhouse...."

"No, no. You don't have to apologize. This is sumptuous and beautiful and probably crazy expensive, and I love it."

"You can even wear it over pants!" Irine said.

"And I can even wear it over pants." She chuckled, low. "You know me so well."

"I hope, a little."

That left... "But this, though." She was almost scared to pick it up, but it deserved to be seen. She would have called it a crown before she'd come here, but she'd seen Liolesa in a crown, standing on the hill looking down on Athanesin's army. 'Crown' meant a serious band of metal and precious stones, something heavy enough to sink your heels a few inches into the ground. This was more ethereal: a fillet of what was no doubt real gold, or maybe something more terrifying, like gold-leafed platinum. There were three stones in the center: two cabochon rubies the size of Reese's thumb-nails, and between them, a tawny fire opal with play-of-color in splashes of red and green, and if it wasn't at least the length of her thumb, she'd eat her data tablet.

"Oh," Araelis breathed. "Oh, House cousin... don't tell me some of them were saved!"

"He had some in keeping in the palace vaults," Liolesa said. "More than you think, Araelis. I think you will be gratified."

"It's... I can't... this is...."

"You must, Theresa," Liolesa said firmly. "It is an appropriate gift from a former Head of House to his betrothed."

"Oh, verily!" Araelis said. "That is the Dolorith opal, Lady Eddings, and I thought it was gone with the fire. To see it again is... oh, it's wonder-ful. By the Goddess, the traitor didn't destroy everything that was once ours!"

"It has a name?" Kis'eh't said, ear fans sagging.

"The gemstones of significant character that have been with us since Settlement do, yes," Liolesa said. "Each House has its own trove, and the principals of the family may bestow those gems where they will, though they rarely do. No, that is a fine gift, Theresa, and deeply symbolic."

"It'll also look amazing on you...!" Irine exclaimed, eyes wide.

"So let me get this part straight... this gemstone is thousands of years old?" Sascha said.

"Most gemstones are," Kis'eh't pointed out, amused.

"Yes, but..."

"You're sure about this?" Reese said, to Hirianthial and Araelis both. "If all Houses carry their wealth as gemstones and Jisiensire just lost most of its... this... you should take it back to rebuild."

"It is his to give," Araelis said softly.

"And Jisiensire is not poor even now," Liolesa added. Something about her voice....

But Araelis didn't seem to notice. "She is correct. And Laisrathera does not yet have any named jewels, and should have at least one. It will lend the House legitimacy in the eyes of those who revere tradition."

"It matches the coat!" Irine added.

What could she say? Except, "I'm honored." She ran her finger along the gold leading back from the rubies. "It's unbelievably beautiful."

"Do the rubies have names too, or are they riffraff gemstones, trying to pass for better?" Sascha said, grinning.

"They have no names, no, though they are as old," Hirianthial said, amused. "They've always been used in concert with other stones. It is when they can stand alone that they earn a name."

"Only here would a gemstone that size not be enough to be set in jewelry by itself." Kis'eh't shook her head. "I can't imagine what your rings must be like."

"Because we rarely wear them," Araelis said. "We use our rings to state our family allegiances. One ring per hand per person is proper."

"We make up for the lack with brooches and pendants and fillets and hair-strands," Liolesa agreed, pleased. "You will look the proper lady now, Theresa, when you go down to your town for the holiday."

"I will," Reese agreed, resting the fillet back in the box. She looked at the last package and said, "Blood, I hope whatever you gave me is less overwhelming, my lady."

"It is at very least less expensive!"

That was somewhat encouraging. But not much, because when Reese opened it she found a choker of apricot-colored moonstones and rubies, faceted this time. "You said—!"

"It is not a historied piece, I pledge it!" Liolesa said with a laugh. "No, no, don't throw my own stuffed toy back at me. I ordered it for you, and I promise it is a modern piece and far less fraught than something out of the vaults of Ontine. You will have to grow accustomed to such gifts, in fact, as the colors you've chosen for Laisrathera are rare in our gem hoards."

Reese lifted it, found it breathtaking, was still terrified. She could have filled the *Earthrise's* holds completely for the price Liolesa had probably paid for something she considered a bauble. Sometimes she wondered how she'd gotten mixed up with these people... but then, she was becoming one of 'these' people. A woman with a castle, a ship, a baby crown, and a Founders' stone? Teenage Reese wouldn't recognize herself now! She shook her head and chuckled. "You really do like buying presents, don't you."

"It is one of the few pleasures of being a queen, and one with a modest fortune."

"Modest!" Sascha exclaimed.

"Alas, I keep having to divert funds into things like importation of foodstuffs, and building of moon bases." Liolesa sighed. "My life, aletsen, is a trial."

"Then absolutely, I should keep this and say thank you," Reese said, tucking it back in the box. "You having so few pleasures in your life." The flash of the rubies in the firelight just before they vanished under the lid made her think of giving this box to a daughter one day. Laisrathera now had a modest trove of its own to pass on to its children. The idea made her smile. "I'll wear it to my wedding."

"Is that everyone?" Irine asked. "Because if it is..."

"Then the Stranger is left with her untoward gift," Araelis said, eyeing Liolesa.

"It was the right time," the Queen replied, unrepentant.

Araelis shook her head, the minimalist twitch typical of the Eldritch, and opened her envelope. There were three sheets in it, separately folded. The first, Araelis frowned at. Glancing over its top edge, she hazarded, "A map?"

"Indeed," Liolesa said.

Kis'eh't, who was sitting closest to Araelis, said, "Looks like a star map."

Araelis had already set it down and was puzzling at the second page. "Names," she murmured. "None I recognize. But they look like offworlders? What are you about, Liolesa?"

"Continue and see."

Araelis sighed, visibly exasperated, and put down the list of names. Reese caught a glimpse of a paragraph on the last page as the Eldritch unfolded it: one paragraph, and a short one, so it couldn't possibly be taking Araelis as long to read it as she was taking. Were her hands trembling? The woman slowly lowered this last page and said, "You are serious."

"More to the point, they are serious," Liolesa said. No, that wasn't Liolesa anymore. That was the Queen again, and there was that battle flag in her eyes somehow. Challenge, Reese thought. And maybe what Araelis needed to pull her from the devastation of her life was challenge, because she didn't back down from the stare.

"Who's serious?" Reese hadn't planned to ask, but she wanted to know.

"But where would we...." Araelis trailed off, then picked up the map again. "Don't tell me."

Liolesa smiled, eyes hooded. Seeing it, Araelis's chin jerked up. She handed the map to Kis'eh't. "Alet. Tell me where this is, please?"

Kis'eh't glanced at it. "I'm not the navigator here. Sascha?"

The Harat-Shar took it from her hand. "Hells, who prints out something three-d like this on paper?" He turned it upside down, then clockwise. "Ah, okay. Yeah, this looks like one of the undeveloped sectors? Not far from here. Nothing's out there, though."

"Something is now," Hirianthial murmured.

"Or will be," Liolesa agreed. "If Araelis is willing."

Reese knew about the world the Alliance Colony Bureau had granted the Queen because Hirianthial had mentioned it to her not long after they'd started work on Laisrathera. It had seemed like sensitive information, so she hadn't shared it, but she thought Sascha had known... was sure of it now, because he leaned back and put his elbows on the seat of the chair he and Irine'd been using as a backrest. There wasn't enough tension in him to indicate surprise. So it was Kis'eh't who said, "You have a roster of strangers and a map. Does that mean you have a colony planned?"

"Not strangers," Araelis said, her voice brittle. "Kin."

"Kin who are Pelted..." Irine trailed off, then brightened. "You said you had adopted a pard! So they're all..."

"Harat-Shar!" Kis'eh't exclaimed, and laughed. "Goddess! What a world that would be."

"Wouldn't it?" Liolesa asked. "It only wants someone willing to emigrate."

Araelis was folding each paper deliberately and returning them to the envelope. "You are," she said, the words slow and clipped, "the most *managing* female, Liolesa."

"Positively interfering, if I recall correctly."

"I think asking someone to start an entire new colony for you is certainly interfering. Writing to my Pelted relations and asking them if they are willing to join me in the endeavor before you've even discussed it with me is even more outrageous."

"But?" Liolesa pressed.

"But... yes." Araelis sighed, then shook her head. "Goddess and Lady, Liolesa. You will drown me in fur."

"Better than sorrows, cousin," Hirianthial murmured.

"So this is real?" Irine asked, awed. "You're starting an entire new settlement somewhere else? With Eldritch and Harat-Shar?"

"I hope you're not thinking of bailing on me," Reese said, grinning.

Irine waved a hand dismissively. "No, you need me too much. But still. That's going to be something to see!"

"It will be something you do see, I imagine," Araelis said. "We will need significant trade with the mother planet for some time before we are self-sufficient. I am hoping you are not saddling me with the rulership of this enterprise, Liolesa."

"Only of your family and the move there," Liolesa said. "When I choose a new heir she will become the viceroy of our colony. But you will have first choice of everything, and it is to you and your passel of pards that I will look to conduct the in-depth surveys, choose the site for the capital, and make recommendations on the development of appropriate resources. Lesandurel will, of course, be at your disposal for creating all the necessary orbital accoutrements."

"Accoutrements," Sascha said, shaking his head. "Like it's some kind of fancy ball gown."

"What a task!" Kis'eh't said, eyes wide. "You're going to be very busy, Lady Araelis."

"That, I suspect, is the plan." Araelis eyed Liolesa, then sighed and smiled. "And it is a wise one. I know what you intend, Liolesa, and... thank you. You give me something to look forward to."

"And your son or daughter something to rule," Liolesa said. "You have responsibilities yet to the succession. Do not forget."

"I don't! And she will inherit something not born from ashes." Araelis trailed off. "I have not the first notion how to begin, in fact. This is an enormous undertaking."

"How convenient then that the pards are arriving in two weeks!"

"Two weeks!" Araelis squeaked.

"I said 'yes' for you," Liolesa said modestly.

"Liolesa Galare!"

"Here," Irine said, handing her the plush. "Throw it at her. And then I'll take it so I can throw it at my brother—"

"Hey! What did I do?"

"Because you knew! You knew they had another planet and you didn't tell me!"

Sascha held up his hands. "It's not my fault! A man hears things when he's tagging along after high level ministers of state! That he's not supposed to tell!"

"You're in trouble now," Kis'eh't said, chuckling.

"This... seems a good time for more coffee," Reese said, getting up. "What do we do next? I can't imagine spending another four or five hours playing card games."

Kis'eh't snorted. "Card games! Ridiculous! The Queen has given us something far more interesting to do until dawn than play." At the blank looks she received, the Glaseah said, "Lady Araelis has never built a colony."

"Neither have we," Sascha pointed out.

"No, but we've started building a modern settlement here," Reese said from the sideboard. "It might not be exactly the same, but I bet we could find a lot of parallels."

"Certainly enough to begin," Hirianthial agreed.

"Is it all right to do work during the Vigil?" Irine asked. "There's no prohibition against that, right?"

"Are you kidding?" Reese said. "This might be work, but it's the fun part."

"I would appreciate the advice," Araelis admitted, smoothing her envelope's edges on her lap. "And it would be pleasing, to look forward."

"The season is about the future," Hirianthial said.

"A future created by the sacrifices of the past." There was steel in the words, but Liolesa softened them with her smile. Was that what it was like to be a queen, Reese wondered? To always be finding the bright side in duty and grief? But then... wasn't that what all people did, who survived? And they were all survivors. "By all means. Let us consider Araelis's little project. I predict the hours will positively fly."

And they did, because it was fun, and it was interesting, far more fun and interesting than any board or card game. Half the gathering fetched data tablets, the others notebooks and pens or pencils, and they covered the low table meant for dainty cups and saucers with maps and sketches and jotted projections. The discussion ranged from trade routes to governance—Reese had plenty to say about how a colony and its parent world should treat one another—and touched on seemingly everything in between, from what language everyone should speak to the ratio of Eldritch to Pelted. Little was decided; much was speculated on. But like so many other things lately, it was a beginning.

"We will need to name the planet," Hirianthial said to Liolesa.

"The colony?" Irine asked.

Araelis shook her head. "Both planets, then."

"Your planet doesn't have a name?" Sascha said, aghast. "This one? The one we're on right now. You're telling me you people never named it?"

"I thought you were just being coy about sharing it." Kis'eh't's brows were lifted.

"No... no, I'm afraid not," Liolesa said, laughing. "When we speak of the homeworld, that's what we call it. 'The homeworld,' or 'the world.' It has no formal name. Now that we have a colony, I suppose we will have to stop putting it off."

"How do you name a planet?" Sascha asked, ears sagging. "I wouldn't know where to start."

"You could vote?" Kis'eh't said.

"Certainly not!" Araelis exclaimed.

"Araelis is entirely correct," Hirianthial said. "This is not a democracy. Cousin, you shall have to shoulder the responsibility."

"Woe," Liolesa said. "Yet another duty! Pity me."

"Do it quickly," Araelis said, brisk. "I would like to call my new home something less withering than 'That Other World' before the name sticks."

"You see how much I suffer," Liolesa told Reese and the others.

"Oh yes," Kis'eh't said. "Goddess forfend we have your problems. Owning two planets, and having to come up with names for them!"

"I still can't believe you didn't give the planet a name," Sascha muttered.

"Things without names are forgotten," Reese said, thinking of history. "So maybe this was the right time. Before it was too late."

Liolesa met her eyes and her lips twitched into a crooked smile. "There is something to that."

"Begin as you mean to go on?" Reese offered.

Araelis startled them both by laughing. "You have taught your offworlder liegewoman well, Liolesa. She has learned all our precepts already."

"The ones that matter, anyways," Liolesa said with a chuckle. "Very good. I will take care of the matter before the year ends."

"Then we can get back to this," Kis'eh't said. "Because I'm curious if you have enough in that overstrained budget of yours for another merchant vessel or two, alet, or if you've gone and cultivated another handful of traders like us?"

"Woe is you," Araelis said to Liolesa. "All the responsibility."

"And all the bills," Liolesa agreed, long-suffering.

With so much to divert them, dawn wasn't long in coming. When Reese's data tablet chimed a muted warning fifteen minutes before sunrise, she glanced at it in surprise. If it hadn't been for the gritty feel in her eyes and the ache in her shoulders, she wouldn't have realized the night was over. "Looks like it's almost time?"

"Nothing like!" Liolesa said. "You must go to the window, Theresa, and wait for the entirety of the sun to rise over the horizon from your vantage."

"From mine!"

"You are the lady of the house," Araelis agreed. "To you falls the duty of informing everyone of the end of the Vigil. When you see the sun has safely risen, then you take the bell and ring it—either at the door if you are at the ground floor, or a window if you're in a room like this one. Then the other women with you take up the spares and join you."

Then she would finish the rite with the glass. And then she could sleep. Sleep suddenly sounded like a very good idea. "All right. I can make it that long. But Freedom, my bed is going to feel good when I get to it."

"Everyone will be sleeping in tomorrow," Hirianthial said.

"Day triumphant over the fears and terrors of the night," Liolesa murmured. "It will be safe to rest."

Reese glanced at her, then went to the window and moved the candle so she could sit on the sill and squint out the clear panes in their leaded glass frames. She was very glad Irine had chosen a third-floor room for this, or it would have taken a very long time for her to finally see the sun with the castle walls in the way. Wouldn't that have been ridiculous: everyone asleep with lunch almost ready for the tables and the bells not yet rung!

The room had a sleepy peace to it now. The twins were leaning against one another, eyes narrowed to golden slits. Kis'eh't had her hands folded over her forelegs, composed almost as if for meditation. Bryer, of course, hadn't moved or spoken much, though Reese had heard more of his hissed laughter than she'd had in years of their acquaintance. Allacazam... she'd left him kindly by the fire, because he liked firelight. Something about it made him tipsy, or at least, as close to tipsy as she thought Flitzbe could get.

The Eldritch were the most alert of the lot. They were waiting on the sun.

Well, so was she.

When it was finally time, she opened the windows, mindful of the

61

beautiful but antiquated catch. Kis'eh't had brought her the bell; peering past Reese's shoulder, the Glaseah said, "Looks good to me, too."

Reese nodded and ran her finger along the golden metal rim of the bell. Then she stuck her arm out the window and rang it, expecting a clang and hearing instead a bright chime, so pure it made her ears tingle and the hair on the back of her neck rise. As she rang it again, Irine took one of the spares and gave the other to Araelis. They opened the other two windows and added the pure clear tones of their bells, one higher, one lower.

And then, like magic, all across the courtyard other handbells answered. How many families had been sitting this vigil to make such an amazing chorus? The goosebumps that flashed up Reese's arms and sides had nothing to do with the cold and everything to do with the unlikely beauty of it: the voices of this perfectly tuned chorus, sounding across an iced-over courtyard grown through with sweet winter roses.

She was almost done. Setting the bell down on the floor by the window, Reese crossed to the fireplace, and the glass. This part of the rite was not codified: it was supposed to be her choice, the choice that revealed her to her people. There were no words, nothing she had to recite. Her only job, Val said, was to make sure an empty cup was displayed by the firebowl. Most ladies handed the glass they received from the men at Vigil, still full, to servants, and trusted them to empty it before setting it up on the pedestal. It was, however, permissible to drink it.

"But should you?" she'd asked him. "I thought this was some special men-only drink."

"It is," Val said. "If you drink it, it is transubstantiated, and becomes the blood of the sacrificed." He paused, then grinned. "But if you slam the whole glass back, that's considered bad form."

The Eldritch and their unspoken rules, she thought. Well, this was one she understood. Mars had begun with blood in the soil. Laisrathera had too: twice over, if you counted its first incarnation as the castle Corel had taken from the first Queen of the Eldritch, and how could she not when history shaped so much of any people?

Kis'eh't had been right: gentleman's punch packed one, a hard-liquor burn that made her eyes prickle and stung her nostrils and throat with the fumes. But it was spiced and complex, too, oranges and cardamom and cinnamon sweetness, with hints of other things she didn't recognize yet but knew one day she'd have names for. The wine that served as the base for it was dry and full and probably expensive, and yet nothing could be as priceless as what it represented. She closed her eyes, letting the liquid lie on her tongue, then swallowed. One sip, to show that she honored the sacrifice, but that she wasn't trying to appropriate the mysteries that belonged to men. The rest of it she poured in front of the dim glowing embers of the fire, watching it pool and sink into the ashes like blood.

Sascha nudged Irine gently. "Time to go, sis."

Irine yawned and straightened. "I'm ready."

"I think we all are," Reese said, and handed Allacazam to Irine to cart back to a safe place. She stopped Kis'eh't and handed her the glass. "Goes in front of the firebowl. Or leave it for Felith, she'll know what to do with it."

"All right." Kis'eh't hugged her. "A wonderful night. Good night, Reese."

"Good morning, more like!" Sascha said, much to Irine's evident dismay. One by one her crew trickled out of the room toward their beds.

Araelis curtseyed. "Theresa. Thank you for having me."

"Any time," Reese said. "I mean that."

Araelis smiled. "I shall take you up on it. We have similar works to do now; I have no doubt we will benefit from consulting one another on them." She inclined her head and then headed down the hall: a transformed woman, Reese thought with gratification. Not less sad, but no longer irresistibly drawn by the singularity of her grief. Another present, she thought: this evidence that there was hope, and a second chance, and a third and fourth and fortieth one. As long as they were alive, there was hope for a rebirth.

The hand Liolesa rested on her wrist surprised her out of her reverie. "A magnificent Vigil. I don't remember the last time I was so happily entertained."

Reese managed a huff of a laugh. "You are a holy terror, lady, between your presents and your comments." More seriously, "I'm glad I got to meet Hirianthial's cousin for a night."

"Goddess willing you shall see her more often." Liolesa smiled at her and let her hand slide away. "Speaking of... be well, cousin. I see you anon." She kissed Hirianthial's cheek. "Happy the day that finds you once again a Lord of the Vigil."

"Lord and Lady be praised," he murmured. "Go well, Lia, with our love."

...and that left her alone with him, when she was far too tired to do anything about it, that brittle tired that meant she was either going to fall

unconscious the moment she tripped onto her far-too-large Eldritch bed...
or be up all night staring blearily at the ceiling. Except that the moment
he cupped her face in her hands, all that fell away: the tension, the fatigue,
everything but a calm so perfect she wondered if this was his last gift
to her.

"I would not want you to pass the morning poorly," he murmured, his
mouth close enough that she could sense the cinnamon on his breath as a
tingle on her lips. Softer: "Theresa. You drank from the glass." And then
he kissed her.

She was keeping count of the kisses they'd shared so far. She...
couldn't remember the number, because she was tired. And because this
one was the best yet. The last one had been the best yet, until this one.
When he pulled back he was chuckling, a low, happy sound.

"Number... thirty...ish?"

He kissed her between the eyes. "Thirty-ish and one."

Reese's laugh was a little on the shivery side. But she said in response
to his earlier words, "I had to. You know I did."

"Yes. And it is one of the many reasons I love you." He smiled against
her brow. "My Courage. Go to bed now. And... Happy Dawning."

"You too," she murmured, and drifted to bed in a contented haze. Irine
had left Allacazam by her pillow, along with the promised box: a new
nightgown just like her old one (but not falling apart), and under it, a set
of surprisingly modest underwear in ivory satin, pretty without being
fussy. Reese petted one of the straps, hesitant, and wondered how she'd
fallen into so many blessings.

It was exactly the sort of thing she would ordinarily have 'discussed'
with Allacazam, but when she climbed into bed alongside him the only
thing he had to offer was a vague impression of bubbles floating past a
kaleidoscope of dim and slowly changing pastel colors. Her Flitzbe, she
thought, was drunk. Grinning, she fell asleep.

ACT 2
LADY'S DAY

CHAPTER 5

The Tam-illee, it turned out, hadn't celebrated a Vigil at all. They'd gone up to the ship to join Lesandurel in preparations for a Christmas ball: not a Hinichi Christmas either, but a bona fide human edition, with donkeys in the manger instead of wolves. Lesandurel had met the Tams' ancestress, Sydnie Unfound, the day before her office holiday party, and gone to that dance with her in silver to her gold. Ever since, the Tams had celebrated that meeting and the holiday together with a dance that had only grown in size with every passing generation, until now it was an enormous affair with hundreds of Tam-illee, most of them wearing something gold or silver to honor Sydnie or their Eldritch patron.

Reese would have liked to see it. Maybe next year she would wrangle an invitation. For now, though, she was mostly concerned with the final preparations for her trip to the village, and for that she wanted Felith as much as she wanted Taylor. Which gave her the opportunity to ask some questions which, naturally, led to awkward answers.

"Why were there so many bells ringing during the Vigil?"

Felith was with her, sorting through the crates of supplies sent down by the Fleet vessels. Exhausting work but gratifying, since she kept coming up with small and useful things that she'd had no idea were useful until she'd started setting up a modern city from scratch. Who knew that genies needed special adapters to be connected to low power gem grids? Reese did now!

"I beg your pardon, lady?" Felith said. "There were as many bells as there were groups of Eldritch waiting for their men."

"But I thought... that was just... you know. You. And me for Hirianthial...."

Felith glanced at her. "You do know we employ Eldritch servants here, milady?"

"Yes?" She did, more or less. She'd given Felith carte blanche to hire as she saw fit. "But I didn't think... they're not local, are they? I thought you got most of them from the capital. Wouldn't they have gone home for the Vigil?"

That won her a hesitation, and then a sigh. Felith found a crate and sat on it, hands grasping the edges for balance. As this was as informal a pose as she'd ever seen from the woman, Reese wondered just how worried she should be about whatever cultural faux pas she'd triggered this time.

"No, no. It is nothing bad, I pledge you. You are correct, in that I have chosen our staff from the capital. They have moved here, lady, that is why they didn't go home... this is now their home. But the situation weighs on me because I have since seen the census records that Sascha brought back at High Priest Valthial's request. And the remaining families in your village are descendants of this castle's servants."

"That's... bad, then," Reese guessed. "Because we didn't go down there to hire them, and I'm guessing that there's some Eldritch thing where you vow your family to your noble liege until the last person in it dies."

Felith's eyes widen. "Your instincts are very good, milady!"

Reese winced. "Right. So... we didn't do that because...."

"That was my fault, I am afraid," Felith said. "I know the servant pool in the capital. We talk amongst ourselves, you know. And it was much easier for me to know who would find employment for a foreigner agreeable, and who needed the work, so...."

"No harm done. Yet, anyway. I'm guessing we're not fully staffed?"

"Not yet. There is not enough to do yet," Felith said. "Or rather, there is too much to do, but little of it can be done by us."

"Well, that's something that's gotta change," Reese said, and opened a new crate to see what else Soly had sent her. "We can't all be engineers, but there's a basic level of competency in just... living a modern life that the engineers should be teaching all of you. We should probably be looking for Eldritch who'd be interested in professions in engineering and medicine and modern technology, too. Now, before Liolesa snatches them up."

"My lady! You would have us poach from the Queen!"

Reese looked over her shoulder and arched one skeptical brow, and Felith giggled.

"I suppose I should not be surprised."

"No," Reese said. "Besides, Liolesa's got plenty of people. She can share. So tell me about these Eldritch down in the village?"

"That is the astonishing thing," Felith said. "They comprise all four of the necessary types of service. The families that remain were those that gave the castle their seal, manse, land, and beast servants."

"Trust you all to complicate things. I figure the beast servants took care of the horses, and the land servants did... groundskeeping?"

"And patrolled the province, and noted the state of the roads, suchlike. The beast servants also cared for any other creatures."

"So, chickens, I guess. Or sheep. We have sheep."

"We do, and they are dearly in need of management," Felith said, stern. "They have become a nuisance with their wandering."

"We'll get someone to pen them," Reese promised. "What's the difference between manse and seal servants?"

"Manse servants maintain the physical building and the other servants," Felith said. "So you would find both your cook and your cleaning maids there, as well as repairfolk. Seal servants take care of the noble family. That is both guard duty and chamber duty, dressing, keeping appointment books, so on."

"And who manages this army of servants?"

"The chatelaine," Felith said. "She reports to the lady and manages the staff, the stores, and makes sure anything the lady wishes done is done, from planning for large events to hiring for expansion of the grounds."

"Oh, good! So that's you."

"I beg your pardon!" Felith exclaimed.

"You've resisted my every effort to turn you into one of Laisrathera's nobles," Reese said, satisfied at the stare she'd shocked out of Felith. "Since, if I'm remembering right, you didn't want to be far from the castle and accepting something like that would require you to go ride out to some village and take charge there. But you're far too good at managing things to be wasted in a position with less responsibility. And you're already doing all this for me, so... that makes you it, doesn't it?"

"But... but this is a position you should not bestow without careful consideration!"

"I've considered it the only way it should be," Reese said. "By saddling you with most of the job and seeing that you can handle it. So are you going to keep arguing or let me give you a ring of keys?"

"A... a what?" Felith said, starting to laugh.

"I read romances," Reese said loftily. "I know what a chatelaine is. And she's inevitably got a ring of keys on her belt." She frowned, making a show of tapping her lip. "Of course, around here there aren't going to be many doors that latch with physical keys, so I guess I'll have to get someone to synthesize you a data wand. Those are antiquated compared to reading biometric fields, but God and Freedom know when we're going to get those installed. The Tam-illee tell me the power plant isn't ready for anything that strenuous."

"Lady! You are... you are outrageous!" Felith wiped her eyes and suppressed—poorly—another gurgle of mirth.

"So are you done arguing with me? I know you feel obliged to pretend you're not worthy of the honor, but maybe we can consider that done already and move on to the 'thank you, Reese, I'd be glad to be Rose Point's chatelaine and keep you from making any more ridiculous cultural faux pas for the rest of your natural life' part?"

Felith collapsed into another giggle and pressed her fingers to her mouth until she could control herself. Then, meekly, eyes dancing, she said, "Thank you, lady, I'd be glad to be Rose Point's chatelaine."

"What about the rest of it?" Reese said. "That part's important!"

"I can only commit to preventing you from making the problematic faux pas, I'm afraid. The ones I think necessary I may let you commit, the better to... rearrange... any problematic customs that might benefit from a fresh approach."

"See?" Reese said. "You're already showing the discretion and wisdom necessary for the position. Now, here, this is the thing Taylor said the heaters would need! Let's find at least four more."

———

Restraining the Tam-illee turned out to be more work than the actual preparation for the trip, because apparently Val had told Sascha which of the houses were abandoned and he'd snuck Taylor into one of them so she'd have a feel for the project facing them. Taylor had come back with a fire burning in her eyes: she wanted to rip all the houses down and start from scratch because it was "disgraceful" that anyone should be forced to live that way, and it was unsafe and unsanitary and a million other pejoratives that would have made an engineer take up arms and go to war.

It became Reese's job to explain, as someone who'd been poor most of her life, that you couldn't just go in and rebuild someone's house and have them thank you for it. That in fact, you couldn't go in and make *any* substantial changes without their permission, or they would resent you until their dying breath for not only taking away one of the few things they had—control over their environment—but also humiliating them by showing them how backwards they were. This was not an argument that found much favor with Taylor. "Fine, they're emotional about it. But aren't they also emotional about their babies dying of pneumonia because it's too cold in the house? I'd think that would matter more than whether their house looks exactly the same as it has for generations."

Reese had finally recruited Irine's help and used the ultimate Harat-Shariin argument against the plan, which by then had mutated into the nuclear "swooping in and re-homing all the inhabitants of the village" option; confronted with the tigraine's reminder—that consent had to matter, or how were they better than any two-bit despot?—Taylor gave in. But only because Reese promised her that given some time, she was sure they could bring the villagers around, and her army of Tam-illee would end up with permission to renovate the place to their heart's content.

"I hope I'm right about that," Reese said glumly to Irine. "Knowing how stubborn Eldritch are, it's just as likely they'll decide never to speak to us again."

"On the bright side, if they do, they'll probably move out in search of some purer Eldritch noble family to serve," Irine said. "Then you really can flatten the entire place and redo it from scratch."

Reese rubbed her head. Initially, she'd greeted the revelation of Lady's Day's existence with enthusiasm, as a way to give useful things to people who needed them. It was only after thinking it through that she'd realized how fraught the whole thing was: not only did these Eldritch not know her, but they hadn't been consulted on whether they wanted their hereditary jobs back at the castle, and now there was the challenge of figuring how to give them what they needed without offending their pride or dignity, both of which the Eldritch had. In spades.

This would be her first real piece of diplomacy as Firilith's new noble keeper... and she would have to do it through a translator. It was probably going to be a disaster. But, looking around her study, Reese thought that her disasters had found ways of working themselves out, so maybe this one would too. Mistakes could be fixed. Nothing, though, came from not making an effort.

CHAPTER 6

L ady's Day dawned cold, and it was a wet cold that crawled all the way down her throat into her lungs. It was at least sunny, Reese thought as the horses were coaxed onto the back of the ground transport. As blessings went, that had to be a major one, because she couldn't imagine making her first appearance in town in a cold rain, snowstorm, or even under a sky cloudy enough to make any superstitious tenants decide she was some sort of demon. Blood, *she'd* be superstitious at that point.

"This is a lot of trouble," Kis'eh't said, arms folded. She was overseeing the assembly of the cavalcade in the Rose Point courtyard with a jaundiced eye. "Don't the Eldritch say you should start things the way you mean them to continue? You are starting this with a lie."

"It is not a lie!" Irine exclaimed as she joined them. "It's a story!"

"It's not a lie or a story," Reese said. "It's the truth, which is that under Laisrathera's management, we're going to have a hybrid of Alliance and Eldritch ways. I'm going to ride a horse into the village, because that's what you do. And because horses are kind of pretty, once you get over their bad points. But I'm going to get the horses most of the way there on a flatbed because it's faster, and easier on them, and because we've got baggage in tow."

Studying the gifts already stowed on the truck, Kis'eh't said, "Taylor's not happy."

"Taylor wants to remake the world in a Tam-illee engineer's image," Reese said. "If I was an Eldritch living here, I'd take up arms to keep her off my property. The Eldritch are right about one thing, arii: we have to start things off on the right foot, or we'll have to clear the wreckage before we get started on the real work."

"Hey, Boss!" Sascha yelled from the flatbed's door. "We're about ready to go!"

Reese sucked in a breath and opened her arms. "How do I look?"

Irine adjusted the fillet and brushed off the shoulders of the new coat. "You look wonderful."

"And warm!" Kis'eh't said. "I will watch over Allacazam for you. I promise, no rolling into trouble."

"Or the firebowl, or the glass..."

"Or any of those things." Kis'eh't grinned. "Go. You too, fluffy."

Irine grinned and hugged her, then bounded off to join her brother.

"You'll do well," Kis'eh't said to Reese.

"God, I hope so."

The flatbed cab was more than large enough for their entire party: Hirianthial, of course, as future consort of the noble House, and Felith to translate, and the twins because they'd insisted, and, oddly, Bryer, who'd said, "I am so strange-looking, you will look normal."

...which was... hard to argue, really. The priests had stayed behind, and Reese guessed that made sense: you couldn't have male priests hanging around on a day devoted to the Goddess and Lady, particularly since they had a female priest waiting for them in the village to officiate at the ceremony. Reese looked at the paper in her lap and recited the responses for the ceremony until Irine plucked it out of her hands.

"It's like a test," Irine said. "If you study too hard, you'll forget everything."

"I'm already forgetting everything!"

"That's why you have me and Felith to remind you with well-timed whispers." Irine looped an arm around her shoulders and squeezed. "Stop worrying so much. It'll go fine."

"And if it doesn't?" Reese asked.

"Then it goes badly, they all leave in an offended huff, and we repopulate Firilith with Tam-illee."

"And Harat-Shar," Sascha said absently from the driver's seat.

The idea of being trapped between the Tam-illee's zeal to renovate and

74

the Harat-Shar's passion for partying made Reese dizzy. "Blood. Let's hope *everything* goes *perfect*."

———

Sascha stopped the flatbed a credible distance from town so Reese could climb up on her horse—with help this time, because while she could get into a saddle in pants, doing so while managing a coat was beyond her—and ride the final stretch the way a lady was supposed to, with an entourage carrying all her offerings. She didn't let herself linger on Taylor's opinion of literally carting those gifts into the town square; personally, she thought there was something satisfying about bringing the modernization of the Eldritch world on its own old-fashioned conveyances.

And she liked the town. A lot. Not because she recognized the architecture or felt any affinity for the countryside, but because the dilapidation spoke to roots deeper than any of those things. She'd come from a place that had sagged at the corners, and she remembered the pride she and her fellow Martians had taken in the fact that they'd clung to their settlement despite its challenges. These Eldritch, too, had persevered in the face of increasing hardships. They'd been abandoned, whittled to the bone, and left to fend for themselves, and they'd stayed alive and kept their church bells tuned... something she could hear for herself after the youngest member of the community spotted her and dashed back to warn everyone they were coming.

Reese squared her shoulders and exhaled a plume of white breath into the moist, cold air. "This is it," she muttered.

"You faced down pirates, slavers, and traitors," Hirianthial reminded her, his voice a low murmur.

"Fleet took care of the slavers, you killed the pirates, and they were someone else's traitors," Reese said, but her mouth was quirking.

"Ah, I see. You were just bystanding. War tourism. Very fashionable."

Reese sat on her burble of mirth and settled for glaring at him. As expected, he was wearing a bland expression, fit for a haloed saint, so she ended up snickering after all.

"Much better!" Irine said from behind them.

"Hush, fluffy."

"Yes, ma'am!"

75

But if she worried that she'd be unable to shake off an unbecoming levity before she reached the square, she soon threw that concern off. As they gained the main thoroughfare and their party passed through the crumbled remains of what had once been proud houses, her thoughts turned again to the Sol system, and the spaceports there that had seen better days, or that were falling prey to entropy for lack of time, money, manpower. Reese loved the Pelted... loved them in the abstract, as the family that had adopted her when her own had failed to nurture the dreams she'd needed to thrive, and in specific, in the individuals she'd embraced on the *Earthrise*. But the longer she stayed on the Eldritch's nameless world, the more she felt these people were blood kin, estranged but familiar.

The Pelted wanted her, but didn't need her. The Eldritch, though... they needed her, and didn't want her. And she knew how that felt in her bones.

The center of town was the only part of it that showed upkeep, and Reese could only imagine how much trouble it had cost. She'd been imagining a literal square when Felith explained the ceremony to her, like an enormous plaza faced with buildings. Instead, the small church opened onto a stone circle, and from it spread a village green complete with small pond and what had probably once been charming shops and public halls. They were abandoned hulks now, painstakingly maintained but hollow where they should have been filled with laughter and light. Only three buildings were obviously tenanted, festooned with garlands for the holiday, but surrounded by so many derelicts they looked vulnerable and lonely. Reese cast her eye around the village as she guided her mare toward the small crowd awaiting her by the church. Fully inhabited this place had probably not seen more than five hundred residents, but that was a far cry from the twenty-eight that remained.

But twenty-eight did remain, and they had turned out in what was probably their finest, the women in embroidered woolen gowns—those sheep!—and the men in tunics edged in ribbon. Even men regarded as little more than peasants by Eldritch standards still wove trinkets into their hair, Reese noticed, though they kept their hair much shorter than the Eldritch she'd seen at Liolesa's court. The one teenager who served as the village's youngest child was already old enough to be dressed in a man's raiment, and while Reese had never thought of herself as a maternal woman, the lack of any children or babies felt ominous and sad to her. It felt like endings.

Well. She was here to change that.

The priestess was standing in the forefront of this gathering. Reese supposed she was old, but until they were almost senescent all the Eldritch were uniformly tall, elegant, thin, and ageless. It would be easy to resent them if she didn't know they were washing with cold water in unheated homes that didn't have real bathrooms.

As Reese halted her horse, this dignitary stepped forth, her rose and white robes swaying around her. Touching her fingers together, she curtseyed and said something in a clear, carrying soprano.

"She is welcoming you," Felith murmured. "And asking the Lady's blessings on this day, dawning so favorably after the ending of the men's Vigil night. She is adding something now about how particularly fortunate this year finds them, because it has finally brought a new lady to Rose Point to oversee long-neglected Firilith."

"Did she actually say 'long-neglected'?" Reese whispered, surprised.

Felith wrinkled her nose. "It is a nuance, lady. But... yes. More or less."

Reese studied her new priestess, wary but intrigued. There was no rule that said a priestess couldn't look a noblewoman in the face so boldly, but somehow Reese doubted most priestesses did. Was it the fact that Reese wasn't Eldritch that was inspiring the defiant look? Or was it too long spent ministering to a flock no one had cared enough to help in centuries? If Reese had been abandoned that long, wouldn't she have an attitude too?

Silly question.

"Her name is Ijiliin, Lady."

Of course it was. Because nothing rolled off the tongue like four identical vowels, all separately voiced.

Reese scanned her newest tenants. They were staring at her with those supernal Eldritch masks, the ones they retreated behind because showing excessive emotion was vulgar. They'd been assigned a new lady without warning, and she was an outworld freak, small and dark and strange, a mortal who couldn't even speak their language. After clinging to the remains of their dignity and their lives in this town, to suffer this newest injury: to be forced to give themselves into the hands of a stranger.... oh yes. She had no doubt they were hiding any number of unruly emotions behind those expressionless faces.

"Tell her that we are ready to observe the mass," Reese said, because that was the next step... and she was glad, because she needed to think.

The inside of the church reminded Reese of Rose Point's chapel, with a low ceiling but walls of stained glass windows depicting scenes Reese didn't need a scripture to interpret: beautiful men spearing monsters, beautiful women bathing their wounds, elegant mothers with their new babies, stern fathers with adolescent sons wielding their first weapons. The back of the church, though, had the most stunning window of all, a man bent over the body of a woman bleeding among a profusion of roses, all ruby and frosted glass. Reese glanced at Hirianthial, who managed a faint smile at this monument to the story of Corel. She managed not to scowl. She would have thought the extremely matriarchal Eldritch wouldn't be interested in enshrining a woman's wilting sacrifice to save a man's soul, but she guessed if their love for common sense had outweighed their worship of tragedy and high drama, they wouldn't have reached this impasse in the first place.

Reese settled on the pillow assigned to her, to the right of the altar and in front of the congregation, and prepared to wait out the ceremony without her translator, who'd been relegated to the audience with everyone else. Her participation in the rite was thankfully minimal, and involved her joining the congregation in response to five different exhortations from the priestess. Despite Irine's warning she did not, in fact, forget the phrases. She did find herself wondering when, if ever, she'd be able to understand the language. She wasn't one of those people who took to languages, and supposedly the Eldritch tongue had been designed to be twisty and hard to learn. On purpose. Naturally. There was no translator function for it in the Alliance u-banks, nor would there be unless something changed, because one of the treaty stipulations involved a fleet of patrolling codebits that swept the entire Alliance computer network for anything relating to the Eldritch so that it could be deleted. Instantly and permanently.

There were times Reese wondered how the Eldritch had survived their own paranoia. Those times comprised 'most of the time' now that she was here.

Her new tenants were carefully not staring at her. She returned the favor, and focused instead very intently on her folded hands, so dark a brown in her lap against the apricot velvet of her coat... too dark for an Eldritch lady's, but with a ring far too expensive for a Martian trader's. She couldn't help sympathizing with the unease of the residents given the perils of reconciling all the contradictions of the woman who now held power over them.

That was the mood that wrapped her like a second cloak when she followed Ijiliin out onto the stone platform outside the church. The residents gathered around it on the green, several steps below her, leaving

only the priestess to share the dais with Reese and all her unlikely atten-
dants: Irine and Sascha, Bryer and Taylor, and only two, very confusing
Eldritch at her side, because Hirianthial was dressed like a lord but coiffed
like a boy, and Felith was wearing very fine clothes, but they were obviously a chatelaine's, not a noble's.

The priestess was speaking now. Behind and to one side of Reese,
Felith whispered, "She is opening the part of the ceremony where the
Lady's bounty is shared with Her people... that's your introduction."

"Right," Reese said. This was it. There was no script from here out. She
remembered being puzzled about that... the Eldritch loved their formal
rituals so, and while this one seemed the perfect opportunity to do something spontaneous and warm, something that connected a liegelady with
her people, she couldn't imagine the Eldritch going for anything that
intimate.

She, though, was no Eldritch. "Good afternoon, everyone. My name is
Theresa Eddings Laisrathera, and I am honored to be your new—" Over-
lord? Landlord? Boss? "—lady." She paused to let Felith catch up with her.
"I've come bearing the gifts of the goddess, and I think they're long
overdue in Firilith."

She paused after the translation to see if she'd overstepped by stating
the obvious and tried not to clench her fists when one of the women on
the green lifted her chin. This was it—this was the moment they chal-
lenged her right to be here.

"We do understand Universal. Lady."

How had that managed to be both a welcome and an insult at the
same time? Only the Eldritch. And these Eldritch in particular, who must
resent the hell out of the fact that they had to accept her, and were probably attempting to prove they didn't need any charity. From anyone. What
was the safe response to a gambit that blatant? Bland cordiality? She'd
never been any good at diplomacy. But then again, when had diplomacy
ever worked with Hirianthial?

She did what she did best with Eldritch and bulled ahead. "I should
have guessed you learned it two or three centuries before I was born."

"Something like that," her speaker said.

"That makes my job easier, then." Reese started to fold her arms
before she remembered that guarding her chest was probably not the best
way to suggest her intentions weren't adversarial. "The Queen gave me the
deed to Rose Point and the surrounding lands and charged me with the
maintenance and improvement of the grounds and the lives of the people

living on it. As you've no doubt noted, I am not Eldritch." Was that a flicker of a smile on the teenage boy's face? Maybe she had one ally, then. "Most of my family isn't either. With the notable exception of my betrothed."

That finally got her the incredulity she'd been expecting from the start. Almost as one all twenty-odd of them stared at Hirianthial.

"Yes, him," Reese said. "That's Hirianthial Sarel Jisiensire. The Jisiensire sealbearer."

"The soon to be former Jisiensire sealbearer," Hirianthial said, modestly.

"But the current and future Eldritch Lord of War," Reese finished, because she didn't mind hanging on his coattails if it made it easier for these people to accept her. "So I imagine the Queen's going to keep him very busy. That leaves me to the management of Firilith, and that includes this town... and all of you." She paused, then added, quieter, "I hope you'll stay. I know you were part of Rose Point's life once, or your parents and grandparents were, and it would be a shame to lose that continuity. I might be a mortal by your standards, but I believe in the importance of history."

This silence wasn't encouraging. It wasn't precisely discouraging either, but she'd hoped for a little more animation from them by now.

"So, in that spirit," Reese continued, gamely, "I have brought the Lady's bounty." She cleared her throat. "First, to the priestess of the Goddess and Lady, who with her leadership has seen this town through its long darkness." Taylor handed her a small clear hemisphere and she offered it to Ijiliin, who hesitated before plucking it off her bare palms. "A light," Reese explained. "If you tap it..."

The priestess did and her eyes widened as it glowed.

"Because the Lady brings the morning after the Longest Night, and you are Her representative here."

Ijiliin eyed her with just the faintest hint of speculation. Reese figured that was better than outright rejection and took the next gift from Taylor. "To the matriarch whose family once tended the manse." She waited for this woman to step up and offered a box. "You were charged with the comfort and safety of those who dwelt beneath the lady's aegis. I give you back that charge again. This box has ten space heaters in them. When you turn them on, they warm the room. Please give them to those who need the heat most, and if you find you don't have enough, return to me with your requirements."

Reese had hoped this woman would ask her how they worked, but she only received the box and stepped back into the crowd.

"To the eldest male whose line once tended Firilith's land, I have this gift." She waited for the man to come to her, then presented him with a pair of binoculars. He turned them in his hands, obviously familiar with the concept... but she thought if he used them, and he obviously was having trouble not interrupting the ceremony to try them, he'd be pleasantly surprised. It wasn't as good as a heads-up display, but it wasn't far off. "Once the stewardship of land is in your blood, it never leaves. I hope these will help you to extend the limits of that stewardship."

"Thank you, lady," he said. Surprising everyone, including his relatives, whose narrowed eyes indicated disapproval.

Reese ignored them and said, "I address now the eldest female of those who once served the seal... and the youngest male."

This summoned the woman who'd corrected her about Universal... and in keeping with her seeming personality, she started moving before Reese finished the sentence, and the additional request caused her to twitch. Fortunately, she didn't stop outright, and the two of them joined her in front of the dais, the woman radiating her agitation and the boy, wary curiosity.

The light explained itself, the binoculars didn't require instruction, and the heaters were simple instruments—if the Eldritch could read Universal as well as speak it, operating them would be self-explanatory. This, though, was the biggest gamble of all her chosen gifts, and she'd vacillated for several days before deciding to run with it. Naturally, it ended up going to the mouthy one, which only heightened Reese's nervousness. So she offered the data tablet with the bravado that had once been her habitual response to fear. "The seal's servants knew a great deal about their lords and ladies, their needs, their schedules, the lives they lived. This is the proper tool for such servants... or will be now, at Rose Point."

The woman accepted it with a frown, and watching her examine it Reese remembered the argument she'd had with Taylor and Felith. The data tablet wasn't difficult to use, but it required curiosity and a willingness to engage with technology. Felith had suggested it would be useless without guidance; Reese had felt that forcing an Eldritch to accept a 'mortal' teacher would be humiliating and that leaving them to figure it out on their own was more likely to lead to acceptance. Taylor had thought it a waste of a data tablet, predicting the Eldritch wouldn't bother with it at all.

81

Staring at the woman would definitely provoke a response. Rather than gamble on it being a good one, Reese turned to the teenager, who was looking at her with a lot less wariness and more interest. She suppressed the urge to exhale with relief: here, at least, was someone who wasn't poised to reject her on principle.

"Your gift and the beastmaster's are kin," Reese said. "So I would have the eldest male of that line stand with you."

That caused an older male to join the youth, both of them considering her with far more engaged expressions than she'd gotten from any of the women. Was it because Eldritch men were more used to bowing to a woman's power that they were less combative when confronted with her? Maybe they felt they didn't have anything to prove. Who knew? She was just grateful to be down to the last two personal gifts, which Taylor delivered to her hands. She offered them on her open palms, one for each.

"I couldn't get the actual animals here in time," Reese said to them apologetically as the older man lifted the collar. "But some of them should arrive by the New Year's Feast. I've been told that long ago, when the world was new, men were once companioned by their hounds...."

The older male inhaled sharply, lifting his eyes to hers.

"...but that almost no dogs survived the first few centuries of your Settlement, because of how bad the basilisks were. So, to you," she addressed the older man, "I give the keeping of our new line of sheep-herding dogs, because Goddess and Freedom know if we don't get the sheep in line I'm going to murder them all."

He suppressed a huff she suspected might have been a chuckle from the sudden twinkle in his eye.

"They're sending five breeding pairs," Reese continued. "I hope that's enough, but if it's not, you tell me and I'll get enough more that we don't have to worry about the babies."

"Puppies," Irine muttered.

"Puppies," Reese corrected herself. "And if that works out, maybe we can talk about a third kind of dog, because you..." She turned to the youth. "Are getting the second kind: our first two Hinichi Guardkin. I did the research, and they breed the best dogs for defense in the entire Alliance. They're smart and fast and big and once they accept you as pack they'll die to save you. I figure that's what you've lost. And that's what you need back, because the seal servants also defend the family."

"Oh!" the youth exclaimed, his breathing quickened. "You cannot mean it!"

"I do. And you'll need the senior beastmaster there to help you with training them, I imagine. And eventually, hopefully, breeding them. I'm guessing the land servants will want them too..." She glanced at the man with the binoculars, who was stunned enough to show it.

"He'll want them," the beast servant agreed. More cautiously, "Real dogs."

"The best dogs I could find." Reese smiled crookedly. "Maybe eventually we can sell some of the puppies to other Eldritch Houses because each one of them is costing me a small mint. Especially the Hinichi ones. The Hinichi don't sell those, they require you to pay adoption prices for them. People adoption prices."

The beastmaster looked at the collar in his hands. His voice was low as he said, "The Lady's bounty is great."

"It's there to be shared." Reese stepped aside and gestured to the hand-cart beside Taylor, which she'd had loaded with fresh produce. "Here is an advance on the New Year's feast, which I offer as a promise that Firilith will once again observe the festivals, honor the God and Goddess in both Their forms, and enrich its people."

The priestess said, "We accept the gifts as evidence of the Goddess's blessings."

She said it in Universal too. Reese wasn't sure if that meant she was getting somewhere or if they were rubbing it in. But after that, the ceremony closed without fanfare. Felith had told her that in some settlements the lady remained to speak with the residents, bless their children, even mediate disputes, but Reese had no doubt that the people here wanted to see the back of her. Which was fine: staying would only solidify their antagonism. She'd ruffled their feathers by existing, by not being Eldritch, and by giving them the holiday gifts they'd foregone for so long they'd forgotten how to accept them gracefully. The winning strategy here was to leave them with the puzzles of her particular presents, and what she'd implied with them.

Taylor had groused about it. Felith had hesitantly predicted failure. Only the twins, of the people she'd consulted, had wisely held their peace. They'd understood, she thought. She wasn't trying to show these people that they needed her. She was trying to show them that she needed *them*, and that she trusted them to make decisions for themselves, and for her, and for the good of Firilith as their families had once done. In the end, all the glittering technology that made the Alliance so wonderful... it was just a tool. None of it mattered without a person to wield it, and an Eldritch could do that just as well as one of the Pelted. She had to demonstrate to her Eldritch residents they could be partners in the future they were going to share with the Alliance, or they would go into it the way Earth had, struggling beneath the burden of inadequacy and shame. A beginning like that could be overcome, but why invite extra suffering if a little mindfulness could prevent it?

So she'd chosen her presents as invitations to autonomy and paths back to gainful employment, knowing that rejection would hurt them all far more than if she'd given them simpler gifts. But if there was a thornier way to do things, Reese inevitably found herself stumbling down that path rather than the easier one, and maybe that had made her tougher— she could hope anyway! Leading her party out of the village, Reese had no idea how the situation with her tenants was going to turn out, only that she couldn't have done anything differently.

She hadn't had the courage to ask Hirianthial for advice... or maybe she hadn't wanted it. Maybe she'd wanted to make the mistakes herself, find her own path, see if it worked. As they rode past the village's boundaries, she did glance at him, though.

"What do you think?"

He shook his head just a touch, the shorn hair swinging against his jaw. "I think you have a knack for this, Theresa."

"A knack," she repeated, finding the colloquialism endearing, spoken in that cultured accent.

"But will it work?" Felith asked, hesitant.

"It had better work," Taylor said. "Because there aren't that many people left back there, and there'll be none left soon if they don't change."

Reese shared a pained look with Hirianthial, whose expression grew grave.

"Well," she said, fixing her gaze forward, "here's hoping."

ACT 3
NEW YEAR'S DAY

CHAPTER 7

Preparing for the New Year's Feast wasn't as straightforward as Reese had hoped. Her plan had been to 'serve food' until a call with Liolesa had explained exactly how food happened on the Eldritch homeworld: which was to say, it didn't, not really. With the exception of Nuera's small holdings in the Galare lands, none of the Eldritch provinces could feed themselves off their own fields. The Queen imported everything everyone ate, and distribution of those stores hadn't taken into account a new holding full of visiting aliens. Liolesa had been planning to increase her purchases in the new year to compensate for Firilith, but obviously they'd all been a little distracted and that hadn't happened yet.

Which wasn't a problem, because the woman seemed to have more money than God—one day Reese would have to ask how she managed that little miracle—but it made planning the feast a logistical challenge. The *Earthrise* wasn't crewed yet, and the orbiting Fleet ships couldn't leave since their job was guarding the planet. The only ships available were Lesandurel's, and they'd been pressed into service building the new orbital and lunar stations and bulking up the heliopause defenses. The Tams had one ship standing by for the Queen's use, and it was already in the Alliance running her errands—and Reese's. And the one week they had wasn't all that long from the point of view of moving interstellar cargo.

The alternative was stealing power plant time from all the many

87

projects that needed it to use the genie to create food. That had sounded easier than hoping that single Tam ship could run to the Alliance and back in time until Taylor had presented Reese with the power plant's list of dependencies and asked her which she wanted to delay. She'd wanted to complain that synthesizing food couldn't possibly take this much time, but it wasn't about time. It was about the size of the generator and the amount of power it could produce. Genies were notoriously energy-intensive, which is why everything wasn't created with one; Reese had known that vaguely because she'd never had the energy budget to have on installed on the *Earthrise*. But it shocked her to learn just how much power you could waste genie-creating a turkey. She understood suddenly why people bothered to raise animals and crops for food. Nor was the borrowed Fleet battlecruiser much help; Soly had offered its genies for their use, but it turned out a warship's power plant was even more constrained than the kind of generator you could build on a planet, even the tiny one Taylor had cobbled together to get them going.

In the end they decided on a painful compromise: they'd withdraw some of the food they needed from the Bank of Liolesa, signal the Tam ship to bring food along with everything else and please arrive *before* the holiday ended, and they'd synthesize a small amount of raw materials that Felith and Kis'eh't could use for a variety of dishes: butter and almond flour, sacks of salt and sugar, and so many very, very expensive eggs that Reese immediately put chickens on the to-buy list. Only to be told by Liolesa that chickens didn't thrive on the local insects, so if she wanted chickens she'd have to build greenhouses that could support an artificial ecosystem.

Reese put that on the list after everything else, and then whacked her forehead with her data tablet.

She hardly had time to wonder how her residents were doing, managing all this. But two days after Lady's Day, Irine poked her head in Reese's office and said, "Those Eldritch are here."

"What Eldritch?" Reese asked, massaging her temple.

"The teenager, and the man you gave the dogs to?"

"What?" Reese sat up straight. "Here? Like, in the castle?"

"In the courtyard, anyway. They're asking for—" Irine stopped as Reese jogged past her. "You. Right! Off we go!"

The two males really were in the courtyard, and in defiance of the usual Eldritch reserve they were staring at the activity going on around them. In their defense, it was worth staring at: the chapel had already been repaired, or as repaired as Reese wanted it anyway, but the new chapterhouse to teach the mind gifts was going up along with Hirianthial's hospital; the Tam-illee had repaired the fallen castle tower only to start tearing it all apart again to install the gem grid and modern amenities that the rest of Rose Point also still needed. Bryer had made significant headway on the overgrowth of the garden, but there were still more winter roses in places than there was clear ground. Plus, the bleeding sheep, getting into everything and then vanishing again....

"Hi!" Reese said. Which... wasn't very ladylike of her, but she was in her beat-up old *Earthrise* uniform of vest and pants, to which she'd added a short jacket to combat the cold, and she didn't really look the part anyway. "I didn't expect you, but welcome!"

"Lady," the elder of the two said. "We've not been formally introduced. I am Shoran, and this is Talthien. You said the dogs would be coming, but you didn't know when?"

"The Guardkin should be here soon," Reese said. "I'm hoping before New Year's." On the same Tam ship that was bringing them the food, she hoped.

"But not here yet," Shoran said, with one of those abbreviated nods you could miss if you weren't watching for it. "Thank you, lady. Come, Talthien."

And then they turned to go. Shocked, Reese said, "Did you walk all the way up here just to ask?" Which... wasn't the most tactful thing to say. But it was over ten miles. How fast could people walk? How many hours had they been on the road? Just to get here, ask a question, and leave? And now they had to walk all the way back... "On your feet??"

The two glanced at one another. The older man looked discomfited, but the younger one flashed her a grin, as if he expected her to come up with some new and dazzling surprise. "Yes?"

"No, wait, stay here. Irine! Ir—oh, blood, don't stand right behind me like that!"

"It's not my fault you don't pay attention to anything when you're anxious," Irine said, pressing on the ear closest to Reese's exclamation. "What?"

"Wait here," she told the Eldritch. Then, thinking better of it, "No, come with me."

Shoran glanced at the teen again, then said, "Of course, lady."

Reese led them to the stables, determined. The horses had been some of the first things to arrive for reasons relating entirely to the Eldritch mania for them. She hadn't been planning on hosting actual animals until she'd gotten the *Earthrise* set up with her new crew, but Liolesa had made separate arrangements with Kerayle and Laisrathera's first horses had arrived with that shipment. She thought they were nice animals—a little intimidating at first, but you got used to them—but she hadn't realized what they'd mean to the males she led into the stables until she heard the gasp behind her.

"My lady," Shoran breathed. "These are yours?"

"*All of them?*" the youth added.

"God and Freedom help me, yes. Only the first of the bunch even. The Queen wants me to breed them for her, so I'm going to end up with even more of them. An entire herd of them." She trailed off and eyed them both, the elder in particular. Being a trader had taught her to recognize avarice on even the most schooled of faces. Shoran wasn't hiding his that hard. "We're supposed to have multiple types? I don't know the first thing about breeding horses."

"I guess that's a servant to beasts thing," Irine added, staring up at the ceiling with her hands folded in front of her hips.

"They're magnificent," Talthien said, hushed. "The one you rode, lady... we'd never seen anything like it. To see so many others just as beautiful!"

"How about this one?" Reese said, stopping in front of one of the spares. She and Hirianthial had horses of their own—that's what happened when you lost bets—but they'd gotten a handful of others to start their herd and no one was attached to any of them yet.

"To breed?" Shoran asked, coming to stand alongside her.

"For you," Reese said. "Or... if there's one you like more? Just not the two in the front two stalls. Those are mine and Hirianthial's."

At last she shocked a real expression out of the man. He was gaping at her. "My lady! No, you cannot mean it! I... own a horse... I haven't..."

"Ever?" she asked, concerned. Maybe she'd gotten this wrong?

"Owned a horse?" he said, stunned. "Such an expensive... no! Never! No servant would! Care for them, yes. I did that long ago. But our last horse died over a century ago. And even then it wasn't mine."

"Whose was it?" Irine asked. "Wasn't Corel dead by then? And all the nobles who lived here?"

"Yes," Shoran said. "But servants don't own anything. Everything belongs to the sealbearers. Even if the sealbearers are dead."

"Well that's—" Irine stopped short, which was good because Reese suspected the next word was going to be 'stupid'. Instead the Harat-Shar said, "That's not how we do things here. And when Reese gives you something, you can keep it."

"Which I am," Reese told him, starting to find the conversation amusing. Mostly because the teenager was beaming. "But only one of them. You need one; how else are you going to get here every day, if you're going to insist on coming to ask about the dogs?"

"But—"

"Shoran-alet," Reese said firmly. "I don't have the first idea what to do with these things. Right now the Tam-illee are checking on them, because some of them learned horsery on some farm Lesandurel keeps for himself on Earth. But they can't do it forever. I need them for other things. You, on the other hand, know about horses. Maybe you can come fix this problem for me?"

"And the breeding part," Irine added. "I've started researching that —"

"You have?" Reese interrupted, bemused.

"I like babies!" Irine folded her arms. "Anyway. I've started, but I could use someone with experience to advise me." Her ears sagged. "Ah... a lot of experience. I like figuring out breeding stuff, but I know more about people than animals."

This made the youth stare at her, which Reese supposed was a reasonable reaction from someone who probably thought Irine looked more than half-animal herself.

Shoran cleared his throat. "I could not begin to choose one of these for myself—"

"Without riding them!" Talthien crowed. When his elder glared at him, the youth said to Reese with a grin, "Can we ride a different one to and from the castle every day? By the end of the week we'll know."

"*We'll* know, is it?" Shoran said, with narrowed eyes and one lifted brow.

"Please, lady?"

Reese laughed. "Sure. Try before you buy and all that. Except you're not buying this horse. You're accepting it as part of your wages for working here, because you can't work here without commuting, and a seven hour walk is not acceptable."

"Three hours," Talthien corrected.

"Three hours is too much," Reese said. "So pick one out for today and tack it up—do you know how to take care of saddles and things? That would be another load off my back—and go home. And come back tomorrow."

"Can I too?" Talthien asked.

"I'll employ anyone who'll work at a useful task," Reese said. "And you can tell everyone that."

"But what's useful to you, lady?" the youth asked.

"At this point? Everything." She nodded to Shoran. "I'll let the two of you get on with it then."

As they left the stables, Irine said, "You're trusting them to teach them that they're worthy of your trust, aren't you."

"It worked on me," Reese said, tucking her hands in her pockets.

Irine slipped her arm through Reese's. "It really did."

Reese looked at her, at the golden profile with the amber eyes. She'd known Irine for years, and yet, how well did she really know her? "You were serious? About the breeding thing?"

"Oh, sure!" Irine nodded. "I've started family trees for all of us. I've got our genealogy—me and Sascha's, I mean—but I don't know much about anybody else's yet besides Hirianthial's. That's a matter of Eldritch public record, more or less, so I've requested it from the Ontine archive." She grimaced. "The original copy of that was at Jisiensire's estate."

Reese winced.

"Yeah. But the Queen keeps copies, so..." Irine shrugged. "I've always loved the idea of generations rolling over, and having people continue through time that way. That's why I've always known I would settle down somewhere and have a family of my own. It's a relief knowing that I don't have to be here for something of me to still be around, you know?"

Reese glanced at her sharply. "That's... profound."

"Is it?"

"Most people want to live forever," Reese said, feeling her way around her love for Hirianthial and what it implied for their future.

"I don't," Irine said firmly. "It's not that I'm not scared of dying, because I am definitely scared of dying. But... I'm young and even I can see a point where I'll be tired and glad to let other people do things for a change. That's how the universe keeps going, arii. It makes itself new in every generation that discovers it for the first time." The tigraine looked up at the walls of the castle. "Maybe that's what the Eldritch need most. Staying here... it's bad for them. More than any of us they have to see new things, and discover as much of it for themselves as they can. And when they run out of new things to see, they need to surround themselves in people who are constantly finding things out for the first time so they can remember what it was like."

Reese said nothing for a while as they walked toward the castle doors. Then, quietly, "I guess I should get with the baby-making."

"You know what the Queen would say...."

Reese snorted and tried for a mimicry of Liolesa's fancy accent. "'See to the succession, Laisrathera.'"

The tigraine giggled. "Exactly!" They heard hooves, turned... saw Shoran and Talthien sharing a saddle on one of the gray horses. The elder waved a hand and Reese waved back.

"I don't know about the rest of your plan," Irine said, ears perked, "But that part's going *great*."

Reese grinned.

———

The following day Hirianthial came home, for no reason other than to steal a little time from both their schedules, "as we will soon be quit of this year and it seems a pity not to cherish its final hours." Which was just the sort of thing he'd say, and she didn't mind at all if it meant she could put down her data tablet and put off her meetings. For a few hours, anyway: that was all she could afford. She wondered sometimes at the source of that whisper, the one that said she was running out of time and had to get things set up sooner rather than later... and then she remembered the dragons.

Fleet was here. But they weren't going to stay forever. The sooner the world had some modern defenses, and the modern mindsets to use those defenses, the sooner all of them could exhale and maybe concentrate on growing things at a saner pace.

"You look as if you need the holiday," Hirianthial said as she left her office.

"I think we all do," Reese said. "But... it won't always be this hectic."

"No," he said. "We will have time, God and Lady willing."

She smiled up at him, grateful for the reminder, and followed him down the stairs.

Their path took them through the great hall; Hirianthial paused there to look at the firebowl, which was still burning (as was required) via science (as Kis'eh't had insisted). The empty glass had been set on a foot-stool alongside it because Irine had thought it suited the symbolism better, as if it was just waiting for someone to come have a seat and ask for a refill. There was a residue at the bottom that had become a granular red splotch. Reese liked that, too. It was a visual reminder that the party wasn't over yet. Not until New Year's Day... and the bleeding feast, which was giving her so many headaches she'd had Taylor bang a few hooks into the corner of her office so she could hang her hammock and take a proper nap. With Allacazam. When she could find him, because lately he'd been rolling into weird nooks. Did Flitzbe explore? Could they get lost? She hoped not.

"All good?" she murmured to him when he remained transfixed by the sight.

Shaking himself, just a little twitch of shoulders, her fiancé said, "More than good." Glancing at her, he added, "Horses?"

"Horses."

She'd gotten used to their outings involving horses because Hirianthial loved them, and because Reese was starting to associate them with getting out of her office and doing something that wasn't working. Besides, she was getting a little fond of the horse Hirianthial had chosen for her. She'd been disturbed at first when she'd discovered that Kerayle allowed buyers the option to design their purchases' personalities... nothing specific, of course, but predilections toward passivity or aggression. This reminder that genetic manipulation was a mature technology—more or less—and that humans had put it to use for less savory reasons also relating to the wishes of consumers had been unwelcome... until Sascha had shaken his head and opined that it wasn't necessarily a bad thing to make sure the animal she got wasn't going to have a tendency toward panic attacks.

The last thing she needed as a person with no experience riding was an animal that outmassed her probably a million times over with an anxiety complex. Or an aggressive mount who knew how to use all the pointy ends.

Hirianthial had taken care of the last of her objections by noting that any animal they bred onworld would be a natural-born creature with whatever personality God decreed. So she'd relinquished her grip on her objections and resigned herself to having a tailor-made mount, chosen specifically for the sweetness of her disposition.

And the mare really did have a sweet face, with large dark eyes fringed in extravagant lashes. Irine had mentioned the mare using those eyes to plead for carrots, and ever since Reese had noticed similar behaviors.

Apparently the engineers on Kerayle hadn't thought to code against predilections for begging, and Penny was an unrepentant beggar, using her lashes to advantage on anyone who'd look at her. It made Reese like her more, for somehow having found a loophole in her designers' contrived personality template.

"Vain thing," she told the mare with a grin.

"Who wouldn't be, looking as she does?" Hirianthial said, amused.

Reese got her tack down—she had her own, stamped not just with her initials but with the Laisrathera crest—and let him put the saddle and bridle on for her. She wasn't confident of her ability to dress the horse yet, nor was she highly motivated to learn if it meant she could watch Hirianthial murmuring to the animal, running a pale hand down her arched neck and looking every inch the fairy tale prince. She thought he looked more dramatic on the horse she'd bought for him, a black-coated stallion he'd named in true Eldritch tongue-twister tradition: 'Iecuriel,' which meant "Steadfast." More or less. There was some nuance there he hadn't explained, but that caused Liolesa's mouth to twitch when she heard about it.

Reese had more prosaically named hers for the bright copper shine of her coat, and for the superstition her grandmother had once shared with her, about how if you found a Terran penny you should keep it because it meant you'd never be poor. Penny was Terran, valuable, and the right color: close enough.

"Shall we?" he said when he was done.

"Let's go," Reese said, and accepted his help up. Penny was a lot taller than the horse she'd ridden on Kerayle. She tried not to think about that; it kept her from dwelling on what it would be like to fall off. At least with the Fleet ships in orbit she had access to real medicine, and soon enough she'd have it in her own courtyard. Plus a doctor who'd already rebuilt her esophagus, so a broken neck wouldn't surprise him. Hopefully.

"You won't fall," Hirianthial assured her.

Reese chuckled. "You're only saying that to make me feel better."

"Yes." At her skeptical look, he laughed, guiding them out of the stable and into a day gone a damp and cottony gray. "Because if you believe you won't fall, you won't. She's paying attention, you know. If you convince yourself, you will convince her, and your prophecy will fulfill itself."

Reese shifted in the saddle, making sure her toes were pointed in the right direction in her stirrups. "I know. Terry's told me a thousand times during our lessons."

"The lessons have been doing you good. You look more comfortable."

"You notice?" She glanced at him—which was also something new. She'd had to work hard to figure out how to look to one side or the other without accidentally signaling Penny to go that way.

"Certes. I would dare to suggest it suits you..."

Reese laughed. "I wouldn't go that far. Not yet, anyway. But thank you for noticing."

He smiled at that. His horse was more restive than hers, but he handled it with the ease of someone who'd been riding for centuries; Penny ignored the noises in the courtyard with a sort of long-suffering tranquility, only occasionally twitching an ear toward something. Reese was grateful for her apathy, and had secreted a few sugar cubes in her pocket for after the ride.

"Speaking of noticing... I see one of our herd is missing."

Trust him to catch that. "I'm giving one of them to the beastmaster. Shoran, he said his name was."

"You are *giving* one?" He cocked a brow at her. "But have not yet."

"The kid said they needed to try all the available ones before they decided which one they wanted."

His mouth twitched. "I see."

"I like him," Reese added. She grinned at the memory. "He and the beastmaster came up yesterday to find out if the dogs were in yet. I think Shoran wanted to know about the dogs, but I'm not sure he would have come on his own, without Talthien prompting. I'm completely sure he wouldn't have said yes to the horse without Talthien accepting for him." She glanced at him. "Was it wrong to offer? Shoran said servants weren't allowed to have expensive things. I'm guessing horses are expensive."

"These horses are astronomically so."

Something in his voice though... she knew him well enough now to know there was more, or maybe he was letting her hear it. Either way: "What?"

"Value is contextual," Hirianthial said as they passed through the castle gates. "Liolesa paid a great deal for these horses, because they are rare purebloods resurrected from archived DNA. They are... antiques. Collectibles, in the Alliance."

Reese nodded. "Which makes them expensive in the Alliance. You're saying it's different here?"

"Historically, horses here were the privilege of the wealthy," Hirianthial said. "They are very expensive to feed and maintain. They don't live long—compared to us—and maintaining a ready supply of them requires breeding programs that only the idle have the time to oversee. That puts them out of reach of those without money and land. Horses are also transportation, and speed, and communication, and those were advantages the aristocracy wanted to preserve for themselves."

"So they had no reason to change the status quo."

"No." Hirianthial patted his horse's neck. "Now, however, things have changed. The Pads are not ubiquitous, but Liolesa will ensure that all the provinces are linked by them to the capital. You will bring shuttles... to Firilith, at very least, and no doubt some of Liolesa's allies will want conveyances of their own once you have demonstrated their value. And the orbital and lunar stations, and the ships that will be visiting... those will afford even more opportunities."

"So horses will end up pets. Or status symbols." He didn't say anything; she could tell the idea disquieted him. So she continued. "I thought the beast servant should have one. I want more of my people to have their own... well, property. Possessions. I want them to be invested in Firilith's success, but not at the cost of all their autonomy. Maybe because I want them be able to leave if they hate what I'm doing here, and how can they leave if they don't have the resources to go?" She stared at the path, framed by Penny's bright ears. "This feudal thing... some parts of it work for me, and some parts of it won't."

"I am already enjoying what you're making of it," Hirianthial said, smiling at her. "And I don't think you've done any harm with your gift. No doubt it is the subject of every discussion in town. No one will know what to make of a woman wealthy enough to hand out horses to servants."

"They might not think I'm rich," Reese said. "They might just think I'm crazy." She imagined the conversations, then grinned. "They might not be far off."

"If you must claim madness," he said, "then you must share it, Lady. What you're doing here is necessary. I believe in it... moreover, Liolesa does as well."

"Thanks," she murmured, flushing.

He smiled and didn't press.

Their path took them toward the shore, an easier one than some of the courses they'd taken into the fields because she could see the terrain better. It let her concentrate on the minutia of riding that she still didn't have down: her wrist and hand tension, her seat, how her feet were set in the stirrups. She'd arranged a daily lesson from Terry, one of her temporary Tam-illee grooms, because horses came with the sealbearer job and while she didn't intend to fuss with all the trappings she'd thought it a good idea to accede to at least some of them. Since Hirianthial loved horses, this choice had been easy.

Riding, though, wasn't simple. She'd figured that out on Kerayle, and increased exposure had only confirmed the impression. But strangely, it was relaxing. Once she'd gotten used to the idea, she found it appealing: something about the creak of leather and the solidity of the animal under her, and the fact that she had to focus on something real and immediate instead of fretting about the next meeting, or the next problem, or the next schedule she had to rearrange.

Part of it was Penny, though, with her doe eyes, and her determination not to let her genetic predisposition toward docility become colorless obedience. Reese could sympathize with that level of obstinacy.

Once they'd been pacing the shore for a while, and they'd both had a chance to enjoy the hushed roll and boom of the surf, she broached a topic she hadn't known was nagging at her until it came out of her mouth. "The boy—Talthien—he's not, I don't know... sixty or seventy years old, is he?"

"What?" Hirianthial laughed. "Goodness, no. Though I am forced to concede the assumption is reasonable. We mature at the rate humanity does, Theresa. Until we reach adulthood, and then the process slows."

"How... how does that work?" Reese asked, confused. "You'd think if you started out with human lifespans and stretched them... wouldn't it stretch the entire thing equally? Why only the convenient part before your knees start aching and your eyesight gets wobbly?"

"I don't know," he admitted. A little more wryly, "Though I did not avoid the aching knees for as long as I'd like." She glanced at him sharply enough to draw Penny's attention, but he was still talking. "It is one of the things I would like to research, once we have a secure facility here to do so."

That startled her even more than the idea that someone so perfect could have joint pains. "Really?"

His smile was wan. "The notion will outrage some part of the populace, admittedly. Even among Liolesa's partisans. But I would like to understand our physiology better. And if not an Eldritch doctor, in an Eldritch hospital, on our homeworld, then... where? And who?"

"Good questions," she muttered, frowning. She flexed her fingers carefully on the reins; the wet cold off the ocean was biting straight through her gloves. "So Talthien's as old as he looks."

"I would guess fourteen or fifteen. Perhaps older, given the probability of nutritional deficiencies. No more than eighteen, certainly—he'd be growing his hair by then."

"Explains why he's on my side already," Reese said. "He's a teenager. He's probably bored."

She'd expected that comment to win her a chuckle, but Hirianthial turned thoughtful instead, and she glanced at him askance... and then her gaze lingered, because Goddess and freedom, but he was gorgeous: the stallion, black coat gone matte as a silhouette beneath a cloudy sky, pacing the gray sea with Hirianthial gracefully astride, bronze cloak fanned over the horse's back. This picture, she thought, she wished she could keep forever. Except she'd have a chance to see it every day if she wanted. Lucky her!

His face had been turned down, consumed with his own thoughts... but now his eyes slid to hers with a twinkle, and one brow lifted, as if he knew exactly what she was thinking.

"Can't blame a girl for coveting," Reese said, ignoring her blush.

"I'd blame any other," he said lightly, which only made her blush harder. But he grew sober again as he continued. "You do not understand what you offer a boy like Talthien, Theresa. Eldritch women are reared to rule—their families, if not a castle or a nation. They are born with duties that distinguish them and give them pride, and those duties remain relevant even in small towns, like Rose Point's, and among those of diminished means. One need not have money to have authority over one's husband, children, grandchildren, house. But men... men are expected to serve." He cast his gaze over the sea. "What is there left to do here, with the monsters gone? No man is sent out to ensure his family's safety anymore. If there are crops to be tended, that is labor without reward, for our farms are barely viable. Beasts, equally difficult to keep alive almost anywhere. Buildings can be maintained only if one remembers how it is done, and if one has the tools to do it. Do you suppose such tools—or the knowledge to employ them—remain in Firilith?"

"Not with the houses looking the way they do," Reese said, disturbed.

"So, then. What future for a youth? Talthien is the youngest of the population of Rose Point's castle town. He lives too far from other townships to know their children, or he would if Firilith had them, which it does not. He grew up without playmates, and now has no peers. His only society is that of men who have nothing to give him: no path to dignity or utility, no tools, no apprenticeship. All they will have offered is a legend of what life was like when there was work for men to do, work that gave them self-respect and an honored place in their community. Reared on stories of men he cannot emulate and deprived of the chance at their future, what do you suppose he felt?" Hirianthial inhaled. "And now here you are. You bring changes, where his future was once sealed. You bring work: work that men can do as well as women. You promise him dogs, like the ones that once companioned heroes on the hunt. Do you find yourself surprised that he might cleave to you?"

"No," Reese said, hoarse. She cleared her throat, tasted sea spray on her lips. How had it never occurred to her that life for most of the Eldritch was as much of a dead end as hers had been on Mars? Her heart hurt for them all now, urgently. "That would explain why the men were more interested in the gifts than the women, I guess."

"You will have won them already just by suggesting that Rose Point might wake again. With this offer of a horse, to go with the dogs?" Hirianthial shook his head, and that chuckle was happy, was him focused on the future and finding it beautiful. "You will have them on your doorstep sooner than you think."

"They're only half the problem, though," Reese said.

"Mayhap. But a household with productive members is a more pleasurable one to manage than one without a future. The women may take longer, Theresa, and I fear you may have to wait for longer than you hope for them to come around. But they will."

"You're a lot more confident of that than I am," she said, but she was smiling. So when he looked at her like that—indulgent, confident, loving —she was ready to accept the gentle reproof. She lowered her head, flushing, and added, "I'm allowed a little bit of doubt? After all the mistakes I've made, I'd think I've earned it!"

He kneed his horse closer and reached for her hand, a lot more steadily than she would have had she been trying the same maneuver. "Theresa. Not everyone you lead will love you; Liolesa will be the first to tell you so. But believe me when I say that most of your people will. Women and men both."

"I guess if I convinced one Eldritch not to pitch me out, I can handle twenty-eight."

He snorted. "As I recall, I was the one who had to do the convincing. There were times I was certain you were ready to toss me out an airlock."

"You were insufferable," she said, mouth twitching.

Hirianthial laughed. "Insufferable!"

"But only because I fell in love with you the moment I saw you and I had a stupid habit of throwing away anything that might be good for me." Reese squeezed his hand, then let it go so she could pay attention to her reins again. "I got over that habit. Maybe I can help the Eldritch figure out how to do it too."

"You are making a good beginning." He glanced at the horizon. "That, though, is a poor one. Shall we return before we are inconvenienced?"

Reese followed his gaze and winced at the dark rim on the stormfront the wind was blowing in. "Yeah. I don't want to be caught out in that."

"We go, then." He smiled at her as he turned Iecuriel. "Too little time with you, my Courage. And yet, a little too much, to also be forced to remain so apart. I will be glad to be wed."

Was she blushing? She was definitely blushing. Blood and freedom, but she was blushing. At least it made the cold easier to handle? Or maybe it made her notice it more. She was babbling, and he could probably hear it. "Me too."

His grin made it all worthwhile. Even the impossible trot she had to try to post all the way back to the castle.

––––––––

They had no sooner ridden through the gates when Bryer demonstrated just how phlegmatic Penny was by swooping to the path in front of them. Hirianthial's horse did a little prancing plunge that he handled with his usual skill, but Reese almost ran Penny into him: she was so busy staring at the sight of the Phoenix *flying* that she forgot to give the horse instructions. Like 'stop', maybe. But Bryer could fly here, and it was magnificent and surreal. Birds flew. People didn't. People-sized birds? She was still staring when Bryer strode to them and said, "Bad storm comes."

"That?" Reese glanced back toward the seashore.

"Off ocean, yes. Go check satellite."

"Right," Reese said. Curious, she added, "Do you know when it'll hit? I guess this is some thing you just... know. Because of the winds?"

He cocked his head, the feathers of his crest splaying. Confusion? Interest? There were nuances to Phoenix body language she still didn't know after years of Bryer's acquaintance... because, she now realized, the life they'd been living hadn't given him much impetus for it. When every day was 'another cargo, another minor but expected crisis,' how many facial expressions did you need? Her own standard had been 'scowl' for so long that smiling this much all the time still made her cheeks ache.

"Yes," he said. "There is a great deal in wind. One must be very still inside to hear it." Of course. "Have maybe most of day. Depends."

"Understood. Thanks for the warning."

He nodded and jogged away, and that jog became a sprint that flung him back into the sky. This time Reese remembered to stop Penny so she could stare, jaw agape.

"It is awing," Hirianthial said, baritone low.

"Yeah." Reese straightened in her saddle. "But it's not so bad, flying by machine."

He smiled over at her. "Not so bad at all, no."

She nodded and sighed. "But, duty calls. You staying?"

"I can see us back to the stables, at least."

If Reese remembered right, Kisses Number 12, 16, 19 and 27 had happened in the stables. She ignored her blush and said, "Sounds good to me." Pointing Penny's nose in that direction, she fumbled in her vest pocket for her telegem and flicked it on. "Give me... um... Taylor." A chime.

"Goodfix here."

"Hey, Taylor? Do we have any weather people tracking a storm on the satellite feed? Can you tell me how bad it's going to be?"

"Oh? Oh, yeah." A pause. "Okay, I see it. It's not a hurricane if that's what you're worried about."

"I might have been born on a dust bowl but I know hurricanes happen when it's hot out."

"Blizzard, then. Just a bad squall line. It'll be nasty for a day or so. Might actually get snow!"

"Really?" Reese said, wondering if she was looking forward to that or not. She was leaning toward 'not' given how much of the castle still needed sealing.

"Or it might get too cold for snow." A chuckle. "We'll be fine, alet."

"But the villagers might not be," Reese said. They had reached the stable, so she cut off the Tam-illee before she could start suggesting the inevitable fixes the Eldritch wouldn't accept. "I guess they've handled weather like this before, though. Keep an eye on it for me, please?"

"All right. But alet—"

"I appreciate it," Reese said. "Thanks, Taylor. Reese out."

Dismounting in front of the doors, Hirianthial said, "Neatly done."

"A little obvious, maybe, but I don't want to fight with her about it." Reese sighed. "I just hope she doesn't take it into her head to rush down there and put up storm shutters."

"She won't. You were correct when you guessed such weather has come through before and will no doubt again." He tossed the reins over a post in a way that looped them—stylish, that, she wondered if she could figure out how to do it—and came around Penny's side to help her down. Technically she could could make it off Penny's back without help now, though she wouldn't take any bets on how good she looked doing it. But she wasn't about to say no to those hands wrapped around her waist.

They were probably glowing like two people who were impatient with their self-enforced premarital abstinence when they entered the stables and interrupted the catechism there. Urise was perched on a hay bale with Allacazam in the puddled robes of his lap; Belinor was hovering at his side like an overprotective parent. Seeing him with his mentor made it clearer how much older Belinor looked; Reese hadn't known him that long, but the events onworld had matured him enough that she found the scene endearing as well as humorous. She could see the shape of future-Belinor's personality and thought he'd make an excellent priest, if Eldritch priests considered themselves stewards of their flocks.

Their students were Shoran and Talthien, also seated on hay bales. Val, of course, was slouching against the door of a stall. Petting a horse. Because all Eldritch inevitably were horse-mad, and had a penchant for coming to rest in poses that would have made lovesick teens swoon. When Reese had been learning how to brush out Penny's coat, her mare had liked to lean over and leave spit all over her braids. She bet no horse ever did that to an Eldritch.

Maybe she was a little annoyed to have been planning a tiny sliver of alone-time with her fiancé only to have walked in on a religious thing. Complete with celibate priests.

Hirianthial's mouth was twitching. "Later for you," she told him, low. To the priests, "Are we interrupting anything?"

"Not at all!" Urise said, beaming. "We were just discussing the mysteries."

"I... shouldn't be here, should I."

"No, lady," Shoran hastened to say. "We were doing nothing formal."

"We haven't been able to talk to any priests in a long time," Talthien said. Thought better of that and said, "Well, Shoran hasn't. I've never talked to a priest in my life."

"Long past time," Shoran said. "A temple should have both priest and priestess. And you have brought us three, Lady!"

"More or less," Reese said, stepping aside so Hirianthial could guide the horses past her. "Though I don't know how much time Val will be spending with us, given his position."

Val snorted. "I'd rather be here than somewhere else."

"Even two priests," Shoran said firmly, standing to take Penny from Hirianthial's care. "Talthien, help please." As the boy sprang up, he continued, "It is good to hear the words from an elder. And to see that there are good men in training yet."

"I promise we'll get the chapel full staffing," Reese said. "Meanwhile, I have a message for you to take down to the village."

Both Shoran and Talthien looked at her at that.

"There's a storm coming," Reese continued. "It'll probably blow over in a day, but it's going to get cold later. High winds, too, probably. You should tell everyone to get ready."

"I'll go!" Talthien exclaimed. "The dapple wants a run. I'll take her."

Shoran eyed him. "And what makes you believe I'll let you carry such a message?"

"Because you're the one who's best with the beasts!" Talthien was already going for a saddle. "Who'll stay with them through the storm if not you?"

That gave his elder pause. Reese watched the byplay, wondering at the subtext. Catching Hirianthial's eye, she asked a silent question; he canted his head so slightly she might have missed it had his much shorter hair not swung out from his jaw. So, he'd noticed it too. How best to shore up the situation when she wasn't totally sure of the currents?

When in doubt, trust. Wasn't that what her crew had finally taught her? And she had to start with herself, and her own instincts. "You're the son of the seal's servants," Reese said to Talthien. "I think warning people of danger is your duty, anyway. Particularly since Shoran really is better with the animals."

The two glanced at one another and this time they were both caught off-guard. She hid her grin.

Shoran recovered first. "Very well. But help me with the lord and lady's steeds first. You know better than to go tacking up some new beast before the others are settled. Unless the errand is urgent, lady?" He looked at Reese.

"No. You've got time."

Nevertheless, the two finished the chore far faster than she would have. When Talthien led the gray mare out of the stable, Reese strolled after him and watched him swing himself into the saddle. He went up like the knowledge was genetic even though he couldn't have had more practice than her since the only horse in the village had died before he was born. It worried her enough that she broke character and said, "You know how to ride that thing at a gallop, right? It's hard enough to stay balanced at a trot!"

He grinned at her. "Never fear, lady. I have been practicing with the horses you graciously lent us. And I rode the postpony religiously from the day I got my first." He gathered the reins up and said, his manner more stilted, "Thank you. For this errand."

"You're the right man for the job," she said, and from the way his shoulders squared she'd gotten that part right. Maybe that had earned her enough capital for a question? Nothing to lose by trying, particularly with the youth... he'd been the most flexible of the bunch so far. "So what was the real reason you wanted Shoran to stay?"

"You noticed?"

"I think everyone noticed," Reese said. "I'm betting the only reason he didn't fight you about it was that he didn't think I saw what you were doing. So what am I not supposed to know?"

Talthien grimaced. "He's not old, mistress. Not at all. But he gets pain in his joints, and it's much worse in the cold. Your stable is warmer than any of our houses."

Something Hirianthial could fix? It would have been an easy problem to deal with for human or Pelted patients. But who knew with Eldritch biology? "I get it. Good thinking, then." She smiled. "He must like you to let you boss him around like that."

"Oh, no! He almost never allows me to be impudent!" Talthien said. "But I think he liked what you said. About me having a duty." He tilted his head, an uncanny mimicry of Hirianthial's gesture earlier. "You meant it? Will I train one day to guard you and your heirs?"

"Talthien," Reese said, "I wouldn't have arranged for your dogs otherwise." She patted the horse on the neck and stepped away. "Now go, and don't break your neck. There's a transceiver in the saddle pad and a different one in the horse. If we start getting suspicious data, we'll come find you."

"God and Lady!" Talthien said. "You won't have to, I pledge it! And I will tell you myself when I arrive."

"Those transceivers don't let you talk, you know."

"But the data tablet you left with us will!" And with a triumphant grin, he said, "I go, mistress!"

And he did, leaving her staring... and not just because he'd apparently been hard at work picking up the technology she had been praying his elders would use. The boy really could ride a running horse. How the hell did he do that? Why had he picked up in a few days what she was still struggling to learn?

Then again, she remembered being a lot stronger and more supple in her teens, too. And a lot more headstrong. She prayed he didn't do anything stupid, or that she hadn't by sending him, and made a note to doublecheck the transceivers in a few hours. Wandering back into the stable, she asked, "What's a postpony?"

All five Eldritch men looked at her. Hirianthial chuckled. "A postpony. You might call it a rocking horse?"

"Except they aren't on runners," Val said, grinning. "You mount them on springs."

"If you're fortunate, you get one every year as a toy, so that it's the right size to challenge you as you grow," Belinor said. And hastened, "Mind you, it is a toy for those without the expectation of real horses. Men with titles must learn to ride from the time they are old enough to walk."

"Real horses are safer," Hirianthial said, wry.

Reese looked at Shoran, who said, "He has a talent. He will need it, if he is to serve his duty."

"Mmm," Reese said. "Well, then, I gave the right jobs to the right people. And that means I'm going to leave you to these horses, Shoran-alet —and the discussion of the Mysteries—while I see Hirianthial off." She lifted a finger at Val. "Don't say it."

"I haven't even opened my mouth!"

"I know," Reese said. "But knowing you, you were about to."

Val's mouth twisted but he managed a straight face. "Enjoy your... seeing off, Lady Eddings." As she turned, he finished, "All the priests are here rather than in the chapel. I know you've realized this small fact but I thought you might appreciate having your attention called to it."

She paused, then grinned. "Okay. Maybe I'll change my mind about letting you talk."

"I wouldn't," Belinor muttered.

Hirianthial laughed and pushed open the door. "Go, lady. Before they keep us."

The chapel was, indeed, empty. It smelled like storm winds blowing, and winter roses. She and Hirianthial, on the other hand, smelled like horses. Reese didn't mind. Or, after a little bit, notice.

———

Reese had grown up on a planet, but Mars's domes supported an atmosphere as artificial and stable as the *Earthrise*'s. Given that, she'd expected the storm to disturb her for longer than the twenty minutes it took for her to stop noticing anything but the most sustained of gusts. The thickness of the castle walls muffled the noise until it became a vague reminder that she was safely insulated from the severity of the weather. It was actually kind of... cozy. She understood now why people liked to curl up with blankets and read books during bad weather. In fact, after spending a fruitless hour at her office trying to catch up with paperwork, that's just what she did. The room they'd used for the Vigil was still decorated, and she had no trouble with the fireplace since the Tam-illee had long since swept through Rose Point and added burners everywhere they found a flue. With an old, familiar blanket stolen from her hammock and Allacazam in her lap, plus a big mug of hot chocolate snitched from a genie—there were compensations to being in charge—she settled in the rocking chair with her data tablet.

It had been a long time since she'd been able to relax and read one of her romances. She'd been half-afraid that living through a romance to shame a bestselling author would make her too critical to enjoy them, but, no... it turned out that being in love made her even more engaged with the subject matter. She cheered for the protagonists, empathized painfully with their communication failures and angsts, and sighed in satisfaction at the rapprochements. The only parts she found more difficult to read were the bedroom scenes, because now they made her mind wander.

There were far worse problems to have.

So it was a pleasant evening. Talthien used the data tablet to assure her that he'd reached the village safely, so she didn't have to worry about him needing rescue. The rest of her crew was snugged up somewhere in the castle; Hirianthial was at Ontine, where the weather was fine. For once, no one needed her attention. She read until her eyes blurred, sipping the rich chocolate while Allacazam burbled his inebriated firelight dreams in her lap. The wind seemed very far away, and even though the shutters gave the occasional creak she felt safe enough to start drifting to sleep in the chair.

She thought of her tenants, and hoped they'd managed, and tried not to wish she could don shining armor and ride in on Penny's back to fix everything. She knew better than to think that ever worked. Besides, knowing her riding skill she'd probably fall off... and then she'd really catch it from Hirianthial. She could almost hear his voice: 'It was not enough to require a new esophagus. You had to apply to me for a new head as well?'

Reese fell asleep, cheeks mounded up in a smile.

CHAPTER 8

The morning revealed a world gone raw with melting frost. The wind had scoured the earth, exposing its layers in wet, dark streaks and littering everything with broken vines and branches; on the seaward side of the castle the walls were spattered with either sand or salt or both. The sky seemed very far away, its tall bowl filled with torn clouds that were moving fast on a steady breeze. It smelled good, oddly: clean and clear. But the moist cold made her throat and chest hurt and seeped past all the layers of clothing she put on.

"Could have been worse," Bryer opined when he found her in the courtyard.

Joining them, Taylor said, "Much worse. A sustained storm might have delayed construction significantly. Or even damaged the property."

"I don't know, the mess looks bad enough to me."

Taylor surveyed their surroundings. It was cold enough to have induced her to wear something over her vulpine ears, which on a Tam-illee meant wool-lined cones in bright red and orange, topped with pompoms. They were the brightest colors in sight with the world gone gray and sullen and damp. "It'll be a pain to clean up, but things could be worse." She shook out her shoulders. "I'll go get some people on that, in fact."

"Thanks, alet."

It was morning, and with no emergency waiting for her, that meant lessons with Terry. Reese went obediently to the stable and found Penny already tacked up and waiting for her.

Shoran was too. Reese wondered where he'd slept—in an empty stall? And on what? She couldn't imagine what the conditions were in the houses in the village to make him so bright-eyed and limber after sleeping on a hay bale in a stable. But he showed no signs of dismay or pain, and at the sight of her he bowed and exclaimed, "My lady! These horses! They are extraordinary!"

On the other side of her mare, Terry flashed her an amused look.

"I guess they came through the storm all right?"

"Without even a flinch," Shoran assured her. "And this stable! I have never seen its like. It is a facility fit for a Queen's herd."

"Appropriate, I guess, since Liolesa's the one who charged me with breeding her horses for her," Reese said. The awe in the man's eyes prompted her to say, mischievous, "I don't suppose you think any of the ones we've bought so far would suit her?"

"Suit... suit the Queen, Mistress?" Shoran stammered.

Reese pursed her lips. "You're right. One horse is probably not enough. She needs three or four, doesn't she? Something for parades, something for casual riding, something for war maneuvers...."

"Is she planning any war maneuvers anytime soon?" Terry asked, ears flattening.

"I hope not," Reese said. "But knowing her, I wouldn't make any bets either way. She has contingency plans for her contingency plans."

The wonder on Shoran's face was almost funny. Almost. Reese said to him, "It's not urgent! We have time. And thanks for taking such good care of the horses during the storm."

"Mistress. It was my duty and I was honored to perform it."

Another bow. Reese accepted it and let Terry lead her out of the stable. Once they were out of earshot, the Tam-illee said, "He wasn't quite sure what to make of me, you know."

"I bet. Did you change his mind?"

"I didn't," Terry said. "Everything else did." When Reese glanced down at him, the tod chuckled. "Horses in the Alliance are luxury items, alet. The only people who keep them in the Core are wealthy, and rich people don't like mess or chores. The hay was amazing enough to someone who's never seen it baled, much less so much of it in one place. But the stalls not getting dirty? When I showed him how that worked, he got very quiet."

"Bad quiet?" Reese wondered.

"No," Terry said, grinning. "The 'dreaming of the implications' quiet."

Reese laughed. "Okay, yeah, I can see it." She tilted her head. "How does that work?"

"Self-cleaning stalls?" Terry shrugged. "It's not a big stretch. If you're rich. A computer to decide what to leave and what to reduce, a specialized grid..."

"Blood, am I rich? Because that sounds like a lot of trouble for horses when we don't even have gem grids for the entire castle...!"

Terry laughed. "It's nowhere near as complicated as a gem grid, alet, don't worry. And honestly, you wouldn't have been happy with the workload if we hadn't set it up properly. Particularly since you really are breeding horses."

Reese chanced a look back toward the stable. "So he's listening to you?"

"He's listening to me. He's not sure what to make of me personally, but he's accepted that as far as horses go, I've got some good ideas. And speaking of which... it's time for us to work on your thighs."

"Do we have to?"

Terry's ears flicked forward and he grinned. "Your horse won't be the only one who thanks you for your dedication."

Reese eyed him. "I don't even want to know where you learned talk like that."

"We all want you to have a splendid wedding, no matter our species," the Tam-illee said, amused. "So... toes up, captain. That's better. Now put out your arms and let's do some balance exercises."

———

No matter how cold it was outside she was always sweaty by the time she was done with her lesson. After a rinse in the shower—thank the God and Goddess the Tam-illee had taken care of the bathrooms *first*—she was back in her office with Irine, going through the final plans for the feast while ignoring almost everything else that needed her attention. Since all those things had needed her attention yesterday, a week ago, a month ago, she figured another few days wouldn't hurt them. Half an hour into their meeting, her data tablet chimed with the news that the Hinichi had arrived insystem with the dogs and that meant:

"Thank the angels!" Irine did an impromptu dance in her chair. "The food got here!"

"Even if it hadn't, we were planning on mostly using Liolesa's stores," Reese said.

"Yes, but it doesn't seem right to start the new year by borrowing from the old. Right? 'Begin how you mean to go on?'"

Impressed, Reese said, "You've been listening. Or eavesdropping."

Irine laughed. "Both? Big family, remember? You have to have sensitive ears. If you don't know who's fighting with who and who's sleeping with who, you make your life a lot harder."

And she really was good at that kind of thing. Even on the *Earthrise*, she'd served unobtrusively as Reese's right hand. Reese had never noticed it because her brother had the job that usually went with the position; Sascha's far more commanding personality had overshadowed his sister's less obvious contributions, which had mostly involved keeping them all from strangling one another. Flustered, Reese toyed with the fancy Eldritch pen she still thought of as more of a prop than a tool. "Irine... I gave Felith the chatelaine job. I didn't even ask you if you wanted it. I didn't think about the fact that you'd be good at it, and you would. If you want the job..."

"Oh, Reese." Irine leaned over and covered Reese's hands with hers. "No! It's all right. You have to have Felith in that position because it needs an Eldritch. I'm flattered that you think I'd do a good job, but I don't need it."

"Are you sure?" Reese glanced at her. "I want you to know that... well, I finally see some of what you've been doing all along, and it's important."

"And I'm going to keep doing it, title or no title," Irine said, smiling. "Felith's got a whole castle to handle, and all the staff. I don't want any of that. The only person I want to fuss over is you." She canted her head. "Well, and Sascha. And possibly Narain. And if Narain has a sister...."

Reese covered her face with a hand.

"You get the idea."

"I get the idea," Reese said. "And I'll think these things through before I do them next time."

"That usually works out better than leaping for them," Irine said. "But... not always. So don't second-guess yourself too much, all right?"

"All right." Reese sighed. "And the dogs will be here in two hours, so... let's get back to this."

"That sounds good! We can do that after we see why Kis'eh't's flagged us a priority message."

Reese frowned. "That's all we need. What's exploded now?" She spread it and paused. "Okay, well, maybe nothing. Or everything?"

Irine leaned over the desk to squint at the message. "Talthien's coming back. With one of the Eldritch women?"

Reese checked the transceivers: steadily making their way up the road. "Looks like they'll be here in half an hour."

"You want to meet them downstairs?"

"You're assuming they're here to see me."

Irine awarded her a skeptical look.

"All right, the chances of them being here for any other reason are tiny," Reese admitted. She sat back and rubbed her head, the beads capping her braids clicking. "If I was Liolesa, I'd probably be sitting here thinking 'what's more advantageous—to go down there and meet them so that they can figure out that I'm a lot less formal and a lot more interested in their welfare than the average Eldritch noble? Or to stay up here and make them travel through the castle to find me so they can see what I'm doing to the inside and get covetous?'"

"You're not Liolesa, though," Irine said. "Do you really want to model yourself on her?"

Reese rested the data tablet on the table and folded her arms. Did she? On one hand, you couldn't argue with success, and Liolesa was probably in the dictionary next to the word given everything she'd managed to accomplish in the face of opposition. On the other... Liolesa had chosen Reese because of who she was. Granted, who-she-was needed some work. But who-she-was had also been molded by some of the more romantic values she'd found in her quasi-historical romances, many of which were congruent with Eldritch mores. So what did Liolesa want out of her? The woman who'd run the *Earthrise*? Or the woman who'd fallen asleep in a rocking chair over the happily-ever-after of her book?

"You're overthinking it," Irine suggested.

"No... I don't think so."

Both of Irine's brows went up. Ears perked, she sat back. "Okay, this should be interesting. What's going through your mind?"

"Well, I've run the *Earthrise* in the past. Not very well, but well enough to keep you all from deserting me, and not to be completely in debt. Not counting... you know. This." Reese waved a hand at the study.

"Right," Irine agreed. "It's too bad not all debts end up getting paid by foreign queens who eventually make you into princesses."

Reese eyed her.

"Can I also have a unicorn?" Irine added, and this time Reese knew her well enough to see the mischief under the earnest request.

"Be careful what you ask for," she said instead. "I might give it to you. Now! As I was saying." She looked out the window at the horizon. "The *Earthrise*... that was small change compared to what I have to handle now. This isn't just six people and a ship. This is... this is a handful of towns full of people—"

"Eventually!"

"Eventually," Reese allowed. "But it's in the plan. And it involves offworld assets too. The *Earthrise* used to be my only concern, arii, and now it's so small a part of my responsibilities that I've had to delegate it to someone. I don't want to become another Liolesa because I don't want to run an empire, and Freedom knows I'm not as devious as her and won't ever be. But... I need to learn how to do this from someone who knows how, and that means I have to figure out how to... manage people. Better than I do." Irine's eyes had been steady on hers throughout this speech, and her golden-eyed regard made Reese self-conscious. "That probably sounded ridiculous."

"No. No, I think it's one of the most introspective things I've heard out of you. I'm... it's..." Irine shrugged helplessly. "I didn't expect it, that's all."

"What did you expect? Or should I ask?"

Irine's ears sagged. "Umm... more of the putting yourself down sort of talk?"

Reese exhaled. "Well. Yeah, I can see that. But the stakes are a little higher these days, right? A lot of people are counting on me. I owe them not to cut myself off at the knees before I have a chance to run the race for them."

That put both fuzzy ears up so hard they trembled. The expression of shock was so patent Reese found herself laughing. "You did say I've been growing up."

"Not in those words!" Irine managed a winsome—and apologetic—smile. "But... more or less, yes. I'm glad, so glad that you're trying not to beat yourself up anymore. Especially since you're not into that sort of thing." She paused, grinned. "Sorry, had to say it."

"Harat-Shar," Reese muttered.

"Harat-Shar," Irine agreed, amiable. More seriously, "But you've brought up some really important questions, and only you can answer them. There's nothing wrong with role models, though you've got more than one. The Queen's a really good one, but... that's like... you're an apprentice and instead of trying to copy a journeyman's efforts, you're trying to copy a master artisan's. It might be better to start lower first."

"And who do you suggest?" Reese asked, wry. "Araelis? Also head of a large household?"

"Sure," Irine said. "Or... you know, your fiancé? He ran Jisiensire, too. That's part of what marrying is about, right? You share your strengths, your experiences. You help each other. He's there for you to lean on."

Reese nodded slowly, her eyes traveling from the data tablet to the anachronism of the Eldritch pen, with its bottle of ink and blotting pad. "That's a good idea. But... I want to be careful there. You know? Araelis just lost everything. And Hirianthial... him too, twice over. Liolesa might be a safer role model at this point—I'm not likely to accidentally depress her."

"You sure?" Irine asked, for once uncertain herself. "They were her people too, you know."

"I'm sure she's upset about it," Reese said. "But I think she's too driven to 'fall into despond.' So... yeah. I think for now I'd rather be asking her. Maybe... Hirianthial next." She grinned. "I'll leave Araelis to the Harat-Shar to rehabilitate. Once she's established her harem, I'll write her long letters asking for help."

Irine laughed. "All right. As long as you know you've got options." She drummed her fingertips on the edge of the desk, thinking. "So. Anyone who has to lead has to figure out how they want to handle people and politics. There's no avoiding that. It's just a question of how."

"I don't want to be fake," Reese said, feeling through her ideas.

The tigraine's brows went up. "You think the Queen is fake?"

Did she? "No. It's just... she's playing the game so far ahead of everyone that it makes it look like she's manipulating you." Reese nodded. "I see what you mean about jumping directly to the top of the class. If I tried to act like her, it would be fake, because I'm not that...."

"Don't say 'smart'," Irine warned.

Since that was exactly what she'd been planning to say, Reese hesitated, then finally went with, "Experienced."

"I'll accept that."

"Thanks," Reese said, rueful. "Given that... I don't know how to make decisions like this, where I have enough time to think about all the possible ways to handle it. If I'm surprised by something, I seem to do pretty well. It's the planning part that I trip on."

"Are you sure?" Irine said, tilting her head. "Because you handled all the planning for the holiday really well. You put a lot of thought into the gifts for your tenants, and I think they were the right gifts. Plus, all the other decisions you made, including the way you dealt with the glass from the Vigil? Don't underrate yourself. You have good instincts."

Put that way....

"The only question you have to answer right now," Irine said, "is what do you think the Eldritch from town need to know more. Who you are, or what you're offering."

Reese let the words sink in.

"First reaction," Irine prompted.

"They've already seen who I am," Reese said. "Too much more and I might frighten them away. I'm not Eldritch; they need to get used to that, and pushing it in their face is a good way to back them into a corner."

"Personal experience there," Irine guessed, grinning.

"Maybe I should just assume they're all going to react like me and act accordingly," Reese said, chagrined.

"So, what are you going to do?"

"I'm going to stay here in this office and figure out the rest of the details for the feast," Reese said, determined. "And if they want to talk to me, they can come find me."

Irine rested a hand on her wrist. She enunciated all the words very clearly, and there was no doubt in her eyes... no doubt, and a lot of pride. "You're doing great."

"So far so good," Reese said, exhaling.

"Begin as you mean to go on?"

Reese laughed. "You're always telling me what I need to hear. So now you can tell me about why you think I should be worried about utensils."

They worked for another twenty minutes or so before Kis'eh't poked her head in the door. "Busy?"

"We're mostly done," Reese said. "Why?"

"I thought you'd want to know a woman with modern heaters has arrived to ask how they can be recharged." Kis'eh't sounded smug. "She's with Taylor now."

Irine and Reese looked at one another; Reese broke into a grin first. "She did, huh?"

"I took her to Taylor's office," Kis'eh't said. "The long way."

"There is no long way to Taylor's office," Reese said, eyeing her. "It's off the main hall."

"I was creative! She liked the firebowl."

"Did she like it or did she stare at it because it was weird?" Irine asked.

"Both? She said it was interesting." Kis'eh't preened.

"For an Eldritch, that's pretty effusive," Reese said. "I hope Taylor doesn't make her feel dumb explaining how to recharge the things."

"I think the danger is more that she'll overwhelm the woman with her enthusiasm. She was so excited that someone was willing to embrace any of the technology that she was practically bouncing out of her chair."

Reese thought of the ear-warmers with their pompoms. "I bet that was an unforgettable experience." Shaking herself, she said, "If the woman's here, then Talthien is too? I should go down and tell him to stay since the dogs are almost here."

"This I'm definitely going to have to see," Irine said. "Hinichi dogs!"

————

Fortunately, Talthien was still present when they made it outside: loitering in front of the stables, in fact, which wasn't a surprise given how often he and Shoran did their chores together. But he wasn't alone, which *was* a surprise, and so was his companion; the senior seal servant was with him, and they were having an impassioned conversation that Reese wished she could understand. Had she come with the senior manse servant? Or had the seal servant brought the heaters herself? And if so, why?

The discussion was becoming heated. Just as Reese was wondering whether it would be rude to interrupt, Talthien looked past the other Eldritch and said, "My lady!"

"Talthien," she said. And inclined her head to the woman. "Alet."

"Lady," the woman said, and there was nothing in her voice to cue Reese about her feelings at all... which was its own tell.

So Reese kept her attention on the youth. "The dogs should be here within an hour. I'd like you to be here to greet their handlers with me. You can get instructions directly from them that way."

She'd always thought the whole 'eyes sparkling with excitement' description was poetic license. Staring at Talthien's, she couldn't pinpoint how his face had changed to make it seem like he'd lit up like a firecracker, but he had, with an eagerness so obvious she couldn't help her grin. "That's fine with you, I take it."

"Of course, mistress!" And hesitated, glancing at the other woman. "In an hour?"

"That's right."

"I'll... need to prepare, then!" he said, but this sounded less like enthusiasm and more like defiance. Or an excuse. For a long moment she wondered what was going wrong, and then she looked at the two of them. And then she knew.

"I'll let you do that," she said. "Shoran's in the stables?"

"Yes, mistress."

"Then I'll go inform him as well. He'll want to make a start on those preparations while you finish up here."

This time Talthien bowed. "Yes, mistress."

Reese walked around them into the stables and had that conversation with Shoran. She thought about bringing up Talthien's problem—the youth hadn't had any qualms sharing Shoran's, after all—but remembering how she'd been as a teen, she restricted herself to a single question and that was enough for her. By the time Irine slipped inside to join her, Reese was sitting on a hay bale, thinking that it was warm and the horse-and-leather scent in the air was actually kind of nice.

"Well!" Irine said. "Poor kit."

"Yeah."

The tigraine canted her head. "You figured it out?"

Reese smiled a little. "Let's say I've had plenty of experience with my own family heaping abuse on me. Enough to recognize the body language. That's his mom out there, Shoran says."

"I don't know if I'd call it abuse," Irine said, perching alongside her. "He wanted her to stay and see him meet the dogs. She told him it wasn't proper, and that she had a duty back at the village."

Reese's eyebrows tried to climb off her face. "Should I ask when you started picking up the language?"

"No, because you're not surprised?" Irine hugged her knees, socked tail resting over her feet. "I like languages. And Val offered to teach me. Plus, I asked Felith to start requesting baby books for the forthcoming heir—"

Reese burst out laughing. "You didn't!"

"And that delighted her so much I thought she was going to explode," Irine finished and grinned. "You done?"

"Not... quite." Reese rubbed her eyes, waiting to see if the incipient tickle in her chest was going to turn into another round. "Blood and Freedom, arii. That was low. Raising her expectations like that."

"I wasn't! You are planning to have kits eventually!"

"Eventually isn't the same as 'quick, let's start decorating the nursery and knitting baby blankets!'"

"It is for an Eldritch! We're positively hasty compared to them! They'd be dithering about kids for half a century." Irine hesitated. "You're... not going to wait that long, are you?"

Was she? "I hope not," she said. And, a little more carefully, "I... kind of hope we'll start soon. And have a lot."

"How many's a lot?"

Reese paused, then laughed. "Not enough to make *you* think it's a lot! Three? Or four? Maybe?"

Irine grinned. "You're right. That's positively cozy." She rested her head on Reese's shoulder. "Don't worry. I'll make up for it with Narain's sister."

"I... don't think Narain's sister is capable of helping you with that particular problem."

Irine giggled. "No, I mean she and I will have enough to make up the numbers."

Reese rested her nose in the fluffy golden hair. "You don't even know if Narain has a sister."

"Can't stop a girl from hoping!"

Reese grinned. Then thought of Talthien. "So... I'm guessing that was 'I want my mom to be proud of me.'"

"'And see me as a man and not a kit,'" Irine agreed. "And that was mazer refusing. But she was determined to take the heaters back to the village because they were needed. I can't tell if that's just them being Eldritch—you know, 'duty before everything'—or his mom being... well, obnoxious."

"We might not know that for a long time. Or even ever."

Irine wrinkled her nose. "She's taking the heaters back. That has to mean she's at least willing to change, right?"

"Maybe. But as you've no doubt noticed, Eldritch don't do anything very quickly. And I bet they take changing even slower." Reese shook her head. "Hirianthial says the women might not come around as soon as we wish. But... we've got time. And pushing them will just make it take longer."

Irine huffed softly. "You should tell Talthien that."

"Maybe I will, when I know him better." Reese grinned. "So, as long as we're stuck here waiting for the dogs, tell me what you know about the language."

"I don't know as much about it as I want yet, but I will say this: if there's a way to make a word longer, they'll take it."

Some ten minutes later, Talthien joined them, and hearing the conversation topic gleefully weighed in. Reese wasn't sure she learned anything, other than the very real possibility that she'd never master her fiancé's language, but she enjoyed listening to Talthien coach Irine between enthusiastic linguistic tangents. It amazed her that he could sit so still, with his hands clasping his knees and his posture so impeccable, while still giving the impression of wild gesticulation. When the telegem she had in her pocket chimed, she was almost disappointed. Almost.

"The dogs are here. Someone should find Shoran—"

"The dogs!" Talthien exclaimed, darting for the door.

"And Shoran!" Reese called.

"Too late," Irine said, amused.

"He heard me." Reese headed out, squinting up: most of the clouds had cleared, at least, and the sky was now a shocking powder blue, clear and light. The world looked a lot less raw with the sun out.

Reese had never had the money for a Pad for the *Earthrise*, so she hadn't considered any of the logistical issues surrounding them. When the Queen had offered her one for Rose Point, she'd said 'yes' and figured since it was portable she could just move it wherever it needed to be used. That plan had lasted all of half an hour. Her guard, consisting of a handful of Liolesa's Swords on detached duty, plus Bryer and Sascha and, of course, Hirianthial, had been adamant that the Pad not deliver people directly into the middle of thoroughfares, particularly indoors. Beronaeth had wanted the thing installed outside the castle gates so that visitors had to pass through a checkpoint there before advancing inside; she'd put her foot down on that one. Who would service the thing and make sure no one ran off with it if it was outside the castle? But while Pads could be locked down so that they could accept requests from specific originating Pads, there was no guarantee that, for instance, the Ontine Pad couldn't be commandeered by some assassin who somehow got through palace security.

So rather than putting the Pad in the great hall, which was the room people had to use to get anywhere else in the castle, her team had decided that the Pad belonged in the courtyard. And not just inside the courtyard, but at the farthest end of it from the keep. Since she wasn't willing to put it outside the gates, it would be installed just inside them, so that her over-paranoid security could shoot any assassins full of arrows before they got to the doors.

To be honest, as embarrassing as it was to imagine asking Liolesa to brave the exposed elements to get to her doorstep, Reese couldn't help remembering that Surela had managed a coup from inside Ontine. She was willing to deal with a little mortification to make sure no one tried to put another dozen holes in Hirianthial's back.

The dogs, then, came from Ontine over the Pad, having taken the shuttle from the Tams' courier to the palace. Reese stopped in front of the steps leading up to the great hall's doors to wait through their long walk to the keep, where she was flanked by Irine, and then Shoran and Talthien.

"How many of these did you buy again?" Irine whispered.

"Adopt," Reese said. "I adopted them. And two. A female and a male."

"Right," Irine said, and Reese didn't blame her for her uncertainty, because they were being advanced upon by seven people. There really were only two dogs, but seven people? And very stern people too: the Hinichi were a handsome race but they tended toward gravity. After years of dealing primarily with the twins, not even Hirianthial's reserve prepared her for the formality of the delegation approaching her. She suddenly wished she'd changed into a fancy dress. Or at least a newer vest.

The deputation stopped a few paces away and the wolfine standing between the two dogs said, "Theresa Eddings?"

"That's me," she said, nervous. She stepped forward and offered her hand palm up. "Welcome to Rose Point, aletsen."

"Thank you," he said, covering it with his own, larger one. "I'm Benneit Drummondly. We spoke about your adopting Graeme and Moire?"

Before Reese could say anything, Talthien breathed, "Oh, what beautiful names!"

The Hinichi glanced at him, and to save everyone mortification Reese pretended as if the Eldritch hadn't spoken out of turn. "This is the Seal Servant Talthien, who has been charged with the comfort and welfare of your kin."

"Oh?"

Talthien straightened further—if that was possible given the ramrod perfection of Eldritch posture—and said, "It is the traditional duty of my family." And, staring at the dogs with unabashed longing. "And I want to."

Reese was looking at the Hinichi, not Talthien, so she caught the faint softening in his eyes. She didn't think the youth could have hit the core Hinichi values any better if he'd tried: duty, family, kids. More kindly, Benneit said, "Then perhaps you would like to meet them. Come." As Talthien started forward, he added, "These are not ordinary animals, Seal Servant Talthien. Don't let their four feet and mute throats fool you. They are as smart as you or me."

Talthien went to one knee in front of the animals, and Reese didn't blame him for holding his breath. They were magnificent: enormous creatures that shared their lupine faces with their keepers, and if their eyes were doglike rather than humanoid, the intelligence in them was still unmistakable. One of them was an amber-eyed ivory with dorsal fur the yellow of buttercups, and this dog seemed to scintillate in the early winter sunlight; the other was much larger, gray with an elegant black mask, back, and tail, and warm brown eyes. Benneit stepped forth to introduce them formally to Talthien, but the gray dog made his own choice. He paced to the Eldritch and pressed his nose against the pale neck with a huff that blew the short hair back from Talthien's jaw.

For a breathless moment, neither moved: the boy on one knee, the dog leaning into him. Then the tail wagged, a hard, fierce twitch.

The noise Talthien made... such elation, to be so strangled. He buried his face in the dog's ruff, white fingers lost in dark fur. And then he raised stunned eyes and said, "Graeme says they've been waiting for someone like me all their lives."

The Hinichi froze in place. Behind him, one of the others said something sharply in their tongue—Reese hadn't even realized the Hinichi had a language of their own—and he responded in kind before saying in Universal, "He spoke to you?"

"Of course!" Irine said, ears trembling with excitement. "He's a touch-telepath, right? Like all the Eldritch?"

The ivory dog, meanwhile, had joined her mate in Talthien's arms, and the three were lost to the world as far as they were concerned. Reese glanced at Benneit and offered, ruefully, "At least they like each other?"

The Hinichi had the look of someone who'd been doused with a bucket of ice water. Reese sympathized; the Eldritch made her feel that way all the time. "This is... this is not a ramification I had considered when you made your offer, alet."

"I... hope that doesn't mean you're thinking of retracting it?" Reese asked, careful. The thought of separating Talthien from his newest friends....

"No! No! You don't understand. It's always been one of our regrets that the Guardkin can't talk. We didn't want to breed the intelligence out of them, but we didn't want to change them either, to be more like the Pelted. Not without their permission, and we never felt we had it. That's... you understand, that brings up debate among us, about playing God, about consent, about the rights of those divinely endowed by their Creator with the ability to perceive Him." He glanced at her. "You might not understand, not being Pelted...."

"Not totally, no," Reese said. "And I won't pretend that I do. Is it a bad thing then that Talthien can hear them?"

"The opposite," Benneit said. "It seems the perfect solution, in fact, to a problem we never knew how to solve." He smiled crookedly. "How would you feel about becoming the host to a breeding hub, alet?"

"Of dogs? Why not? I'm already doing horses." Reese grinned at him. "Why don't we go inside and talk over some hot chocolate."

"As long you also have something stronger," the woman who'd spoken to Benneit earlier said. "Because I'm afraid I might need it."

"Spiked hot chocolate is the best hot chocolate," Irine said. "Let's go inside where it's warm."

———

What followed was one of the stranger meetings Reese had ever had. It began with her and Irine and the Hinichi, grew to include Kis'eh't and Felith, and then the dogs themselves wanted to listen, which inevitably involved Talthien and Shoran. It was a wonder anything got decided, and yet a great many things did. By the end of the talk, the Guardkin had a place to sleep and preliminary duties, Talthien and Shoran had their schedules and care arranged, and the Hinichi had asked for and been granted permission to remain for a few days until they could receive a response to their query, because "now that we know, it's likely other Guardkin may want to emigrate."

Felith led the Hinichi to their guest rooms while Reese sent word to Ontine that the delegation wouldn't be back immediately, along with a separate note to Hirianthial about all the craziness that had been going on, and also that she really wanted to see him for New Year's for Kiss Number Forty. Or Thirty-Nine. Did he remember the count?

She smiled writing that part, knowing that he'd laugh while reading it.

Talthien and the dogs had managed to fall asleep in front of her fireplace despite the commotion—or perhaps in response to it, now that it had abated. The quiet hum and crackle of the fire was enough to lull anyone now that all the talking was over. Reese paused in her work to glance over the top of her data tablet at them: so unexpected to see an Eldritch sprawled, though of course they did it elegantly. Talthien had one arm over Graeme's dark back, and his white hair spilled over the dog's ruff in shocking contrast. Moire was bracing him on the other side, resting her muzzle on his thigh. She opened one golden eye to peer sleepily at Reese, then closed it again.

Returning from their separate errands, Felith and Irine stopped at the threshold of her study.

"They're dead to the world," Reese said, keeping her voice low. "Or at least, they have been for an hour now. Too much excitement, I'm guessing."

"It's almost dinner," Felith said. "We came to fetch you."

"I'll be down in a minute. Just finishing one more note here. The Hinichi all tucked into their new rooms?"

"They were," Felith said. "Now they are downstairs awaiting the call to eat and talking with the Tam-illee."

"It's a big party down there," Irine added with perked ears.

"That'll be fun." Reese set her data tablet down and folded her hands on it. "So... Felith... the senior seal servant was here with the senior manse servant's gifts. Should I be offended by that? Is there some re-gifting protocol I don't know about?"

Felith cringed. "So that rumor was truth."

"It was, yes. You didn't talk with her?"

"No, milady. And she should have sought me if she had been inter-ested in the role bequeathed to her with her bloodlines." Felith's mouth firmed. "The gifts given by the lady on Lady's Day are supposed to be shared among her people, but yours were very specific. I do not know why she might have taken them, but it seems a discourtesy to me."

"Like her not talking to you?" Irine guessed.

Reese shook her head. "It's all right. Maybe she's not ready."

"But I don't understand it," Felith said. "The senior seal servant... we are about to host the largest social occasion of the year! Perhaps of the century! How often does the Queen's cousin marry, after all? And Lord Hirianthial, at that... no one expected him to ever re-marry. Begging your pardon, milady—"

The comment did sting, not because she hated to think of Hirianthial's first wife, but because it hurt to think of him grieving, and hearing about Laiselin inevitably made her imagine his reaction to her loss. Irine saved her from responding by charging into the breach. "You're saying that someone like that shouldn't want to miss the chance to be involved with a party that size? Because of how important everyone is. But does everyone know Hirianthial? This place is nowhere near the court, and even farther from Jisiensire than it is from Ontine. It's not like there's been much communication here since Rose Point was abandoned, either, so how would they have heard of him? Right?"

If Eldritch could ever be said to stare at someone agape, Felith was doing so now. "Lord Hirianthial is the Queen's *blood cousin.*" When Irine's expression didn't change, Felith said, slowly, "The Queen has set aside her heir and has not yet chosen another suitable adult to replace her. Until she does so, *he* is the heir to the throne."

Irine frowned. Thoughtfully. As if she didn't find the thought that Reese was engaged to a man who could end up king alarming. Reese wished for her lack of concern. The tigraine said, "I didn't think men could rule here."

"Ordinarily not," Felith said. "And the likelihood of the Queen dying before choosing a new heir is remote, of course. But in the event of that tragedy, the crown would certainly fall to Lord Hirianthial, either directly or in trust for his daughter."

"That would be Reese's daughter," Irine said. "Just to clarify."

Felith glanced at Reese almost apologetically. "Correct."

Reese covered her eyes.

"So you see," Felith finished, "this is not a wedding a woman dedicated to social events should miss."

Studying Reese sympathetically, Irine said, "I'm betting he didn't tell you any of this."

Reese parted her fingers just enough to look through them at Felith. "No one said anything about the heir having been set aside yet. I thought she was going to stay the heir until the Queen replaced her."

"Alas, such a plan would not work," Felith said, lacing her fingers in front of her. "You forget, lady. I have seen Lady Bethsaida. What she is now could not serve."

Irine's ears sagged and Reese winced. "I'm sorry, I didn't mean to..."

"You didn't," Felith said. More briskly, she continued, "All the same, milady... the sooner the Queen sees to the royal—imperial now, I suppose! —succession, the better for us all. You particularly, as I know Lord Hirianthial has no such ambitions."

"No, he doesn't," Reese said. "That part I do know."

"So that just leaves us with the mystery of why Talthien's mother doesn't want to run the whole affair," Irine said, puzzled. "You'd think this would be an impossible temptation. The wedding of the generation!"

"But to a human, and attended mostly by foreigners," Reese

murmured. She sighed. "We need to give her time. And speaking of which, I want to finish this note so I can go to dinner."

"So many dogs," Irine said, amused. "Between the Tam-illee and the Hinichi, it's going to be a swarm of big ears and short tails. We need to invite some catfolk."

"Luckily, Araelis's friends will be here in time for the wedding," Reese said, and waved them out before Irine could dish out the inevitable saucy reply. The last thing she needed was to get trapped in more banter—she was almost ready to go downstairs and be a good hostess. She had just picked up her stylus when Talthien said, low, "My mother means well, mistress."

Reese set the stylus back down again.

He flushed. "I apologize. I was listening."

"And heard most of it, I guess." Reese sighed. "I'm the one who's sorry, Talthien. I didn't mean to talk about your family around you that way."

Petting Graeme's fur with an air of palpable self-consciousness, the youth said, "I heard nothing a lady should be ashamed of having said. It is your duty to understand your servants' problems."

Which was no doubt why he'd brought Shoran's joints to her attention. It was as obvious an opening as any she'd heard from an Eldritch; Talthien was too young, maybe, to have graduated to the subtlety—or nebulosity—of his elders. "Do you know why your mother brought the heaters instead of the senior manse servant?"

Again, that blush, incongruously like rouge against salt-white skin. "She thinks if someone is to have any interaction with the castle, mistress, it should be her."

Sensing the unfinished statement, Reese prompted, "Because?"

"Because she thinks the others are too eager to throw in with you." He lifted his chin. "I heard her fighting with Sela about it."

Reese nodded slowly. "So she wants to be the buffer between them and me. So that they don't get too attached."

"Yes." He looked down at the fur under his hand. Hesitantly, he said, "Have you ever wanted a thing, mistress, and then received it but not the way you wanted it? And then you couldn't figure out how to be glad, or how to accept it anyway?"

"And your mother has wanted to be the seal servant to an Eldritch noblewoman all her life, but now that she has her chance it's with a woman who's not an Eldritch, not a noblewoman by her standards, and going to die in a hundred years?"

He winced, and Graeme lifted his head, rotating his ears.

"It's all right," Reese said, more quietly. "I understand what she's going through. I've gotten a lot of things in my life that I wasn't sure whether to be thankful for either. And this is important, Talthien: I'm not upset at your mother for not rushing in with open arms."

"You're not *now*," he said. "I don't know how you'll feel when I tell her I'm not leaving the castle anymore and she becomes wroth."

Reese grinned. "Well. Kids do move out eventually."

"Eldritch children don't," he muttered. And got a tongue-swipe over his jaw that made him yelp. He pushed at Graeme's head and said, indignant, "I am *not* being sulky."

Behind Talthien's back, Moire raised the furred ridges over her eyes: they had little comma-shaped marks over them, white on the golden fur, and it made the motion more obvious. If the dog could have rolled her eyes, she probably would have.

The laugh she smothered—Reese probably deserved a medal for it. "You're fine, Talthien. You've got a lot of work ahead of you and I know you'll do it well. Particularly since you've got good help—that's you two, Graeme, Moire, in case you're wondering. And we'll get started on that work now by going down to eat."

"I get to eat dinner here?" Talthien said, excited. "But... with you? I thought the servants ate apart?"

"Maybe one day they will, if we have so many they need to work in shifts," Reese said. "But for now, we're all eating at the same table. And you might as well get Shoran too. If we're doing to do culture shock, we might as well do it right."

CHAPTER 9

How they managed to plow through the week leading up to the new year, Reese couldn't remember; between the dogs and the horses and the construction and her concerns over storms and recalcitrant Eldritch and the very important duty of counting and recounting the kisses she'd received to make sure she hadn't missed any... well, it was a wonder anything got done. But she came downstairs the morning before New Year's to find Sascha and Bryer at work—with the Hinichi—moving tables into the great hall. The Tam-illee were streaming past with food, a lot of food, which meant: "I guess everything's come over the Pad?"

"Yep," Sascha said. "Including us!" He swiped his forelock off a sweaty brow and folded his arms. "We barely got in before Felith put us to work."

Staring at the tables, Reese said, "I don't know why I thought this would happen outside."

"Outside!" Felith said from behind her. "Where the dishes could grow cold? It is winter, milady!"

Irine dashed past the Eldritch to leap into her brother's arms. Ignoring them, Reese said, "I thought... I don't know. A bonfire?"

"Of course," Felith said. "But that's what the bowl is intended to symbolize." She nodded toward the firebowl, now sitting by one of the far walls. "Tomorrow we let it go out. Or... we would if it was fed in a normal

129

fashion. I shall have to ask Kis'eh't if she would arrange for it to appear to die."

"I guess that makes sense. But if the firebowl's important, why did you move it?"

"Because we need the space in the center of the hall," Felith said. At Reese's blank look, she said, "For the dancing?"

"Dancing!" Reese exclaimed, dismayed.

"Of course. It is a celebration, milady!"

"Why so glum?" Irine said, pulling Sascha over. "I've been with Felith looking at the menu, everything's going to be great!"

"There's dancing," Reese told her.

"Dancing!" Irine clasped her hands together. "Hooray, I love dancing! Wait." Her ears dropped and she eyed Felith. "Is this 'we can't touch' dancing?"

Felith stared at her. "Of course." And then, daring to chide in a way Reese hadn't heard yet, "You have been among us for at least a year now, have you not? Including your acquaintanceship with Lord Hirianthial? You should not be so surprised. It is not done!"

"I thought maybe it could be a class thing?" Irine said. "At least, I was hoping it was. You know, fancy aristocrats with too much time to kill have all the crazy rules while normal, sensible people can at least hold hands?"

"Goddess and Lord!" Felith said. More gently, she continued, "No, Irine. Touching is uncomfortable because we sense one another's feelings, do you not recall? It doesn't matter, peasant or lady. But... if it mitigates your disappointment even a little, I will say that the dancing done at New Year's is not the mannered and stately sort practiced typically at the court. There is some energy in it."

"Some," Irine said, skeptical.

"I'd like to see it!" Sascha said.

"Obviously you have to teach us," Irine agreed.

Reese was expecting Felith to cavil—was hoping, actually—so she was alarmed when her chatelaine said, "Oh yes, you must be taught. Such dances will also be expected at the lady's wedding, and as there will be as many of you Pelted as there will be Eldritch, you will have to know the conventions. As soon as the tables are arranged...?"

Sascha pressed a fist into an open palm. "I'm back to work, then!"

"I'll help!" Irine said.

Watching them join the Hinichi, Reese said to Felith, weakly, "Dancing?"

The Eldritch's expression was touched with compassion, obvious enough that Reese wasn't sure to be embarrassed or relieved. "I take it you have never learned."

"It's... not something I would have needed to know in the past, no. Come to think of it, no one tried to teach me what I should have been doing at the court?"

Felith waved a hand, a brief, brisk gesture. "One does not dance much at the winter court. The great balls are reserved for summer, when the young go to Ontine to find their spouses. And as I said, those are more staid dances. It wouldn't do to show too much interest at such affairs."

"I'm glad I skipped the whole dating part here, then," Reese said, rueful.

Felith laughed. "Yes, milady. I'm sure you are. If you're free, I could show you the menu?"

"I guess you'd better." As they walked past the tables, Reese said, "Where does the glass go?"

"Lady?"

"The glass for the people who died. From the Vigil. Is it supposed to stay by the bowl?"

"There's no tradition," Felith said. "As every lady treats with the custom differently, each household does as well. Do you have a notion of what you'd like?"

Did she? Reese's gaze glided over the room, seeing it as it would look when it was done: tables forming a square around an open space, the fire in the fireplace brightly burning, people laughing and dancing, people eating. "Yes," she said. "Set a place at the table. We'll have an empty plate to go with the emptied glass." She smiled a little. "Just in case a few ghosts want to stop by."

She'd expected the last comment to inspire a laugh, or maybe a shocked look. But Felith said, "Very good, milady," and from her tone, she meant it.

———

What Felith set to teaching the Pelted visitors later was nothing like the ballroom dancing Reese had been expecting. She supposed seeing how everyone had dressed at Ontine had led her to expect that couples would sail together across the enormous ballrooms typical of Eldritch architecture, and it would be beautiful and terrifying because that was exactly the sort of dancing she'd never allowed herself to imagine she'd do and couldn't imagine she'd do well.

But no, Eldritch didn't dance like that, save on very rare occasions. What they did instead was a group dance based on patterns of moves executed in lines, squares, or circles. No touching, of course, save with wands and daggers... there was a lot of pointing and waving, though, which Reese thought looked more ridiculous than touching, but she could think so, couldn't she? Her skin didn't transmit thoughts. She wouldn't want to accidentally hear what Surela's sympathizers thought of her while trying to concentrate on what her feet were supposed to do next, certainly.

Eldritch dancing came in two styles. In the court style, the order of the patterns was dictated by the music, and the result was far more formal and rigid; everyone knew which form came next, so there were no surprises and a lot of opportunity to calcify one's mannerisms. The country style appropriate to their New Year's festivities, though, was far more spontaneous, and involved someone standing at the head of the hall on a pedestal calling out the pattern. It could and did get chaotic, and when Irine suggested that it sounded far more fun than the fancier style Felith only smiled one of those unreadable Eldritch smiles and said it depended on the dancers. And with that set them to standing in rows and started the lesson.

There were, apparently, a lot of patterns. Fortunately, the Tam-illee knew most of them. Between their aid and Felith's, the rest of them soon had the basics down. Reese was forced to admit that even she could figure out how to skip after someone else, or twirl and clap her hands, though she tried very hard not to think about what she looked like while doing it. It was probably ridiculous. It was also just a little bit fun. Especially since she was practicing with non-Eldritch, and could laugh off all the inevitable mistakes that involved bumping into people. Once she'd been on the floor for a while, Felith waved her aside and put her to work calling the patterns, "As this is one of your duties as lady during the feast." Naturally that wasn't as easy as it seemed either, because some forms led naturally into each other and others... didn't.

That inspired a lot of laughter too, and one or two shaken fists as the dancers recovered from her more ridiculous suggestions. Reese couldn't remember the last time she'd grinned so much or for so long. Maybe dancing wasn't that bad after all.

"You have the sense of it now, I think," Felith said. "Which is well because I believe you are about to retire for the evening."

"You are? I am? Oh—" She flushed at the sight of the tall, familiar figure at the door. "Right."

"My lord," Felith said as Hirianthial joined them. "We are pleased to see you. I shall leave you to the lady, and send supper up in an hour if it pleases."

"It does. Thank you, Felith."

Her chatelaine absented herself with commendable alacrity, leaving her standing alongside her fiancé in a pool of quiet at the head of the hall. Reese never tired of looking at him, especially now that she'd noticed that with each passing day he seemed a little more whole. It would take time for him to bounce back from the shocks and griefs he'd suffered, and she knew one of the reasons Liolesa was keeping him so busy was so he could use the work to center himself again. She also knew, without having to be told for a change, that she held some responsibility for that return to health. It felt good to be one of the reasons he felt better about himself after spending far too long being one of the reasons he didn't.

Also, he really was handsome.

"You are staring, my Courage," he murmured as he took her hand.

"You're worth staring at?" she offered, and it was true. She liked the wind-chapped vitality of him, fresh from the cold. His skin showed the flush better than hers.

"And you are a sight to gladden the heart," he said, and tucked her hand into his arm. "I see Felith has things well in hand here."

"She does! Which means you and I can slip out if you'd like. Unless you'd like to dance?"

He watched the revelry, mouth quirking upward at the corner. "I see the festivities have started early. But no, I have had a long enough day, I think, and tomorrow, while joyful, will be longer yet. I would not mind retiring." He canted his head. "Shall I ask what number we are on now?"

"What? Oh. Forty... three? Maybe?"

"You've lost count!"

His eyes were sparkling. She tried to scowl at him and failed. Even her mock-scowl lacked authority. Which was fine. "Let's just round down and you can make up the shortfall."

He laughed. "Done. Shall we?"

"Yes," she said firmly. As they left, she added, "You're here for the remainder of the holiday, then?"

"I am, yes." The sounds of merriment receded as they passed into the halls. Taylor and her team had started work on the center of the castle, so this section was dimly lit by discreet Alliance technology: a warm glow that brightened as they passed and faded behind them. "I have told my cousin that I am done for a few days, and that if she forced me to use my need to finalize details for the hospital as an excuse to stay away, I would."

Reese winced. "You're not going to work on it. Are you?"

He glanced down at her and chuckled. "No, Theresa. Don't fear that I need an excuse for myself as well as Liolesa to be here. This is where I belong on the first day of the new year. You are the lady of Rose Point. And I am—will be—your consort. When you fete your tenants, I should be beside you. And I do so desire it. I promise."

"You didn't have to read my mind to hear that one, I bet," Reese said, rueful.

"A relationship of sufficient length can lead to exchanges that might as well be telepathy," he said. "And while we haven't known one another long by how the days are counted, we have lived several lifetimes in the days we have." He brought her hand to his lips and kissed it again, and this time he feathered his warm breath over her knuckles until she shivered. "Time is relative."

"Yes," she said, sobered.

"So then. What shall we tonight, on the last day of the old year?"

Reese thought about that. About Eldritch sayings and the rightness of things, about new relationships, and old relationships, and talking and kissing. And found herself saying, "Could we just... sit around the fire and talk?"

"Or read to one another?" he suggested. At her glance, he said, "Do I divine correctly that what you want is... to act as if we have that time?"

"All the time in the worlds," Reese said. It felt right to her. "And we will have all the time in the worlds, for the time we have." She remembered the image he'd painted for her of his first wife when they'd taken that walk beside the sea, the day she'd proposed. "I guess you all really do read to one another for entertainment, don't you?"

"We do," he said. "And I would like it if we did."

"Even though...."

"Even though it is something that reminds me of Laiselin, yes," Hirianthial stopped outside the room where they'd spent the Vigil; she hadn't even realized he'd been guiding her to it. "But I think I would like to be the one read to, this time."

"Really?" she said, startled.

"And I believe I know what I want to hear," he finished, and there was mischief in his eyes... and a compassionate curve to his mouth that she wanted to trust, and also wanted to laugh at because he was about to suggest something outrageous...

"All right. Hit me."

"You read a great deal, my lady. I'd like to hear one of your romances."

Her cheeks flamed so hot she thought she could strike a match off one of them. And then she burst out laughing. "Well, why not, right? It's not like you haven't done it all before." She grinned up at him. "You are terrible, you know that?"

He pushed open the door. "Only a very little bit. After you, my lady."

"Would serve you right if I jumped into the good parts first."

His brows lifted. "Now there is an interesting revelation. Are the good parts the blushworthy ones? I am delighted that you might think so!"

She was sure her skin was going to burn off now, but she couldn't help grinning. "Fine. I won't deny it. But remember you asked for it when I read some of this stuff and we still have to stick with the whole 'celibate until marriage' part."

"Fortunately," Hirianthial said, "the wedding is not too distant. All the same, my lady... pick a *long* book."

———

It had been a wonderful evening. She'd curled up in the rocking chair with Allacazam on her lap, and they'd had the supper Felith had thoughtfully sent up, and then hot cider, mulled with sweet spices and a touch of apple brandy. They'd talked on light topics, as if they didn't have tasks of earth-shattering importance awaiting them, and then Reese had obliged her husband-to-be with the beginning of a book long enough that they wouldn't get to the salacious parts too fast; and to get back at him for the request, she'd picked one of the ones about an Eldritch, and made sure it was one of the most ridiculous ones in her catalog. His smothered laugh when the love interest was revealed in the first scene to be an eight-foot-tall centauroid Ciracaana woman had become what she was fairly sure was a smothered oath when the Ciracaana had started having ribald thoughts about the fainting Eldritch lordling she'd fixated on because of his sexy body and languid, helpless mannerisms. Reese felt Hirianthial's pain; when she'd first read this one, she'd spent several traumatic moments imagining how the body mechanics could possibly work and failing. And she wasn't even a doctor!

135

So she'd read, and kept an eye on him to make sure he was enjoying it, and the sight of him leaning his head against the back of the chair, relaxed and smiling... that had been worth the late night and hoarse voice.

There had also been some kissing. It was, he commented, far less fraught for them than for the poor pair in the novel, the Ciracaana having true muzzles and the sharp teeth to go with them. Reese had allowed that she felt sorry for them, and added that she might feel more sorry for them if he wasn't distracting her from contemplating their plight. Since he'd taken that as a challenge she'd been warm and happy and a little effervescent by the time she reached her bed.

It had been a late night, and even knowing that she'd have to wake up for the dawn she hadn't regretted it.

But she didn't wake at dawn. Her door creaked open while it was still dark, leaving her disoriented and muzzy. Blinking a few times, she peered at the silhouette, and since there was only one person that height likely to be in her bedroom she asked blearily, "I'm not late?"

Hirianthial came to the bedside. He was holding a robe, she noticed, so she sat up and let him drape it around her.

"No," he murmured. "Not at all. But you will not want to miss this, Theresa. Come."

Belting the robe around herself, she slipped off the bed and followed.

Most of Rose Point's windows and balconies were on the upper floors; knowing the castle's history, Reese wondered if it had been intended that way for defensibility. The lady's bedroom suite had a balcony that faced the northern vista, in fact, something Reese had often wondered about since the view now was desolate. Had the province been better settled when Firilith's first lady had settled here? Or had the former lady of the castle liked a quieter view? Come to think of it, if Val's stories were true— and she had no reason to believe otherwise—Rose Point had once been the royal palace. What queen had slept here, preferring the emptiness of the horizon for her view?

Reese didn't mind. Either it would stay quiet, and that was fine... or the Pelted and Eldritch immigrants to her new province would fill it, and that was good too. But for now, it was a potential, and she wasn't surprised when Hirianthial led her to a south-facing balcony, because most of the Eldritch of the world were settled to the south of Firilith. He'd chosen the most striking of them, the fourth floor balcony that overhung the great hall's doors.

The Tam-illee had checked the integrity of the entirety of Rose Point, but aside from throwing a few temporary flexglass doors on those balconies that were missing them they hadn't done any renovation. They had plans: furniture, shielding, lighting, heated and cooled tiles and clever bits of technology that controlled the immediate climate. But fancy balconies were very far down on Firilith's priority list, and Reese briefly regretted it when she stepped through the doors and the cold struck her like a wall. She wished she'd worn shoes over her socks because the flagstones were frigid enough to make her toe bones ache and the balls of her feet burn. Tugging the robe closer around herself, Reese approached the rail and stared into the dark.

Not so dark, anymore, at least. There were lights all over the courtyard, the artificial ones installed by the Tam-illee, and they glowed in the shrouding darkness like faraway stars. But it was still, she thought, a wild and unsettled world, and like the future it was spread before her, uncertain and new and breathlessly wonderful.

Hirianthial came alongside her and wrapped an arm around her shoulders—an arm and the fall of his fur-lined cloak. Under it he wasn't wearing much more than she was, though what passed for pajamas for Eldritch was still a lot of clothes. It was just much looser against his skin than she was used to. That part felt wonderful, and so did his body heat when she leaned into him.

She didn't have to ask what they were doing. She was cold, but she was glad she was here.

The change in the sky was so gradual she missed it at first: a hint of green along the eastern horizon. She noticed it because she could find the line between the sky and the sea, dark and misty, trailing the last of the stars. Gradually the sky lightened until the first streaks empurpled the sea. How slowly that halo inched over the horizon's edge! Until at last a golden ray pricked out the frothing pattern of the waves and the lip of the sun shimmered there. Reese held her breath, watching it.

Hirianthial bent close to her ear and murmured, "Listen."

Such a nonsensical request. Listen? To what? She glanced at him; he wasn't staring east, at the sun... but south, his body tense and waiting. So she looked south, too, perplexed.

And then, very distant, she thought she heard... a bell? And another. And another. They were nothing like the sweet, bright calls of the Vigil night, when she'd heard the handbells singing in the courtyard. These were enormous church bells, sonorous and deep, and the sound was traveling toward them because—she sucked in a breath with delight—the bells were ringing in succession. Which meant—

As the sun heaved itself over the horizon, the tide of bellsong rushed through the countryside, sounding from the distant border, then in the village's church, and finally Rose Point's chapel sang out the chorus. Amid their joyous song, Hirianthial said, "It begins in Ontine Cathedral. The priests there ring the bells to share the news, that the new year has come."

"And then everyone who hears them, their churches do it, and then on and on and on...."

"All the way to the furthest border." He drew her into his arms and dipped his head to touch his lips to her brow. "Theresa, my betrothed. Happy New Year."

She accepted the sweetness of the kiss that moved from her forehead to her mouth, and the bells filled her ears and her heart and her mind.

When the sound began to fade, though, she threw her arms around him and gave him a very, very enthusiastic reprise. Kiss Number One had been for sacred vows. Kiss Number Two was a little more personal. He laughed against her mouth and agreed with Kiss Number Three. Number Four was probably a little *too* personal for a balcony, no matter how far up it was.

"And now, before we break with our intentions to remain chaste," he said against her jaw where he was doing far too good a job of convincing her that they should give up on that intention completely, "we should go prepare for the day. Our guests will be arriving soon."

"You invited Liolesa?" Reese guessed.

"And Araelis, and whomever they wished to bring," Hirianthial agreed. He took her clasped hands. "Bright the new day. Shall we go to it?"

"I can't wait."

CHAPTER 10

The first day of the new year! When had she ever cared enough to celebrate it? Dressing in the diffuse light entering through her northern-facing windows, Reese tried to remember the last time. On Mars, maybe—she'd certainly stopped once she'd gotten the *Earthrise*. The Alliance maintained a universal calendar, originally designed to organize their military, but it had spread when traders had found it useful to have a common point of reference; after that everyone else had started hanging things on it, like ornaments on a Hinichi Christmas tree. Reese could have celebrated the new year by Alliance Mean Time anywhere in space, or gone by Mars reckoning had she felt nostalgic. But it had always felt to her like... like she was running out of time to succeed, and every year that passed was a big fat reminder that the return on her investment hadn't panned out. She'd had dreams, carefully unexamined except in moments of weakness, of finding someone to love and settling down after a long and lucrative run as an independent merchant, and when it had become clear she was still trapped in the role of rebellious young adult fleeing her family's expectations, she'd stopped celebrating holidays. On New Year's, the clock rolled over while she slept, and the only notice she gave it involved scheduling the ship's annual maintenance.

Maybe that's why she'd never bothered with birthdays either. Or any of the other celebrations. Between her chronic poverty and the sense that she was a failure, why would she? Reese paused in the act of shrugging on her dress, struck by how much she'd missed because she'd been so closed up in herself.

But then, if she hadn't been, maybe she wouldn't have survived those years of loneliness. Maybe had she been more open, those years would have taken her life.

Reese tugged the dress down over her chest and smoothed the split skirts over her leggings, watching the fabric straighten under her dark hands. This was just another way to beat herself up, she thought. One that her crew and her husband-to-be wouldn't appreciate. She'd made mistakes, sure. Maybe things would have turned out better, but things might have turned out worse too. Past-Reese had done the best she could, just like Present-Reese was. And if Future-Reese made better decisions, well... she had a lot of people helping her make them, so judging herself based on the difference was a little unfair.

She drew in a deep breath and settled her shower-damp braids behind her shoulders, shaking them to hear the beads click. If she could be kinder to others, she could be kinder to herself. It was a new year, after all. Didn't people make resolutions on those? Smiling, Reese finished her toilette and left her apartments, and found herself hurrying down the stairs because... she was excited. Her new castle was unfinished but already beautiful and full of decorations and between that and the feast and all her new friends and guests she couldn't wait to see the day.

She might also have hurried because once she hit the great hall the smell of something amazing was in the air and she was *hungry*.

The kitchens were enormous by her standards, and every time she entered them it struck her again. But one of the features of Eldritch kitchens was a large nook for eating, one that Felith had explained was usually reserved for the staff. It had taken Hirianthial to tell her later that it wasn't unusual for the noble family to sneak down to the kitchen to snitch food from indulgent cooks, particularly the younger members of the household, or those considered favorites by the servants... probably because, Reese thought, they didn't think it beneath themselves to spend time with the chef and their assistants. It had become her habit to stop by when she could and sneak a little food, talk with whomever was cooking. The servants Felith had imported from Ontine all seemed indulgent of her habit... and also unsurprised by it, which made Reese wonder if teenage Liolesa had once kicked her heels in front of her kitchen's fire while nibbling on almond pastries and listening to servants' gossip.

While she knew better than to think she'd be the first person in the kitchen—no one knew how much time cooking took like someone who'd been forced to subsist on protein bars—she did expect to be the first of her friends to make it there. In fact, she was looking forward to being the first because she could have the pick of what Chef set out. But it turned out all the priests had not only beaten her there, but they'd made sizable inroads on the platter too. Urise was furled into a swaddle of robes and blankets in a chair in the nook's corner, beaming. Belinor was putting away what looked an enormous apple fritter, and somehow that surprised her... his behavior was so proper she'd expected him to be a healthy, balanced breakfast type, and here he was eating one of the most fried-looking sweets available and washing it down with—from the smudge on the lip of the cup—hot chocolate.

But they were not the only ones in the room, and at the sight of him, Reese stepped forward before she remembered he was an Eldritch and not huggable. "Val! I didn't expect you here. Aren't you supposed to be ringing a church bell somewhere in Ontine?"

Val grinned and... stepped into her, surprising her. He'd never hugged her before. He was narrower than Hirianthial and closer to her height, and hard as a rock under his robes—how little had he eaten living here, she wondered, to get so lean? Because she knew the difference between hard-from-muscle and hard-from-privation, and he was definitely the latter.

Well, whatever he'd been before, he was theirs now. His starvation days were definitely over. She hugged him tightly, pressing her nose into his shoulder where his clothing was still cool from outside. He smelled like... she inhaled, smiled. Like winter roses, and the fragrant vetiver oil used to polish the wooden bits in Eldritch chapels.

"Finished staking your claim?" Val asked, affectionate.

"I have strong feelings about my people," Reese said, unapologetic. "And you've been one of them since we untied you in this courtyard."

He chuckled softly. "I'm glad you think so."

"He's very glad you think so," Belinor said briskly. "Given what's on his mind."

"Now, Belinor," Urise said. "Let Valthial choose his time."

"It's certainly too late now for that," Val said, wry. "So I might as well ask if you'll step outside with me, lady?"

Reese glanced at the plate; her mournful look was apparently too obvious, because Val leaned over and plucked a muffin from it and put it in her hand. "There. I won't keep you long, so that should tide you over."

141

"All right," she said. Breaking off a piece of the top, she added, "I hope it's not apple. Apples belong in pies."

"It's lemon," Val said just as the burst of zest and flavor woke her palate. "Good, yes?"

"Perfect. Needs coffee though." She stepped outside and waited for him to join her. "So. What's on your mind?"

"I did ring the bell in Ontine, you know."

Reese narrowed her eyes. Val was the most straightforward Eldritch she knew. He dropped enigmatic hints about things—she thought the Eldritch need to do that was genetic—but the only times she'd noticed him being cagey were when he was protecting someone else... and he wouldn't be asking her into the corridor to discuss something he wasn't willing to talk about. So the comment couldn't be a non sequitur. "There are a lot of churches between here and Ontine, but you still must have had to rush to get here on time. Even with the Pad."

"I would have had I used the palace's," Val said. "But the Queen has granted me a budget commensurate with her apparent trust in me, and I used some of it to buy a one-person Pad for the Cathedral."

"So.... you rang the bell there, dropped everything, stepped over the Pad, and jogged over here to help Urise?" She lifted her brows. "Val. Stop beating around the bush and tell me what you want."

He paused, laughed. "Beating around the bush? Is that idiom really still common in the Alliance?"

"It is? Why are you sur—" Some of her older historical novels swam to memory. "Oh. It's a hunting metaphor, isn't it? A medieval one."

He grinned. "Yes. And we still do beat literal bushes here. Since you've asked so properly, then... the High Priest traditionally keeps his office in Ontine Cathedral." His grin dropped from him abruptly. "In the catacombs."

Her skin stippled with goosebumps. "The catacombs where they dragged people to torture the talent out of them?"

"Or execute them on suspicion of having it. I find—" He looked away, the muscle in his jaw visibly tightening. "I find I can't do it, alet. I've had it cleaned. I've had all the old furniture replaced. Then I had all the new furniture hauled out so I could clean it myself by hand. And I still... can't... stand to work there."

Reese broke off another piece of the muffin. "So. Work here." When he looked at her abruptly, she said, "That's what you're about to ask, right? We're building you the chapterhouse for your talent school. It has plenty of space for an office. And you've put a Pad in Ontine, so either you were subconsciously trying to escape or you were already planning for something like this. Since you've got the means to go back and forth quickly, I think it'll work out fine. If the Queen is all right with it?"

"The Queen says I'm the first High Priest she trusts out of her sight, so I'm free to set up wherever I like," Val said dryly.

Reese winced. "Blood, that's...."

"A high compliment?"

"I was about to say a low bar to set," Reese said, rueful.

Val chuckled. "That too, I'm afraid." He glanced at her. "You're all right with it? Truly?"

She ate the next bit of the muffin while she thought through her impressions. Finally, she asked, "Why did you hug me?"

"I... because..." His eyes lost their focus, then he smiled whimsically at her. "Hirianthial lost a brother, lady. I never had one. Sometimes the God and Goddess provide what you need long after you've stopped looking."

She could relate to that, and let him have the heartbeat of silence the admission deserved. But only a heartbeat, because he wasn't the kind of man who liked to linger on the vulnerable moments. "So you think of Hirianthial as family. But you call me 'alet'?" she asked, teasing a little.

He spread his hands. "I didn't want to presume. You're no longer an intruder to my castle."

"I'm the owner of it, yes," Reese said. "But if you're going to adopt my husband as your brother, you'd better call me arii. Or Reese. No more lady-this or lady that and I don't care that the Eldritch use it as some kind of intimacy signaling. I need one Eldritch to treat me normally around here."

He laughed, easy and free. "So that's the cost of my setting up here, is that it?"

"Yep." She popped another piece of the muffin in her mouth and chewed, watching him finish laughing. "Is it a deal?"

"It is. Reese. But in public, during occasions when your authority needs buttressing, I'm afraid I'll have to default to the formalities. If it's any consolation, you won't be alone. I'll have to suffer people calling me 'Most High' and 'Eldest Favored of the God.'"

"Ugh!" Reese laughed. "You definitely have it worse." She reached for his hand and was gratified to receive it. "And thanks. For being his friend."

"I think it fitting that the God's high priest should be fast companions with the first mind-mage acknowledged outside the priesthood since

Corel," Val said lightly, and she knew the casualness with which he said it was hiding how deeply he felt about it.

"Me too. Now that we've settled *that*, I want to see what Belinor's left of my breakfast."

"Belinor is not the culprit you should be seeking! It is Urise you want."

"Urise! But he's so...."

"Old? Serene? Immobile?" Val laughed. "Woe betide you, woman. You've let his kindly demeanor take you in. Elder Urise put away all those missing savories, and so furtively that the cook's assistants never saw him do it. They didn't even offer him a plate. That's how stealthy the man is."

The image was so unlikely she started giggling. And then she added, "Belinor. And donuts. Really?"

"Belinor will eat anything if you sprinkle sugar on it. And don't you dare train him out of it. It's the only thing I can hold against him when he starts telling me I need to reform my ways."

"I'll keep that in mind." She grinned up at him and added, "It was yours first. It's yours again, Val. Welcome home."

His cheeks pinked, just a little. That was all the acknowledgment she was going to get, but it was also all she needed: that and the relief in his eyes.

"I'll find you some coffee."

With Val vanished into the kitchen proper, Reese dropped onto a stool to scavenge some breakfast of her own.

Belinor said, "All done, my lady?"

"All settled," she agreed. And grinned. "Have another fritter."

———

Having put away a cup of coffee and several savory crepes—freshly made to replace the ones Urise had devoured so stealthily—Reese went searching for her resident village Eldritch. That trip took her to the great hall... where she abruptly halted. The evergreens hung under Irine's supervision at the start of the holiday season had been refreshed at intervals as they grew dry; she'd become accustomed to seeing the dark, resinous green of them in her peripheral vision while jogging past, smelling the pine sap pungency of them. Those garlands still bedecked the hall, but they'd been woven through with strands of winter roses tied with silver ribbon. The perfume added a floral top note to the bouquet of evergreen and the scent of burning wood in the fireplace, and it was perfect.

Bryer was standing on a ladder, hanging a wreath over the mantel: evergreen with silver accents and a single red velvet ribbon, a shock of color that brought out the more furtive crimson glimmer of the glass berries hidden amidst the greenery. Seeing her, he grunted and hopped down.

"Oh, Bryer!" Reese said. "It's beautiful!"

"Looks good," he agreed, feathered arms flexing. "You stay a moment."

"All right?"

He was already jogging toward an Eldritch wheelbarrow, the carved panels on it absurdly ornate to be adorning something so pedestrian and antiquated. Sheaves of roses were still mounded in it despite the hall itself looking complete. Had he cut enough for the entire castle? Rose Point would live up to its name then, with the fragrance wafting down every corridor, and wasn't that a wonderful thought? But the Phoenix was returning, and had in his hand a single petite bloom. It was one of the most perfect roses Reese had ever seen, except for a single creased petal, and the stem was trimmed almost entirely off.

"First cut of new year," Bryer said, handing it to her. "For you to wear."

Touching it gently, Reese said, "Let me guess. It's a reminder that every year the roses die, and every year they grow again."

"That too." He gaped his beak at her. "Good application of lesson. Also private message. To the keeper of the aerie goes the gift. It says she is worthy."

The honor of it lanced her in the heart... just before she laughed. "And the flower dies, so that's a reminder too, right? 'Keep being worthy.'" She turned it, smiled. "Wait, there's more too. The little imperfection makes the rest of it look better, right? Or maybe 'it's all right not to be perfect.'" Which one was it? "It's all of it. You put a lot of work into this one present...!"

He folded her hand over it. "All good things are made with effort. Families. Gardens. Worlds. Lives."

"I understand." She dipped her nose to the rose and inhaled, felt the fragrance sweep into her and open her throat and heart. "Thank you, arii. I think I know just what to do with it. But first... have you seen Talthien or Shoran?"

"Stables," Bryer said, talons clicking on the flagstones as he returned to the ladder.

145

Naturally. "Thanks," she said. "I'll leave this here where I can find it again on my way back inside." She set the flower on the mantel before she headed on her errand.

The two Eldritch were indeed in the stables, along with Terry, Sascha, and the two Guardkin. Her arrival caused a cessation in the conversation as every gaze swiveled to her. Reese put a hand on her hip and said, "All right. What new problem do we have to solve."

"I told you she'd know," Sascha said. "Boss, those people from the village have to walk here. All three hours of the trip. Four. Six. Whatever. I suggested we go get them..."

"And I said it would be rude." Terry was leaning back against one of the stalls. Naturally the horses weren't nibbling his hair. It was only her head that they liked to slobber on.

"Is he right?" Reese asked the Eldritch.

Talthien muttered, "It is not rude. It's stupid to think it's rude. The catechism says to find offense where none is offered is violence against the God and Lady. But it doesn't matter because they'll never say yes."

Reese expected Shoran to agree with Terry, so she was surprised when the other man didn't say anything until Moire leaned over and prodded his leg with her nose. He reached down to pet her ruff, smiling. "All right! No more cold nose, please. I'll stop brooding." Straightening, he said, "Mistress, I think... you should send yon tiger. It's a long walk in winter. Not everyone should be making it. Not everyone would, in fact, under ordinary circumstances. They'd stay home. If you sent something to bring everyone back... well, that would be the first time the entire village could attend a New Year's Feast like this."

"But?" Reese said, hearing it in his delivery.

"But I fear Talthien is correct," Shoran said. "It may offend. Your conveyances are convenient and empowering, milady, but... they are very modern."

"Is that the only problem?" Reese said. She eyed Terry and Sascha. "This is such an easy fix I don't know why you haven't figured it out yet. What am I employing you people for, anyway?"

"Our sterling good looks?" Sascha offered.

"Or our heartwarming banter," Terry said, grinning at the tigraine. "But obviously not our brains. Go on, alet. What do you want us to do?"

"Build a carriage," Reese said.

"A... what?" Terry said carefully.

146

Sascha was laughing though. "Oh, that's perfect! You want us to make some kind of fancy princess carriage big enough for a village?"

"I don't think they come that big," Reese said. "So maybe you'd better make a few smaller ones. Don't they haul hay in wagons? Make fancy wagons, attach the horses to them, and go get the Eldritch. It can't take you long to whip something like that together, right?"

"We're engineers!" Terry said. "We can do anything. Except Taylor is going to blow a relay when you tell her you want to waste time on this."

"It's not wasting time if we use it for every holiday," Reese said. "And for... I don't know. Hay rides? Harvest festivals? Do they do that in real life?"

"Hay rides and harvest festivals," Sascha mused, tapping his finger on his mouth. "That sounds—"

"Don't say it," Reese warned.

"Promising! I was going to say promising!"

"Sure you were," Reese said dryly. "Anyway. Can you do it, Terry? I'll authorize whatever disruption of schedule is necessary to use the genie for the parts."

"Oh, we shouldn't need the genie for almost any of it. This will be a great chance to put the machine shop to work." Terry chuckled. "I admit, half of the fun of this job is never knowing what we're going to do next. Anyone can toss together a typical Alliance town. This assignment? I'm configuring a gem grid one day and trying to figure out how to rusticate a well so it looks like someone built it before there were power tools the next. It's a real adventure."

"Is it really that different from what you're used to?" Sascha asked, curious. "After living with your own Eldritch lord all your life?"

"I say that especially after living with Lord Lesandurel all my life—and all his too. He came to the Alliance and adapted to us, you know. This... this is new." Terry grinned, ears perked. "I'm off, then. Give us an hour, maybe two, we'll have what you need, alet."

"Great. And put my coat of arms on it or something! If I end up with the fancy coaches, I might as well get it right."

Terry saluted her and jogged out of the stable, leaving her to deal with the stares of the Eldritch. "I assume that coaches are fine?" she said, suddenly worried. "I can call him back—"

"No!" Shoran exclaimed. "No, it's... just... that ladies usually do not send coaches for their people. We have always walked. It's expected."

"But it should be all right, right?" Sascha asked. "Sending carriages is less 'this is horrible and foreign' and more 'this is strange and eccentric'?"

"Just so."

"I can handle being eccentric," Reese said. "You two will go down with the wagons? Coaches? Whatever."

"Of course," Shoran said. "The dogs have not yet seen the village. They will want to. Yes?" He looked at them, received two nods. Moire had been sitting next to him, following the conversation like any other participant might have; Graeme had as much of himself in Talthien's lap as could fit, with the youth leaning against one of the hay bales.

"Can you talk to them?" Reese wondered. "I mean... can you hear them, the way Talthien can."

"I can, yes," Shoran said. "Though I don't think I can do it as easily." He glanced at Talthien. "This matter with the dogs will take a great deal of negotiation, so it is for the best that they can speak to all of us, if necessary."

"They just prefer not to," Talthien said. "Graeme says it's complicated... something about it being easier to hear one person the more you practice with them? But he doesn't know if that's just him and Moire, or if it will be like that for all the dogs." Graeme glanced up at Reese without lifting his head and puffed out a breath through his nose. "Moire also says she's not anyone's dog. She's Graeme's mate, and she refuses to make an attachment to anyone who would part her from him."

"Makes sense to me," Reese said, and wondered how the inevitable jealousy was going to fall out when the dogs picked their companions. Fortunately, being at the top meant she got to delegate at least some of the initial procedural issues to the people most involved with them, so... "You'll have to tell me how it goes."

"Yes, milady," Talthien said. "And if the coaches are to be ready soon, I should go dress myself and groom my friends. Sir," to Shoran, "you should tell her your choice!"

"Oh?" Reese said, interested. "Did you finally decide on a horse, then?"

Shoran had flushed, but he gave her one of the abbreviated Eldritch nods. "Yes, Mistress. If it will be no trouble to you, I'd like the rabicano filly." At her blank look, he nodded toward one of the brownish horses, a mare that looked like she'd been frosted in white.

"Wonderful," Reese said, meaning it. She'd half-expected Shoran to put the choice off indefinitely as a way of politely wiggling out of accepting the gift. "So what will you name her?"

"Mistress?" Shoran asked, stunned. "You can't mean me to name her! It should be your choice. You intend to breed her... she will be the foundation of a line of foals. She will need an appropriate name to be noted in the books!"

Reese said, "I don't know if you want me in charge of naming a stable full of horses. I had enough trouble with mine... and I named her Penny, after a small copper coin from Terra."

"It could also be a girl's name," Sascha offered. "Short for Penelope." He grinned at her expression. "Hadn't thought of that, had you?"

"No," Reese said, liking it. Bringing herself back to the task at hand, she said, "It's New Year's Day, Shoran-alet, and she's your horse. Give her a good name to start the year with."

"Then... I shall name her Eiluionase," Shoran said. "If... that sits well with you, my lady. It means silvered Beauty."

"Better not rename Penny Penelope, then," Sascha said. "The way things are going, you'll be needing at least one horse that answers to less than three syllables."

Reese grinned. "I think it's great," she said to Shoran. "Beauty it is."

They left a very proud man to finish tending his charges and prepare for the journey back to the village. Strolling alongside her toward the keep, Sascha said, "Those horses are all going to end up with high-minded names. It's going to be a barn full of Courages and Faiths and Duty-until-Deaths."

Reese chuckled. "And one very lowbrow Penny."

He grinned. "Sort of obvious, that metaphor."

Reese snorted. "Don't work too hard, fuzzy. Remember, I apparently hired you for your looks."

Sascha nodded sagely. "I wouldn't want to sprain anything."

She smacked his arm lightly, swayed away from his threatened swat, and wondered when she'd started laughing.

———

The coaches were everything Terry had threatened, frothing with ornament and bedizened with her new coat of arms and covered in scrolling filigree metal, a watered gold that was just right in the wan winter sunlight. Nor was that the only thing the Tam-illee had made, because the horses pulling the wagons wore shining harnesses hung with sleigh bells, fancy blankets... and hats. With feathers. It was the most outrageous equipage Reese had ever seen, and that counted the illustrations from her favorite fantasy novels; confronted with it, the only emotion she was capable of was a stunned awe.

"Ta-da!" Terry said, opening his arms as if summoning with them.

The pressure in her chest was almost certainly the harbinger of a paroxysm of laughter that would end the boning in her bodice. Reese managed to get the words out level. Mostly. "I... I have no idea what to say, alet. It's... astonishing."

"Are you sure anyone's going to want to get into those things?" Sascha said from behind her, skeptical.

The foxine folded his arms, smug. "See for yourself."

Tiptoeing closer, Reese peered into the first wagon and found Shoran and Talthien already in it, exclaiming over the cushioned seats and admiring the clever mechanism that allowed the passengers to winch a cover over their heads during inclement weather.

"You asked us to speak their language," Terry said. "We heard and obeyed!"

Reese pressed a hand to her mouth until she was sure she could maintain her composure. "And did Taylor blow a relay?"

Terry chuckled. "I think the request was so ludicrous she just accepted it. It happens that way sometimes. Little things you fight. The big things have momentum."

"Tell me about it," Reese murmured.

"Are these things really going to get them here any faster?" Sascha asked, arms folded.

"Not by much," Terry admitted. "Walking horses go at a slightly quicker pace than walking people, but your guess is as good as mine about whether they'll make better time while pulling. The wagons are made of modern materials, so they're much lighter than real wood would be—that's in our favor. But the roads here aren't fantastic." He shrugged, swished his tail once in a way that reminded Reese of Graeme and Moire. "My best guess is that we'll be back in the afternoon."

"But with more people than could have made the walk, hopefully," Reese said.

Terry nodded. "Hopefully. But we should get going if we want to keep to our timetable. Sascha? You coming? That second wagon won't drive itself. At least, not with horses attached."

"Coming," Sascha said. "We'll be back, Boss."

Watching the two wagons roll out of the courtyard, Reese wondered just how many Eldritch would decide to return in them. Would Talthien's mother convince the others to stay? She hoped not. But she'd done everything she could not to push them too far, and that was all she could do. If they didn't come, at least she could celebrate with the Pelted, and with her Eldritch family.

Strange to say it that way. Her Eldritch family. But when she married Hirianthial, that would make Liolesa her cousin-in-law. And Val and the priests, and Felith... they might as well be family after all they'd been through together.

Reese headed back up the steps to the front door. It was going to be a good feast no matter what. She found herself hoping, though, that it would be a good feast with her tenants, no matter how much more comfortable it would have been without them.

CHAPTER 11

Thanks to the magic of Alliance technology, the feast began assembling itself in the great hall by mid-morning even though the festivities weren't supposed to begin until the afternoon. But stasis fields, warmers, and coolers were basic appliances in Alliance kitchens, and since none of her Pelted residents were willing to do without them, they'd been among the first of the conveniences that appeared at Rose Point. Reese had wondered if her borrowed Eldritch staff would be familiar with them, given Liolesa's politics... but she'd forgotten that even something as readily available as a warming platter relied on Pelted power sources that hadn't been available in Ontine before the recent renovations had commenced. Her chef and the kitchen staff thought kitchen appliances were several times more awe-inspiring than modern lighting or heating or transportation. A horse could take you down a road. But keeping the soufflés from collapsing? *That* was magic.

Reese traipsed down the stairs and into the great hall, following her nose. She'd spent most of the morning hunting for Allacazam, who'd rolled himself into a dark closet on the second floor, and after that she'd tidied up her clothes and donned the fillet she'd received on Longest Night. Bryer's flower had been tucked into her hair at her ear, using the fillet as an anchor. She thought she looked about right: the dress split over her leggings and boots, which let her move easily, but it was still a dress, and she'd had it made in wine red because it reminded her of Hirianthial's eyes. That was definitely a thought to keep to herself, because the twins would never let her live it down if they heard about it.

When she arrived, Kis'eh't was supervising the procession of dishes and their disposition on the decorated table with Irine's help. The selections already looked amazing, even though the main courses hadn't yet arrived. Right now it was all fruit-filled pastries and almond cookies and two towering cakes on stilts with ridiculously ornate frosting patterns that looked like wallpaper but were actually stamped and molded sugar. There was punch—cold—and cider—hot—along with wine, pots of coffee and kerinne and hot chocolate, and pitchers of water that were remaining artificially cold, though their glass curves were filmed with steam from sitting alongside the warmer drinks. There was pie, inevitably, because Kis'eh't wouldn't have allowed a feast to go by without one, or in this case, several. And so many breads. Braided breads; glazed breads studded with gem-like candied fruits; sweet rolls and salted pretzel-like breads... the smell was overwhelming, intoxicating, yeast and sugar and the deeper, fruitier aroma of decanting wine.

"I guess the dessert team finished first?" Reese said, setting Allacazam on one of the tables.

"They're used to making dessert in advance because it lends itself better to being prepared in stages," Kis'eh't said as Irine gave Reese a hug. "Since they didn't know we'd be putting everything in stasis fields until the guests arrived, they proceeded as normal... and here we are."

"With food for a fleet of people," Irine said. "Thank goodness we have the Hinichi visiting, or we might not eat it all! You look wonderful, arii."

"I do?" Reese looked down, self-conscious, and gathered the fold of her skirt. "You don't think the whole pants-and-dress thing is too déclassé?"

"I think it suits you," said a voice from behind them, and there was Hirianthial, wearing a court coat in a brown as rich as a mink pelt, edged in golden embroidery, and by now she was no longer surprised by the succession of stunning outfits he owned... which is why she was able to look down and notice him wearing *shoes*. Not boots, but actual shoes. They were inevitably opulent, brown suede with embroidery and buckles, but none of that mattered because she could see the line of his ankles and calves. Her expression when she lifted her face made him press a hand to his mouth to hide the twitch at their corners. She started laughing.

Kis'eh't cocked a brow at them both. "Should I ask..."

"No," Reese and Irine said in unison. Glancing at the Harat-Shar,

Reese said again, more firmly, "No. I was just having a moment." She held out her hands, expecting and receiving the kiss he'd wanted to bestow on them. "You look perfect, as usual."

"Practice," he offered, eyes dancing. "One learns to make oneself presentable."

"I don't know if I'll ever get used to the coronet," Reese said, touching her forehead. "But I can see how repetition makes it easier. Once you make the necessary compromises."

"Like?" Kis'eh't wondered.

"Like no corsets. Ever." Reese wrinkled her nose. "And also, shoes I can run in."

"You learned that lesson well, didn't you," Irine said, one ear sagging.

"I'm definitely done being the helpless heroine. As much as possible anyway," Reese said. She looked up at her fiancé. "What brings you down so early? I thought you'd be reading, or relaxing. Like you promised your cousin. And me."

Hirianthial chuckled and tucked her hand under his arm after another kiss, this time on its palm. "Peace, Theresa! I was resting, I pledge you. But it is in fact my cousin who brought me down before time—she sent a message saying she is on her way."

"Early?" Irine asked.

"I'd better see how far along we are in the kitchens, then," Kis'eh't said, and excused herself to jog away.

"I suspect it is for Araelis's sake," Hirianthial said to Irine, quieter. "As she has no one to host for this year."

Reese wondered how he could say that with such equanimity, and guessed that after fifty or sixty years of not being Jisiensire's host, he felt removed enough from it to not miss it the way Araelis must. Poor Araelis! Reese had thought through the loss of her husband, and understood intellectually the loss of Jisiensire's tenants... but she hadn't realized what the New Year's Feast would be like for a lady without a people until she'd had a people of her own. And she wasn't even as attached to her people yet as someone like Araelis must have been, having known her tenants for decades.

"If she's on her way, she's probably already here," Reese said. "We should go meet her."

"Let us," Hirianthial agreed. As they headed for the doors, he said, "Normally we would hear the Queen's arrival announced long before she reached the keep; guards at the gates of noble Houses know to announce

155

the Royal House. I suspect the Pad is allowing her to catch them unawares."

"I bet she likes that," Reese said. "Particularly since her arrival is probably announced with something loud. Like trumpets."

"How well you know us, my lady." Hirianthial paused and finished, amused. "And how well you know the Queen already."

Reese snorted. "It doesn't take long to notice her sense of humor runs to terrible jokes and questionable pranks. What takes time is believing it."

That got her a full laugh, one long enough that she looked up at him and grinned.

"Yes," he said, opening the door for her. "Yes, that is exactly it."

Passing through under his arm, Reese said, "You know what? Leave the door open. Both of them. The hall's not going to get cold anymore, not with the climate control working. I think it's a good symbol."

He glanced behind them at the warm, bright hall festooned with roses and boughs, and the feast taking shape on its tables like treasure, glittering with butter and glaze. "In many ways. Yes."

That was how they received their queen, then: standing on the steps in front of the open doors to Rose Point castle, which so long had stood empty and barren. Liolesa came without entourage, wearing a gown in midnight blue more in keeping with her usual wardrobe, but no crown, and with her head high and her cheeks and nose pinked by the brisk wind. Behind her was Araelis... but Araelis wasn't alone, and Reese gasped when she saw the two women accompanying her. It couldn't possibly be, but...

"Alet," said the Harat-Shar Natalie Felger, author of all of Reese's favorite romance novels, "I am very glad to see you again."

"You know one another?" Araelis asked, surprised.

"We met on Harat-Sharii," Natalie said, and confused and delighted Reese with a hug. Pulling back, the pardine grinned, whiskers arching. "I see you found your way, ah?"

"I did... yes. You helped!" Reese exclaimed. And then laughed. "And it looks like you found yours, doesn't it?"

"The paintings have come home at last, and so have we," Natalie agreed. "I'm glad it happened while I'm still young enough to enjoy it."

"But old enough," said her niece, Shelya, "to sit back and let the rest of us do the hard work!" She hugged Reese with one arm, protecting a platter. "Hello, alet! I hope you don't mind that we brought a cake?"

"Is it the lemon one you fed me before?" Reese asked, and then laughed. "It is, isn't it."

"Authors," Shelya said, "like a certain symmetry to things. I think it's from all the years spent tidying up loose plot ends."

"Of course they do," Reese said. It was incredible to be greeting the two Harat-Shar she'd had dinner with less than a year ago, when that dinner seemed to have happened in some other lifetime. How badly she'd needed Natalie's empathy! And that sense that even normal people could have history with the Eldritch, and come away changed. Reese could still remember the wonder of those cached paintings, so richly pigmented and so intimate in their portrayal of a friendship she'd thought improbable at the time. In retrospect, the questions that night had raised in her had led her, inevitably, to this moment now.

"Yes," Natalie said, satisfied. "You really have found your way."

"I'm home," Reese said, simply, and smiled. "And I'm thrilled to offer its hospitality to you. Please, come in!" She looked into the courtyard. "Is it only the two of you...?"

"For now," Shelya said. "The rest of us are one week out! But Aunt Natalie and I... we've always lived ready to pack up and move the moment we were called." She grinned at Liolesa. "So we were the first ones here."

"Fitting," Liolesa said, "for Sellelvi's direct descendants."

Araelis, Reese noticed, was looking much more present than she had at the Vigil. "Well, let's not all stand out here in the cold! Come on."

The Hinichi had come downstairs while they were outside talking, and the savory courses were filling the tables and adding to the delectable mélange in the air. It was going to be an amazing meal but even with their additional guests Reese doubted they'd finish it all, which made her wonder if there was some custom about leftovers. Gifts to the poor? Of course, Firilith had no poor because it had almost no people, and Freedom knew whether the state of other Houses's provinces warranted that kind of codified charity. And wasn't poverty a contextual thing, anyway? A lot of the Eldritch aristocrats thought they were rich, but they also thought having enough candles to light their mansions at night was the height of luxury.

Truly, she was in the right place. If there was anyone who understood how you could be poor by one standard and rich by another, it was her.

The remaining dishes made it to the tables, and brought with them a parade of Laisrathera's Eldritch servants and priests along with the rest of the Tam-illee. The resulting bustle looked like a miniature of the Alliance under one vaulted roof, and if Bryer and Kis'eh't and Allacazam—and herself—were a small representation of their species compared to the Tam-illee, Hinichi, and Harat-Shar, there were still more aliens in one place than she thought the world had ever seen, and that idea took her breath away.

...but her tenants were still missing.

An hour after the food had been set out, Reese cornered Irine. "Have you heard from Sascha?"

"No," Irine said, already pulling out a telegem. "I assumed he was on his way."

"They should have been here by now."

"Let's see what's holding them up, then." Irine tapped the telegem awake and tucked it against her ear. "Ariihir?" She listened, frowning. "Really?" Another pause. "You're sure? All right, I'll tell her." Taking the gem off, she said, "He says they'll be there in three hours."

"Three hours! They were supposed to be here now! What am I going to do with all the guests for three hours?"

"We could start the feast without them," Irine said, uncertain.

The moment she heard the idea, Reese knew it was wrong. "No."

"I guess it's a good thing we've got the food in stasis fields, then?"

Reese grimaced and looked at her guests. Three hours! What to do? And yet she had to do something. She couldn't keep them waiting with nothing to do but mingle, no matter how much they seemed to be enjoying one another's company. Eventually they'd get tired of it and want to know why they couldn't eat yet, and that would introduce awkward questions.

Fortunately, she'd gotten fairly good at improvising.

Stepping onto the pedestal reserved to the dance caller, Reese said, "So, it looks like we've had a delay. What do you say we take a tour of Rose Point? I'll show you the amenities and talk about what we're planning."

"Show them the horses!" called one of the Tam-illee.

"Show us the horses!" another of the Tam-illee said. "We haven't all had a chance to see them."

"And maybe the gardens?" Reese said, eyeing Bryer. When the Phoenix inclined his head, she said, "And definitely the gardens!"

As the group began to drift toward the great hall's doors, Hirianthial joined her. "Trouble?"

"I hope not," Reese said. "But we've got three hours to fill, and we can't do it with the traditional stuff."

"It will go by quickly, my lady. You will see."

———

Thankfully, Hirianthial was right. Reese wouldn't have thought the Tamillee would be entertained by a trip through a castle they were intimately familiar with already, but she hadn't counted on their reaction to the addition of the Hinichi and the visiting Harat-Shar and even the servants hired by Felith from the capital. All of their guests had questions, and Taylor and her friends were eager to discuss their efforts. If the tour turned into an impromptu brainstorming session strung across half the property, well... that was typical for Laisrathera, and Reese didn't mind. They needed to test their ideas, and since doing so allowed them to imagine a bright and beautiful future, everyone enjoyed it as much as they would have something more obviously recreational.

The entire party was in the courtyard, heading back toward the great hall, when Reese heard the wagons. She hadn't planned on a spectacle, given how delicate the forthcoming scene was probably going to be, but no one showed any signs of wanting to retreat into the hall to oblige her. Reese resigned herself to handling her disappointment in front of an audience and turned to face the gates. She wasn't a fool; if Sascha and Terry hadn't returned immediately, it had been because there'd been a fight. And you didn't win fights with Eldritch... not on the first round, anyway. She'd be grateful if Shoran and Talthien returned with the dogs; more than that, she knew better than to expect.

Hirianthial drew alongside her on the left. On her right, Liolesa, in a rustle of skirts. Reese knew her tension was communicating too clearly when the latter said, "Calmly, Theresa."

"Easy for you to say," Reese muttered. "You've been doing this for six hundred years."

Liolesa's mouth twitched, but she didn't reply. She didn't have to. Reese knew the Queen could have hidden her amusement with those six hundred years of practice. This was the Eldritch liegelady's equivalent of offering her vassal a shoulder to lean on, and if nothing else she'd earned that much. Reese remembered Felith's long-ago explanation of draevilth, the lines of duty that linked tenant to lady to queen; she might not have the lady-to-tenant part down yet, but the lady-to-liege part was working fine.

The wagons pulled up... and scattered all Reese's thoughts.

They were full. Completely full.

As the horses came to a halt and the two drivers hopped down to open the doors and put down the steps, Reese did a quick headcount. Every single one of her tenants had come.

The dogs jumped down first, groomed to gleaming and dressed for the holiday: Moire had a silver ribbon around her neck, and Graeme a red. They sat neatly alongside the steps and watched the Eldritch process out of the carriages, and Reese no longer perceived them as too fancy. They were just right, now, exactly perfect. One by one, the Eldritch lined up in front of her by family, the same way they had in town when she'd distributed the Lady's Day gifts. When they'd all disembarked, the priestess stepped forward.

"Lady. We know we are tardy. If you have hosted the feast without us, we will be glad to deliver our gifts and depart."

"It's New Year's Day," Reese said, meeting her eyes steadily. "I won't eat without my people."

A long pause, one she felt like a wind through the crowd even though no one moved.

"Then, we would give you the gifts," the priestess said, quieter. "And be glad of your hospitality. I shall begin." She set a sprig of greenery wrapped in gold and silver ribbons on the ground in front of Reese. "From the Goddess and Lady's priestess, a sprig of the uliienire, which brings fertility and good health to wives and mothers."

Reese bent to pick it up, deciding she'd have to bring a table next year if they were going to leave her offerings on the ground to keep from accidentally touching her. She found herself concentrating on minutia like this because she was trying not to cry. Hadn't she remembered there being some custom about greenery and kissing? And here her Eldritch had brought something, but even better. The little sprig smelled piquant and bright and the stem's prickly bark chafed her thumb as she rubbed it. "Thank you. All the blessings She can give, I will be grateful to accept."

The priestess nodded and stepped back. She was replaced by the senior land servant, the one she'd given the binoculars to. And he'd brought...

"For you, mistress," he said, proudly, going to one knee to open the bundle in front of her. "There are no monsters in Firilith anymore, God and Lady be praised... but hunting we have in plenty now that so much of the land has returned to the wild."

The pelts he revealed were breathtaking, all in shades of white and ivory and bisque. Set all together like that they were overwhelming, stacked almost as high as her knee: so much fur! Hirianthial was the one who lifted the first. "Ice deer?" he asked, sounding surprised.

"And northern mist bears," the land servant said, satisfied. "These particular pelts have been in our family for decades. We rarely hunt—it is perilous with so few of us—but I think now things might be changing. And if you seek goods of value to trade with other Houses, mistress..."

"Oh yes," Araelis said from Hirianthial's side, drawing abreast. "Those are beautiful. And ice deer! Few people hunt them anymore."

"They are magnificent," Hirianthial agreed, draping one of the pelts in Reese's arms. "But these, my lady, should be made into something for you to wear, as they are a gift to you from your tenants. There will be other hunts. Will there not?"

"Yes, my lord," the land servant said. And bowed. "God and Goddess bless you both for it."

"Thank you," Reese said. "I... I've never had anything so grand. Not until I came here."

Was that too much sharing? Would they resent her for not being rich all her life? But no, in his eyes there was appreciation for her admission. He bowed again and stepped back.

The next man to step into place before her she knew, at least. "Shoran-alet."

"Mistress," he said, smiling. "Your beast servant comes before you now with his gift."

Reese put her hands on her hips. "It had better not be the horse back."

His mouth flexed but he controlled what she was sure would have been a laugh; it was in his eyes when he looked at her. "No. But related, my lady. Your present was generous, but I would not have that gift reduce your herd. With your permission, I would like to give you her breeding rights."

A murmur now, which she ignored; she imagined the rest of her tenants had already expressed their opinions to one another about her overly generous offering to a mere servant. What arrested Reese was Hirianthial's reaction, because he'd become very still. There was a trap in this gift somewhere, but where? She didn't know the first thing about where to find it either—what did she know about breeding and husbandry?

But someone else did. "Irine?"

The tigraine wiggled her way out of the crowd. "Arii?"

"Can you explain?"

Irine glanced at Shoran. "Ordinarily if you own a non-sentient animal,

161

you also have the right to rent their bodies to make babies with other people's animals. If he gives you the breeding rights, then you get to decide what horse has sex with Shoran's horse, and who gets the babies. Otherwise, that would be his decision."

Reese rubbed her nose. Typically blunt, but at least the explanation allowed her to see the trap. "Is that how it works here?" she asked Shoran.

"Yes, mistress. Yon tigress explains it well."

"Which means in another generation—horse generation, not Eldritch generation—we're back where we started, with you horseless and having never been enriched by the gift," Reese said. "Because you're going to outlive Beauty—" Better the Universal translation than to trip up on the Eldritch name—"by centuries."

Behind them, Talthien muttered, "I told you she wouldn't like it."

Shoran inclined his head, just the slightest of nods. "Do you not want the gift, my lady?"

And that was a trap so big even she could see it coming. "No. I honor the gift and I do want it. On one condition. No, two conditions."

The rustle that went through the crowd was loud—or was it that the crowd was otherwise so quiet that any noise at all seemed magnified? Scanning her tenants' faces, Reese said wryly, "I guess conditions aren't usual. But this time, you'll accept them, and then I'll accept your gift, and we all eat happy. All right?"

"Tell me, mistress," Shoran said.

"I'll breed her," Reese said. "And I'll sell her children, or keep them. The first condition is that when she dies, you get to choose a new horse from her line. That way you'll have a horse for the length of your lifetime, not hers. So far so good?"

His nod was more distinct this time. "Yes. Please continue, my lady."

"My second condition," Reese said, reaching for language out of her romances, "is that for every child of your body, you will get an additional horse of Beauty's body, or you can decide not to accept one and accept its market value instead. That way your children will have horses, or you'll have money. Either way your family will be taken care of. And those additional horses will be yours to breed, Shoran-alet, not mine."

That blew the complacent look right off Shoran's face... and every other face too. All her tenants started talking, in fact, and continued until Shoran stammered, "M-mistress! You cannot be serious!"

"I'm very serious," Reese said. "This isn't supposed to be a cast-off piece of clothes, or charity, or some... some bit of noblesse oblige where you briefly share my privilege and then you lose it. I want you—all of you —to have the opportunity to be successful, because the more successful you are, the more we all benefit." She surveyed the entire crowd, then returned her gaze to Shoran. "I want you to take that money, or those horses, and ensure the health and prosperity of your family. That's the real gift. Beauty's just a convenient way of handing it over."

One of her tenants said, tentatively, "We are not supposed to own things of value. All that we have, we derive from our lady. All that we can make, she receives."

"And there will still be some of that," Reese said. "Maybe for a long time. But I want you all to be independent of me, and you're about to ask me why, and I'll tell you: it's so that if you stay with me, it's because you'll have made the choice to stay. Not because you have to."

Hirianthial, of course, knew where she was coming from. And Liolesa... for all Reese knew, Liolesa had planned for the world to evolve into this hybrid feudalism all along. But the remaining Eldritch, including her hires from Ontine, were staggered by this speech. Even Araelis, if Reese was any judge, though more in the sense of 'grappling with intriguing new ideas' than in shock. She let them have a little time to fight with the thoughts, then returned her attention to Shoran. "Those are my conditions. I won't pretend they're minor. But it's your decision, and you're allowed to say no."

Shoran lifted his chin. "I accept, my lady. To you on this New Year's Day I give the breeding rights for Eiluionase, on the condition that I receive a child of her body when she dies, and another child of her body —or its value in coin—for each child of my body."

Reese grinned. "Excellent. Thank you for the gift, alet. I will put it to good use. With your advice."

He bowed and stepped back, joining the tenants, whose consternation was palpable; her gifts, Reese realized, had become as overwhelming to them as Liolesa's were to everyone, and this filled her with unexpected cheer. As her tenants conferred as to who to send to her next, Hirianthial bent close and murmured, "You have made Shoran the most eligible bachelor in the entire kingdom, you know."

She hadn't realized he was unmarried. If he got a horse for every child he had... Reese turned her chuckle into a cough. "I'm sure he can handle it," she replied quietly.

The crowd was still in whispered consultation when Talthien broke out of it and presented himself. Reese didn't have to be Eldritch to know just how big a statement he was making, and that was before he went to one knee in front of her. The two dogs padded up and sat on either side of him, symmetrical and stern, and it was their movement that turned her audience back to her, and to the youth they hadn't noticed leaving their ranks.

"This is what it looks like," Reese said, quiet.

"My lady," Talthien said. "I am the youngest son of the line of the seal's servants, and it is mine to offer. Will you take me into your service, to guard you and your heirs until I fall in that duty?"

Behind him, his mother's mouth tightened and her hand twitched, but she didn't move. Reese looked down at Talthien's bowed head. "Before you can do that, you need training, don't you? How long does that training take?"

Hirianthial said, "I would not release him without ten years of it. But he can serve an apprenticeship with a mentor given a proper grounding. Perhaps five years with the Swords, if you would be willing to allow him to train with them, cousin?"

"Laisrathera's armsmen? I assume there will be more than one," Liolesa said. "Certes. Theresa, you may send your men to me until you have a core of your own to raise them up for you."

...which was when all of Firilith's tenants's gazes swiveled to Liolesa and they realized who she must be. Reese had been wondering why they hadn't made their obeisance the moment they saw her, but then... how would they have known what their queen looked like? This wasn't a world with 3deos and viseos and broadcasts of public addresses, and while richly dressed Liolesa had come uncrowned, as a family member. Reese could only imagine the shock of discovering the woman you'd dismissed as a provincial guest was, in fact, the sovereign ruler of your planet.

Certainly they reacted quickly enough. As one, they bowed or curt-seyed and held the poses, and their silence had a nervous quality even a mind-blind human could read. Liolesa left them there for longer than Reese would have, but then, Reese wasn't making a point, and she suspected the Queen was.

"Rise," Liolesa said at last. That was all. No minatory speeches, no special scrutiny. That was a gift from a queen, when Liolesa could have made them regret their ignorance, and their behavior toward a woman for whom her approval was obvious. Returning her attention to Reese, she said, "Consider the matter arranged, if you wish to accept this gift."

And how could she not? Reese liked Talthien, and knew how hard it was to be purposeless, as the men of Firilith had been purposeless for so long. There was no way she could take away a future from him, particularly one he wanted. But she hated the idea of him getting attached to her and then having to watch her die a natural death while he went on to bloom into his youthful prime.

At least her children would have a guardian of their own... and unlike her, they'd live long enough to give him someone to ward for his own lifetime.

Hirianthial nudged her gently and she looked up at him. The minute twitch of his chin was a reminder not to dwell on the inevitable. "Right. Talthien. I'd be honored to accept the son of the seal's servants back to Rose Point. After the holiday we'll send you to Ontine for your training, and on your return you can take up your apprenticeship until such time as your mentor decides you're ready for your duties." She glanced at the dogs and added, "I assume the two of you are going with him?"

Graeme nodded, ears pricked forward.

"I figured," she said. "At some point we should discuss what you feel comfortable doing in Firilith now that your bonded Eldritch's role has changed. Just because I accept Talthien's service doesn't mean I get yours automatically. The three of you talk it over, all right?"

Graeme stood as if to say something, but Moire reached around Talthien and bumped her mate's shoulder with her nose. He wrinkled his muzzle at her, but flipped his ears back and sighed, an uncannily familiar expression of resignation. Talthien looped an arm around his neck and looked up at Reese, eyes shining but face carefully composed. In that moment, she saw what he would become as an adult: solemn and yet open-hearted. She couldn't help smiling at him—smiling, and praying that there were no assassins lurking in her future to take him down before time.

"We will discuss it, my lady, and I will tell you what they decide."

"Good. Then we'll talk about your travel plans tomorrow."

Talthien nodded and rose, and he and the dogs returned to the crowd... though he hesitated before walking past his mother. She didn't look at him at all.

"Now it is my turn," said a woman in a dark green dress, "and you do not seem to stand on ceremony, my lady. If I may?"

"Please," Reese said. As the woman stood before her, Reese added, "You're the senior manse servant, aren't you. Sela."

"That is correct, my lady," she said. "May I come work for you?"

A blunt request from an Eldritch was so entirely outside Reese's experience that for a moment her thoughts scattered and left her staring blankly at the woman. Then she marshaled herself. Hadn't Felith said the manse servants cooked and cleaned? She already had a fleet of cooks, and the cleaning was already being automated... "Of course you can. We'll find something for you to do, alet."

Sela glanced toward the hires from Ontine and chuckled. "And no doubt you are wondering what. So I will tell you that though I can keep house as is traditional, mistress, what I learned first and best was the herbcraft."

From the tension at her side, that interested Hirianthial, so Reese said, "That sounds like... medicine, maybe?"

"That's correct, my lady. Though I am guessing not as good as what you bring with you. I would be willing to learn, however."

"We would be willing to teach," Hirianthial said. "The hospital will need doctors, nurses, and researchers."

"And I have time to study," Sela said, satisfied. "Will that suit you, my lady?"

"Absolutely," Reese said. "And it's a monumental gift—"

Sela held up a hand. "Ah, but that is not my gift, though I'm honored that you would count it as such. This is my gift." And to everyone's shock, including Reese's, she offered that gift by holding it out, rather than leaving it on the ground between them. A mysterious offering, at that: a slender and ancient key. The ribbon tied to its end was so old Reese was shocked it hadn't fallen apart—as it was, the satin was worn to a shine and the color had faded from a red that would have been as bright as shed blood when it was new.

"The servants of the manse tend its servants... and its grounds," Sela said, eyes steady. "This key came to me through my father's father, to whom it was entrusted when Rose Point still had a mistress. It opens the Firilith burial mound, where the lords and ladies of the past are interred... and the mind-mage that slew them, who began Firilith's decline." She raised her chin. "I know the history of our past, my lady. Of Corel, and how Firilith was once the center of the kingdom. It is not a proper tale for a new year and a bride awaiting her wedding. But after the wedding, if you wish, I will escort you to the burial ground and tell you that history."

Reese had no idea what to say to that, it was so big. From what she'd been able to piece together no one knew the real history of Corel, not even Val, who claimed to be the mind-mage's reincarnation. Or maybe he did know and wasn't telling? She glanced toward him, found him standing alongside Urise and Belinor wearing one of those Eldritch masks. Since he wasn't given to them, she felt a chill. "History," she said, "is rarely a comfortable gift, is it?"

"No, my lady," Sela said.

"But a necessary one," Reese said. "I would be grateful to learn what happened here, alet. And I suspect I wouldn't be the only one interested. If I could bring guests?"

"All that you trust, my lady," Sela said steadily, looking neither right nor left though both of them were very aware of the Queen's and Hirianthial's attention.

Reese nodded. "All right. It's a date." She looked down at the key. "You should hold onto that until then, I think. As a sign that I trust you to keep your word to bring it back. And because you are the senior manse servant, and you've asked to work for me."

Sela leaned back, an infinitesimal motion of surprise. Then she laughed. "You are plain-spoken, my lady! But yes. I will hold it in trust for you until the day you come to me to ask for it. Though after we have gone to the graves, you should give the key to the man you charge with the maintenance of the estate."

"Does it have to be a man?" Irine asked, curious.

"It has been so traditionally," Sela said, without so much as a pause to indicate she found the need to address an impudent alien distasteful. "Because the work is often very physically taxing. I do not know that this holds true for Rose Point today."

Here was a woman they could work with. Reese looked forward to seeing that potential develop. "We'll build that bridge when we get to it. Sela-alet—thank you. I accept your gifts, and Hirianthial and I will be glad to see you return tomorrow for assignment to your duties. Which I'm thinking are mostly going to involve a lot of study, at least initially."

Hirianthial smiled at the woman. "You will find it fascinating. I know I did."

Sela considered him with interest. "I believe I will." She curtseyed. "My lady." And withdrew.

That left... no one, Reese thought. Talthien was a seal servant, so surely he counted for that group, and there wasn't even a rule that said every group had to give her something. So why were they all standing there still? If it was up to her to dismiss them, Hirianthial would probably have nudged her... but they were all looking at one another, and the subtext in those looks was dense enough to incite her sympathy. She wouldn't have wanted to be caught up in that much internal turmoil, all of it unspoken.

She was going to call a halt to it by telling everyone it was time to eat when a young woman stepped up, defiance written in every line of her body. For a moment, Reese saw dark skin instead of light, short figure instead of tall, loose braids instead of crown-woven ones. She recognized that level of hopelessness and the decision to break herself against a wall until she escaped. She had no idea who this woman was, but it didn't matter. She knew her anyway, where it counted.

"My lady," the woman said, curtseying. "My name is Liral. I am the niece of the senior seal servant of Rose Point, and I have a gift for you and Firilith."

"Liral-alet," Reese said, quiet. "Tell me."

"My mother never cared for her mother, so she spent as little time with her as possible," Liral said. "But I loved my grandmother, and to honor that love, my grandmother taught me her trade. My lady, I don't know if you know what it is, because you are an alien. But I can make Firilith meander."

"You can what?" Reese exclaimed, startled. "Like in the stories?" She looked up at Hirianthial. "Like your tabard, that the pirates destroyed."

"Almost like, save that was Jisiensire's meander," Hirianthial said, sounding as surprised as she was. "We are not known for our meander, Theresa. Every fiefdom has—or had—its own meander weaver, and while Jisiensire's was deft, she was not numbered among the masters of the art. Alet, you tell me your grandmother was..."

"Lina of Firilith," Liral said. "Yes."

"Oh my," Liolesa murmured under her breath.

"You learned Lina's craft from her hands?" Araelis breathed, drawing closer.

Liral dug into the seam of her gown, revealing a hidden pocket, and brought from it a little square of fabric that put Hirianthial's old tabard into abrupt perspective. That meander had been beautiful, but this! The random curves and curling lines that gave the pattern its name didn't look messy or confusing; like the most compelling of abstract art, it implied an order in its chaos, subtle and yet powerful. It invited the viewer into it, promised resolution but requested that resolution from the viewer. It was participatory art, and that was the quality that elevated it above the meander Reese had seen. That the material itself was stunning, soft as rabbit fur, with gold thread edging the lines, was just icing on that cake. Tilting it, Reese found that even the areas that had looked plain were actually patterned... just so faintly that you had to see it in the right light.

"Blood and Freedom," Reese breathed. "How long did this take you?"

"A few days," Liral said. "It was a small square. Planning it didn't take long, and the weaving, while tedious, goes quickly when you have nothing else to do."

"Oh, Theresa," Araelis said. "Lina of Firilith's meander was famous! You have no idea how many people would line up to buy it did it become available again!"

Which brought her to the fact that the Eldritch didn't understand modern notions of commerce. There was no way Reese could declare Liral's handiwork hers just because she was the one in the fancy castle, particularly if it was worth as much as Araelis was suggesting. "You have an amazing talent, alet, and obviously you've been trained well. May I?"

Liral dropped the sample on her hand, ignoring the gasps of the crowd behind her. Even without touching, that transaction suggested an intimacy that most of her tenants weren't accustomed to. Yet, anyway. Reese turned the square in her hands, admiring the reverse side, which had been lined so that the strings and knots on the back were hidden. "You can make Firilith meander... that's excellent. I imagine the artistic part of this will keep you really busy. You'd like my business manager to act as your agent, then?"

"You don't have a business manager," Irine whispered.

"I'm about to have one," Reese said. "Hush, or you'll end up it."

Irine's ears flattened and she pressed her lips together. Amused, Reese said to Liral, "Does that sound good?"

"Lady?" Liral asked, confused. "You... want me to sell my own meander?"

"I'd like you to sign a contract with us allowing us to sell your meander," Reese said. "And you would keep most of the money you earn."

She'd been expecting Shoran's reflexive distaste for the idea, so having Liral say, "I would not object to being rich, my lady," was a surprise. But Liral continued. "I would also like to help Firilith, however. Sela is correct in saying we have had a difficult time. Meander is a treasure and sells accordingly... I would be sad if I could not help rebuild our province."

"Well, if that's all you're worried about, I'm sure we can interest you in some investment opportunities," Reese said, grinning.

"Or there's always charitable donations!" Irine added. "We are doing that, aren't we?"

"I'm not sure we can do tax deduction without taxes," Reese said dryly.

"Investment," Liral murmured. "So I earn my money and then...."

"I put in front of you a selection of projects that need money," Reese said. "You choose one to help fund, and then you get a portion of its profits."

"If it is profitable," Hirianthial said. "If it is not, then we will arrange some other benefit, I am certain."

"Founders' Stones for Eldritch!" Irine crowed.

"Would work," Hirianthial said. "We are a people who value symbols."

"We'll figure it out," Reese said. "So... if you're interested in making the gift of a financial partnership between us, Liral-alet, I'm happy to accept."

"Oh, yes! I am ready to have choices," Liral said. "Thank you, my lady. I assume I am to arrive tomorrow, like Sela and Talthien and Shoran?"

"You and everyone else who wants a job, or wants to learn to do a new one," Reese said. "I've got plenty of opportunities, if there are people willing to throw their shoulders into them."

"Then perhaps you should send the charabancs back for us tomorrow," Liral said. "I suspect you will need them."

"If it's going to be that big a group, we might as well put a Pad down there," Taylor said. "Reese?"

"Pads don't grow on trees," Reese said. "We'll talk about it later." She looked at her tenants. "Is that everyone? Because if so, the New Year's Feast is waiting for us...."

She was hoping that Talthien's mother would say something, but it was obvious no such speech was forthcoming. That would have been a little too much to ask for, apparently. Reese smiled a little and said, "Then let's go eat!"

The Pelted cheered and began to stream up the stairs to the great hall. Reese stood out of their way, watching her Eldritch hires from Ontine follow at a more sedate pace. Her tenants moved up the steps last, but they went as a single body, and there was discussion there—some of it agitated, but a lot of it excited, so she guessed that worked out about as well as she could have hoped.

Talthien's mother was lagging behind the group. Watching her, Reese remembered how often people had had to approach her before she let them in. How many times had her crew been rebuffed before their efforts started to knock enough holes in her walls to let the light in? As the woman climbed the stairs past her, Reese said, "Alet. Thanks."

The woman stopped, revealing nothing: just that smooth Eldritch mask, and nothing but a chill formality in her eyes and bearing. "I beg your pardon, lady. I don't know what for."

"For coming," Reese said. "And for letting them come. I know they look to you for leadership."

"I had nothing to do with this," the woman said. "Your gratitude belongs elsewhere." She curtseyed and vanished with the rest of the tenants into the great hall, leaving the courtyard emptied of everyone but Reese, the twins, Araelis, Hirianthial, and the Queen.

"Wow," Irine said, brows arched. "Did she just dismiss herself? I didn't think Eldritch were allowed to do that from their ladies."

"Eldritch," Liolesa said, "can do whatever they please, Irine. Whether other Eldritch find their behavior pardonable... that is a different matter."

Reese winced and turned to face the Queen. "I'm not going to punish a woman for not liking me."

"That would be premature," Liolesa agreed. "She's hardly had any time to get to know you, after all!"

"With my sunny personality," Reese muttered.

Irine hugged her, purring. "It's a lot better now that you're not closed up like a..."

"This metaphor had better end well."

"Like a seed in need of flowering?" Irine offered.

Reese covered her face with a hand. "Ugh, Irine! I am not a plant."

"Fine," Irine said. "Like a fort in need of opening."

"I'm not sure that's an improvement," Reese said. Looking at the courtyard and the distant walls, she finished, "But then, maybe it works."

It was very quiet now, with all the people gone inside. Eerily so: Reese hadn't understood the ubiquity of the bustle until now. While the sun was up, there were people working in the courtyard, helping to erect the new buildings or repair and update the old ones, or in the garden, weeding, cutting, dragging away detritus. That was Rose Point to her: that industry.

But this... this was Rose Point too. She appreciated the ability to see the bones of it, feel the history of it seeping into her with the cold. If this fusion was to be sustained, that was exactly what it had to be: a fusion. And behind her, that group now in the hall amid the mounded trays and platters, the decorations, the heated floor tiles alongside the lit hearth... they were the ones who were going to help her make it happen.

Reese inhaled and let it go. "I guess it can't all go exactly right on the first try."

"You are doing good work," Liolesa said. "Your senior seal servant is a sign of it."

"How's that?" Reese asked, eyeing her.

The Queen was playing with the sliding puzzle the crew had given her during the Vigil, her fingers moving with an absent, lazy grace. Reese hadn't noticed that she'd hung it like an ornament from her skirts, probably because the silver metal reflected the dark blue fabric. "A woman who stands for her principles will always have opponents. It's how you know you're doing it right."

The informality startled a laugh out of Reese. "So, as long as I'm offending someone I'm good?"

"It would be a kind world if we could proceed through it without distressing or agitating anyone," Liolesa said. "A beautiful world, and I know many well-meaning folk who bring much evil into the world by believing we already live in it. But we don't. And so to survive, we must bear a sword as well as the lily of peace. Which brings me to one last bit of business, and here you all are to receive it."

"Oh?" Hirianthial asked. "What are you about, cousin?"

"The worlds need names, as I recall."

"Oh, good," Araelis said. "I am saved from colonizing Planet Buttercup, or That Other World. Do tell, Liolesa."

"Your Planet Buttercup shall be known as Chalice," Liolesa said. "I expect it to overflow with the Goddess's gifts, Araelis, so work hard to live up to the name, ah?"

Araelis snorted. "Ensuring that bounty will be the duty of your appointed viceroy but... yes." She rested a hand on her belly. "Chalice. That is an auspicious name."

"But what about this world?" Sascha said. "The one under our feet."

"This world," Liolesa said, her voice hard as warship battlesteel, "is Escutcheon. Let our enemies brave it if they dare, for they will find a strong arm beneath it."

"Ah," Araelis said, profoundly satisfied. "Perfect."

"It is perfect," Hirianthial murmured. "But I will always think of it as home."

"That's as it should be," Liolesa said. "It is yours also," she added to Reese.

"Yes," Reese said, feeling it. "But... a good home is a shield, isn't it?

From the harsh world you were talking about, the one we wish we didn't have to deal with."

"It should be, yes," Liolesa said. "And ours shall be, if I have any say in the matter."

"That should take care of it entire, then," Araelis said. "For if this moment now is not proof that you have a sure hand on the reins, Liolesa, then no proof will suffice. And that means I am for that feast, because all is in good hands. With permission." She curtseyed and headed up the stairs, heels clicking on the stone.

"Food does sound good," Sascha murmured.

"Go!" Reese said. "I'll be there in a few." She waited until the twins made it to the doors before folding her arms and turning to the Queen. "One more thing, my lady, as long as I have you here."

"It's Liolesa, Theresa."

"No," Reese said firmly. "Right now, it's 'my lady.' Because Felith tells me that this man here," pointing with a thumb over her shoulder at Hirianthial, "is now your heir. When I met him he said he wasn't in the direct line for the throne."

"That was before I lost Bethsaida," Liolesa said mildly. "The other choices right now are less than palatable, so for now he must serve."

"Can you make that 'for now' over really quickly?" Reese said. "I do *not* want your problems. No offense."

Liolesa laughed. "Never fear, my vassal. I already have a new heir selected. I need only groom her for the position first."

"And tell her she's in it?" Hirianthial asked, amused. "I know how you work, cousin."

"If she hasn't realized what I'm doing, she's not the right woman for the job," Liolesa said. "Never fear, Hiran. I know what I'm about."

"I don't doubt it," he murmured.

"Sooner rather than later," Reese added.

"As you say," Liolesa said, eyes gleaming. "I would hardly want to saddle my cousin with an unwanted crown, no matter how attractive it would look on his head. And now I shall flee before I suffer the inevitable reprimand." She grinned, a dazzling expression that lit her eyes, and then left them to head for the top of the steps.

"She's crazy," Reese muttered. "And brilliant."

"And funny," Hirianthial offered, which was such an absurd observation—and true—that Reese started laughing. That laugh lasted until she realized that her eyes had been following the motion at Liolesa's side: her fingers... which were solving the little sliding puzzle and shaking it back into disorder, and then solving it again.

...had she been doing that the entire time they'd been chatting?

"Blood and Freedom," Reese said softly, wide-eyed.

Hirianthial nodded. "You understand now, my Courage."

"Not even the littlest bit," Reese said. "But hell. In for a penny...."

Hirianthial laughed and ran a hand up her sleeve to rest lightly on her upper arm. "Your New Year's Feast awaits, lady."

"Happy New Year?" she offered, hoping for Kiss Number... "Wait, did we reset the counter?"

He paused as he bent toward her to compose himself, but even then she could tell he was smiling when she got Kiss Number Six. Or Number Fifty-six. Or... well, whatever it was, it was glorious and when it was over she was shivering and it had nothing to do with the cold. So when he parted just enough to add, "And to think, all of this has been wondrous practice for organizing our wedding," she didn't hear the words for a moment.

Then: "Hirianthial!"

He laughed. "Come, my Courage. You need wine."

"I didn't a minute ago, but I do now!"

Together they went up the steps and into the warm golden hall, and behind them the first flakes of snow began to fall.

AN EXILE ABOARD SHIP

Surela Silin Asaniefa was convinced she could rule the Eldritch people better than her enemy, Liolesa Galare, and for ten whole days following her coup, she made the attempt—and failed. Resigned to her death as a traitor, she was given a choice by the Queen's newest protege, Reese Eddings: to be executed, or to accept a commuted sentence and attempt to rebuild her life and make amends for her crimes.

To die would have been the act of a dramatic maiden, and as a woman of more sense and years, Surela chooses instead to see what she can make of herself among aliens and mortals. But what begins with cargo runs on an old Terran freighter soon involves pirates and slavers and intergalactic war... and the actions of a traitor might be the salvation of the people she once wronged.

An Exile Aboard Ship kicks off the redemption arc of the villainess from the Her Instruments series. Can Surela earn her wings in the Alliance? Come and see...

Now Available!

APPENDICES

Including the original cover sketch (by the author) for this volume; a short story about Kis'eh't; a map, and assorted other odds and ends.

THE SPECIES OF THE ALLIANCE

Three major groups of sapients are known to exist in the Peltedverse (so far): **the Pelted**, who founded the Alliance, and who are the descendants of animal-human bioengineering experiments on earth; **humans and their offshoots**, the Eldritch; and the **true aliens**, who evolved naturally on alien planets. A fourth, minor group, **AI**, is filled solely by the sapient evolution of AI in the Alliance network.

The following, alphabetically, is a list of known peoples, with graphics.

- **Aera (Pelted)** – This brightly colored race is tall, hare-eared and long-muzzled like foxes, and tends toward nomadic cultures. Some variants also have winged ankles.
- **Akubi (Alien)** – The Akubi are giant bird-like/dinosaur-like creatures, nine to twelve feet tall, with thick razor beaks and large wings. They have three sexes, and the neuters are the ones that tend to travel to see the interesting little mammals. They are excellent mimics and enthusiastic observers of alien culture.
- **Asanii (Pelted)** – One of the more numerous of the core Pelted races, the Asanii are plantigrade people with humanoid faces, but a veneer of domestic feline. They have five fingers and toes, catlike tails, and nails rather than claws. They are excellent jacks-of-all trades, socially and skills-wise, thanks to a culture that emphasizes mutability.
- **Birdsong Natives (Alien)** – Not much is known about the natives of planet Birdsong, who are not part of the Alliance.
- **Chatcaava (Alien)** – A species of shapeshifters, in their natural form, the Chatcaava look like bipedal winged dragons. Some females are also winged, but most have two sets of arms rather

than arms and wings. They sat on the other side of a cold war with the Alliance for a long time, and their Empire is substantially larger than the Alliance thanks to an expansionist warrior culture permeating the upper echelons of their society.

- **Ciracaana (Pelted)** – A race of gengineered centauroids, the Ciracaana are very tall, very lanky, and have furred and pawed lower bodies with long tails and faces with pointed muzzles and large pointed ears. They come in any number of riotous colors and patterns. They were another of the three races created by the Pelted in an attempt to understand their origins.
- **Crystals (Aliens)** – Not much is known about the crystal people, who were found on a single moon and have made no move to join the Alliance or leave their habitat. Their first (and only significant) mention is in *Earthrise*, the first book of the Her Instruments trilogy.
- **D-Per (AI)** – Digital personalities started out as AI assistants in the early Alliance and evolved to more complex and sapient forms.

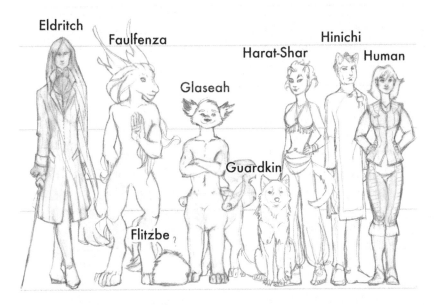

- **Eldritch (Human Family)** – The Eldritch are an offshoot of humanity, altered with greater longevity, light gravity bodies that are long and delicate, and uniform skin and hair color and texture (pearl and fine/straight, respectively). They are one of the only known esper races in the universe.
- **Faulfenza (Alien)** – This heavy-gravity world race is tall, furred, powerfully muscled, standing on digitigrade legs. They have muzzled faces and long ears that fan open, long tails with two tufts, and six fingers/toes. A race of dancers, they are also gifted with the Mindfire, which allows them to burn/heat things with their hands.
- **Flitzbe (Alien)** – The alien Flitzbe are plant-like creatures that reproduce via budding and photosynthesize for energy; they communicate empathically and travel in clods that stick together using their flexible neural fur. In appearance, they look like small furry basketballs that change colors.
- **Glaseah (Pelted)** – The second of the two engineered centauroid races, the Glaseah are compact, dense people with the lower bodies of great cats and a humanoid upper body with a short-muzzled face and feathered ears. All are skunk-patterned; some have membranous wings on their lower body, and some don't. A phlegmatic and practical people, they were the last species created by the Pelted in an attempt to understand their origins.
- **Guardkin (Quasi-Pelted)** – The Guardkin are the result of centuries of breeding for intelligence by the Hinichi, who consider themselves the Guardkin's caretakers. They resemble wolves (or larger wild dogs) and can bond to espers to make their minds known.
- **Harat-Shar – (Pelted)** The party people of the Alliance, the Harat-Shar are big-cat-based, and can be either plantigrade with finger fingers and toes and nails, or digitigrade with four fingers and toes and claws. They can have any big cat pattern, though some are more common than others.
- **Hinichi (Pelted)** – Built primarily from lupine additions, the Hinichi are the wolf-like people of the Alliance, clannish and stubborn and noble. They can be plantigrade, with five fingers and toes and nails, or they can be digitigrade with four fingers and toes, and claws.

- **Human (Human Family)** – Our descendants. Humans from Earth come in the expected shapes, sizes and colors... there are also Martian humans (short but tending toward less mass) and Lunar humans (very ethereal thanks to their light gravity builds).

- **Karaka'A (Pelted)** – The Karaka'A are another felid race, domestic cat-biased, but they're all short, with digitigrade legs and four fingers and toes and claws. Because they were offshoots of the very first Pelted experiments (which were foxlike), they can have fox-like patterns as well as catlike ones.
- **Malarai (Pelted)** – A small populace, the Malarai were built off the Asanii base (humanoid with thin veneer of cat) with feathered wings grafted on. Their feathered wings are too small to fly with in normal gravity, and their original design left them with a predilection toward lower body disorders, mostly nerve but sometimes joint-based.
- **Naysha (Pelted)** – The most alien of the gengineered races, the Naysha are mermaid-like creatures, with the lower bodies of porpoises and the upper bodies of humanoids, with heads that

are somewhat otter or seal-like, with enormous eyes. Lacking the apparatus for speech, they speak via sign.

- **Octopi (Aliens)** – A relative newcomer to the Alliance, the octopi aliens look like enormous octopuses with translucent veils connecting their limbs. They are one of the two inhabitants of the planet Amity; the second, the sapients who lived on land, have died out. Their first contact story is told in the Stardancer novel *Either Side of the Strand*.
- **Phoenix (Pelted)** – The Phoenix are mammalian bipeds with birdlike features, like long beaks and crests and feathered wings and tails. They were engineered by the Pelted, who subsequently found them more alien than many of the true aliens. They come in any assortment of metallic colors.
- **Platies (Aliens)** – Another sea-based alien, the Platies look like colorful flatworms, except without mouths or eyes or any visible organs. They begin palm-sized and can grow to the size of a shuttle. They communicate only with the Naysha, who can't explain how that communication works, and are capable of traveling by folding space (also poorly understood). Some Platies can be found on Fleet warships as adjuncts to the navigation/propulsion systems.
- **Seersa (Pelted)** – The other elder Pelted race, the Seersa are short fox-like people, digitigrade with four fingers and toes and claws. They can have fox or domestic cat patterns, being very similar, biologically, to their sister-race the Karaka'A.
- **Sirelanders (Alien)** – The Sirelanders are a nomadic race of aliens that never stops traveling the universe. They wandered through the Alliance and kept going, though there are Alliance anthropologists who are tagging along with them to study them.
- **Tam-illee (Pelted)** – The last foxish race of the Pelted are the Tam-illee, who are also the most humanoid of the group. They have five fingers and toes and nails, and stand plantigrade, and have human-like faces with fox ears and fox tails. The Tam-illee are also one of the few Pelted races that can often be born completely furless.

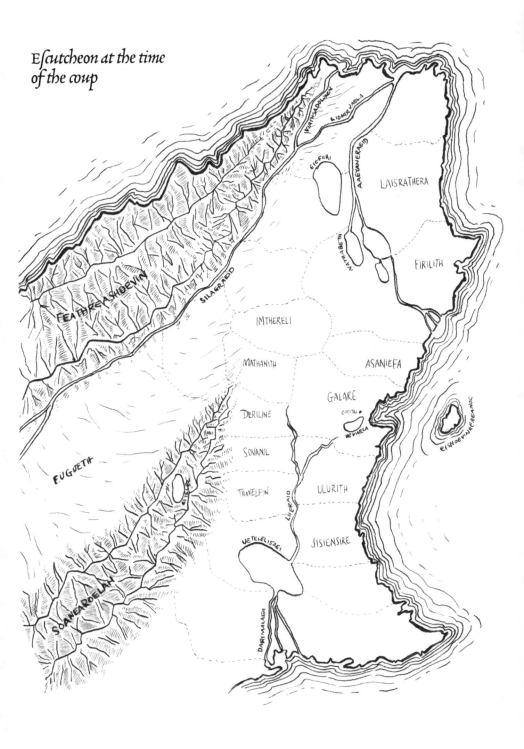

Escutcheon at the time
of the coup

FEATBREASHOEVIN
SILAGRÆD
IMTHERELI
MATHANITH
DERILINE
SOVANIL
THAVELFIN
FUGUETH
SOANEAROELA
UETELELISÆI
DARIMALAÆA
LIVERAID
ULURITH
JISIENSIRE
GALARE
CAPITAL
WEVAELA
ASANIEFA
NAPHABETH
AÆYANERÆIB
IFAITHADNUNEN
LIOMIRJÆLA
ELEFURI
LAISRATHERA
FIRILITH
EIGHDEVINEREANOC

FIELD RESEARCH

"**W**here's Abraham?" Kis'eh't asked as she padded into her lab.

"He's been terminated."

Kis'eh't's hands froze on the strap of her bag. The answer was so unexpected that for a moment she thought of literal termination, of death, of spinning out in the void where only the Goddess could pinpoint your soul. Then logic asserted itself. "Terminated! When? Any termination of my research assistants is supposed to go through me!"

Casey glanced at her, ears sagging. "I don't know. I just know when I got in this morning he wasn't here, and when I asked the receptionist she said he wasn't coming back."

A good student, Casey, but far too demure. She'd have to learn to be more assertive to survive academia. Of course, for that to happen someone had to model the appropriate behavior. Kis'eh't growled and let the strap drop back over her upper torso, the bag bumping against her withers. "I'll be back once I fix this."

It had been almost three years since Kis'eh't had come to Sector Kappa, to Plenitude System's materials research center at Camreigh University. Her degree and the list of honors, papers, and patents she'd accumulated had

189

guaranteed her a job anywhere: she could have taught on one of the Core worlds, gone solo as a lecturer, accepted a high-end position in a company building starbases or orbital habitats. Fleet would have paid her a Maker's ransom to research new materials for battle armor—on starships, or people, whichever she preferred, and would she say yes?

Kis'eh't had said no so she could take a job at the fringe of settled space. Because Plenitude was one of the most exciting places to do materials research, and Camreigh, in orbit around one of the system's enormous gas giants, was on the forefront of that research. There were more exotics in the asteroid belts in Plenitude than had ever been mapped anywhere else, even in the Alliance's vast territory, so much material that people flocked here to prospect, mine, and build despite the lack of habitable planets. The boomtown atmosphere had funded the riotous growth of the academic sector along with the industrial one, and the regulatory environment was lax—not because people wanted to break rules, but because there was so much going on that things fell into cracks.

That open environment had attracted Kis'eh't to the position, because she wanted to do science as unfettered by problematic superiors, politics, and funding problems as possible. Camreigh had promised her that freedom and made good on it, allowing her to hire her own research assistants, requisition what she needed—within reason—and follow her own instincts. For three years, she'd made them money as a byproduct of her desire to chase the Goddess's sacred thoughts into the perfection of chemistry. She had never cared about the money, only the freedom, and she'd given them a great deal of latitude in the former sphere in order to have it in her lab. She'd thought they respected that.

She brushed past the dean's assistant without acknowledgment, and thought it ominous that the young wolfine didn't try to stop her. Even in the lower gravity, her dense, centauroid form would have been difficult to bar, but he should have tried.

Hollyroad knew she was coming, then.

The dean for engineering research stood when she entered: at nearly five feet tall, the Seersa was just under her height, with his race's heavy digitigrade legs, thick-furred coat, and foxlike ears and tail. He was dark gray with spots like a leopard's, and ordinarily she found his agate-brown eyes friendly. Today they were wary, and his shoulders were tense and hands spread on the table. He was prepared for a fight, then.

Well, so was she. "You fired my senior research assistant, Tovin. I want to know why."

He studied her face. She returned the favor: his ears were still erect, but she could just see the tremor at their tips. Not afraid, but jittery. "You said when you came that you wanted to spearhead an investigation of the gas giant's moons."

"And you told me you were rich but not that rich," Kis'eh't said, laying her ears back.

"I got you the money," he said.

She folded her arms. "This is relevant, why? Because you had to fire Abraham to secure it?"

"Yes."

Kis'eh't gaped at him.

Tovin sighed and dropped into his chair, arms going limp on the rests. His eyes had grown cloudy. "Sit down, Kis'eh't. Your looming isn't going to change things."

Her hindquarters slumped to the ground on their own, leaving her staring at him still. "That makes no sense," she said. "What does my research assistant have to do with..." She trailed off, realizing anew what he'd said. "With all the money in the sector, apparently? Tovin? Explain."

"We've got a new company to underwrite your grants," he said. "But they don't like humans. They made their offer conditional."

"On you firing my human assistant."

"On us terminating any human staff that might be assisting you," he corrected. "They don't want any humans associated with the research at all, or benefiting from it."

Appalled, Kis'eh't said, "They're not associated with some lunatic fringe, are they? Anti-Human Leaguers? Skin traders?"

"No!" Tovin grimaced and ran his hand over his face. "No, not that any of our background checks have turned up. They're not terrorists, Kis'eh't. Just... bigots. Bigots with a lot of money."

What could she say? What was she feeling? She couldn't tell. Her primary and secondary hearts were both beating too quickly, and that weird twisting in the pit of her chest was probably nausea. When she spoke, she felt as if she was forcing the words past a numb tongue. "Did you tell him?"

"Abraham? No. I just said we no longer had the money to afford him."

"He's not stupid," Kis'eh't said. "He'll know you were lying."

Tovin shrugged. "I'm sure. But I didn't have to give him a reason to let him go, alet, and under the circumstances I thought it kinder to keep the reason to myself." He managed a rueful smile. "Besides, I wasn't sure I could say it to his face."

"*Our* face," Kis'eh't said. When the Seersa pricked his ears toward her, she repeated, "Our face." She pointed at his, then hers. The Seersa's flat face could have been human, save for the fine fur that felted it and the slight darkening of the pad on the underside of his humanoid nose. And while Kis'eh't had a more animal-like muzzle, the DNA that composed her race had been mined from creatures the Pelted were familiar with: terrestrial animals, like the ones the humans had used to make them. Kis'eh't had always thought of this as a virtuous circle of Making. The Goddess had made humans, using Her mind to nudge them through the process of evolution. Humans had made the Pelted, using their minds to craft them with their skill at genetic engineering. And the Pelted had created another generation of gengineered creatures, Glaseah like Kis'eh't, and the Phoenix, and the other centauroids, the Ciracaana. She had never considered humanity as god substitutes: the power to make was a reflection of the Goddess's divine ability. But other Pelted had more trouble with their origins, particularly the first and second generations that had been the results of Earth's original experiments.

But she could not hold with bigotry, no matter the history that drove it.

"I want him back," she said. "I need him back."

He shook his head. "We need those grants. You don't need Abraham. You made do before he came along, and you can make do without him now." He lifted his brows. "Can't you?"

Was that a suggestion that she was replaceable if she failed to agree to his conditions? "This is disgusting, Tovin. And I resent the high-handed appropriation of privileges I thought were mine alone."

"Things change," Tovin said. And sighed, folding his hands. "I really am sorry, alet, but he had to go." When she didn't move, he said, "Is there anything else I can help you with?"

And now he was dismissing her like an errant student. Her pelt stood up all the way down her second back. "Apparently not," she said, and headed for the door. She was half out it when he spoke.

"There's one more thing—"

She paused, glanced past her shoulder.

"You'll have to remove him from the byline of your last paper."

"WHAT?" She backed up and turned to face him, claws inching from her forepaws. "I can't do that! It's important work and he did half of it! He deserves the credit... particularly if you're cutting him loose!"

He met her eyes, unflinching, and there was the regret again, and behind it, something hard as a clathrate. "Can you tell me where to find twenty-million fin's worth of funding?"

The figure drained the spit from her mouth.

The Seersa nodded. "Thank you for stopping by, alet. I hope we've dealt with your concerns."

What could she say? Nothing. So she didn't.

———

Plenitude's primary habitat had been formed from a cluster of seven tapped-out asteroids towed into orbit, rotated until their living areas faced attractive vistas, and then locked into position with tractors of immense precision and power. Travelers used Pads to step from one asteroid to the next; vessels were uncommon save for travel to other habitats, or to the mining platforms. Abraham had affectionately called the entire arrangement yet another example of the Alliance's arrogance. Kis'eh't merely thought it magnificent. She loved how grandly the Pelted built, and how readily they embraced the alien, whether it came in the form of distant places or strange new species.

It was only people a little too familiar they seemed to find troublesome, apparently.

There had been no working after the news, so Kis'eh't had hopped asteroids, wanting the distance between herself and the campus. She chose a quiet coffeehouse, populated mostly by those working remote jobs, and sat beside one of the vast windows. The casual view would have assumed it looked out on empty space: in reality, it faced the distant glitter of the asteroid belts. If she wanted, she could tap the smart coating and enlarge the area next to her so she could see the ships darting in and out of the spill of gemlike rocks, their edges razor-crisp in the vacuum... but she didn't. She stretched her forepaws beneath her low table, and nursed her coffee, and brooded.

At some point, Abraham slid a refill onto the table's dark surface and sat across from her, his long legs rucking up against the short table.

She'd always liked Abraham, with his shocking white smile, his eyes dark as polished magnetite, and his large bi-colored hands: like hers, but black and pink skin rather than black and white fur. He had a basso laugh, deep and good, and a generous nature, and a mind as quick as the Goddess's. Working with him had been like prayer. She resented losing it.

"So," he said, dwarfing his cup with long fingers, so that it seemed delicate.

"I didn't do it," Kis'eh't said. "They didn't even consult me—"

"Arii." He held up one of those hands. "I know."

That he could call her that—that he still did call her arii, 'friend', rather than the more formal alet—made the fur on her upper back rise. "I talked to the dean. He won't rescind it."

"I didn't think he would." He smiled. Compassion, she thought. For her. "Not after taking the trouble of terminating me myself. Without consulting you." He shook his head. "I didn't blame you, Kis'eh't. I only wondered why. Did he tell you?"

"A group of rich racists dangled twenty million fin in front of him to fire you. They don't want human hands on their pristine science." Kis'eh't bared her teeth. "Their pristine science. Everything we got, we got from you!"

"That was centuries ago, and you Pelted have built it well past what we could have."

"From you," she repeated, upper heart pounding. She poked the table for emphasis. "We would have been nothing—literally!—had you not engineered us."

"And had we not been such bastards that you fled to escape us?" He lifted his brows.

"Not an excuse," she replied. "We don't hold the sins of the parents against the children. Those humans are centuries dead, Abraham-arii. And now we hold all the cards. There's not a thing a human can do to hurt the Pelted these days."

"No," he agreed, his lips curving into a wry smile. "Not the way things are now. But perhaps these bigots want to make sure that situation continues."

"So we turn into the bastards?" Kis'eh't growled. "It's ridiculous. It's stupid. We learn nothing from history."

"We learn that history cannot be turned from, maybe," Abraham said. "There's no use working yourself up over it, arii. I would have liked to stay, but they've set me free... I can move on." His smile was better then. "Maybe someplace with a little more greenery this time. I'd like to walk under a sun again."

"You... you're taking this very well."

He laughed. "Well, it took twenty million fin to make the dean fire me. That's quite a compliment."

"Abraham!"

"Kis'eh't." He shook his head. "Prejudices will be with us always."

"That doesn't excuse racism," she said, ears flattening to her head.

He shrugged, a roll of his shoulder. "It's a big universe, arii... and the Pelted gave it to us. We need to accept they can take it away again." A smile again. "Fortunately, that big universe is more full of Kis'eh'ts than it is full of millionaire racists. I cannot find it in myself to be too worried."

She couldn't count the number of ways that entire statement was wrong, hurt her, lanced her in that place where her conception of the Goddess lived. But she couldn't argue with it either. Humanity had created its half-animal playtoys and broken them in its labs and bedrooms. It didn't matter that they were centuries removed from that pivotal event, and that humanity had since been crushed by its own wars to a point where they were dependent on the descendants of their children for nearly everything. There were Pelted who would never feel safe: they'd been born victimized, and nothing Kis'eh't or anyone like her would say or do, and nothing people like Abraham did or demonstrated, would change their minds.

"Where will you go?" she asked instead, quiet.

"I think I'll head for the Core," Abraham said. "I've always wanted to see Seersana and Karaka'Ana, or Tam-ley...." A pause where they both considered the homeworld of the Tam-illee, an engineer's Heaven. "I don't know. There are so many places I haven't seen yet. One of them will have work for an unemployed research assistant."

"I'll give you a good letter," Kis'eh't said.

"I know." He grinned. "I'll send you postcards. You'll regret living in the middle of nowhere."

She found, painfully, that she already did.

———

Abraham lingered for another hour; they talked science, and family, and science again. He promised to keep in touch after he'd gone, and Kis'eh't wondered if he would. The Alliance was huge, and people easy to lose. It had never mattered to her: on a world full of espers, she'd grown up one of the few Glaseah alone in her own mind, and she'd been accustomed to solitude. She wondered now if she'd been attracted to this post because of its seclusion. If perhaps she had focused too strongly on the chemistry that bonded atoms and molecules and not enough on the chemistry that bonded people.

She could go back to work tomorrow, not just to her routine, but to the excitement of kitting out a new lab, a mobile facility poised to take advantage of the cutting edge discoveries in this system. The research she did on that twenty-million fin tab might affect the entire Alliance one day, maybe even soon. She'd earned that opportunity: her brilliance, her commitment, her willingness to put in the hours. Abraham was already gone. All she had to do to accept this new life was to strike his name from the last paper they'd written together.

She stayed at that table for hours, staring into the perfect blackness of space. Abraham, she thought, had been wrong. The Pelted might have given humanity back the stars, but only because humans had made the gift first. The logic of it was inescapable to anyone who hadn't let fear and hatred cloud their minds.

The coffeeshop's table interface allowed her to tender her resignation without returning to her office, and she regretfully sent Casey a note putting her to work boxing up the Glaseah's things: a waste of the Tamillee's time, and perhaps at some point the girl would find the self-assurance to point that out to someone. Hopefully her next boss would continue to model behavior conducive to survival in academia... better than Kis'eh't had, anyway. The Glaseah snorted. Fine example she'd been. She pulled the strap of her bag back over her shoulder and stood, stretching the kinks from her back legs. It was time for a change of pace. The royalties from her existing patents would keep her fed and clothed; she could afford to be itinerant a while.

As she let herself back into her soon-to-be vacated apartment, she found her thoughts wandering on how the chemistry implied in the infinitely small was reflected up into the macroscopic and human, and humanoid. Making could not be separated from the makers. Perhaps she could find the Goddess in a different field of study, and history would never again leave her flat-footed in response to bigotry and ignorance and hate. Perhaps she could even find another human to show her the way.

A virtuous circle of teaching and learning. Field research—perhaps not involving the moons of a gas giant, but fascinating all the same. She could pick someplace with more greenery this time, or maybe she'd just roam for a while, see a little bit of everything. A wide data sample yielded far better results.

Kis'eh't smiled and started packing.

AFTERWORD

Dear Readers:

Did I expect to write a holiday novel? Particularly one set in the middle of the epilogue of a completed trilogy? No, no, I did not. I planned to write a holiday *short story* about Reese, because Christmas is my favorite time of year and I love holiday stories. So I embarked on this enterprise, and it got longer, and longer, and this is when I realized I was at work on a bridge between Her Instruments and the series that will follow Princes' Game, the series describing the Chatcaavan War that begins with *Even the Wingless*.

There is no extricating the future of the Eldritch from the cast of characters on the stage now. Lisinthir and his dragons from Princes' Game, Jahir and Vasiht'h from Dreamhealers, and Reese and her people in Her Instruments are all building What Comes Next for this sector of the Pelted Alliance, and inevitably the seeds seem small when they're planted. Like a couple of telepathic dogs, or the gift of a single patch of meander to a new —human—liegelady.

That only partially explains *A Rose Point Holiday*, though. The rest of the explanation is that I started serializing this story online when I thought it would be a few thousand words long for the delight of the readers following me on social media. I thought it was an indulgent piece of fluff, but every time I posted, everyone piled in to talk about it. Scenes I thought would interest only me turned out to be just as meaningful to those readers, and I loved watching old hands explain some of the in-jokes from the series to new people just starting. The entire experience was a reminder that we'd taken this journey together, and we all felt we deserved a little indulgence at its end.

The truth about *A Rose Point Holiday* is that I wrote it as a gift. For you all, who've made this series my most successful. And for future-us, because it gives us so many storylines to follow in the future.

Happy Holidays, ariisen.

—M

READ MORE

It's been ten years since the release of Reese's series, and in the time since the Peltedverse has grown! Keeping track of what to read next can be challenging, but my readers have compiled a chronological list you can consult on the Peltedverse wiki here: https://peltedverse.org/wiki/index.php/List_of_Fiction_by_Internal_Chronology

While she never gets another trilogy all to herself, Reese returns in multiple novels and collections. I recommend these stories in particular:

- *An Exile Aboard Ship* - This novel begins the series that is the most direct sequel to Her Instruments, and concerns Surela... so of course, Reese is a big part of it.
- "The Waiting Cradle" - This short story intimately concerns Hirianthial and Reese and a major decision in their marriage, and you'll find it in the collection *In the Court of Dragons*.
- "Teachers and Students" - The opening vignette of this short story catches up with Reese, learning more about the local culture. It's in the collection *To the Court of Love*.
- "Moving Out" - While Reese is only a bit part in this novella, it's one of the first times we see her in company with Sediryl, the new imperial princess. You'll find it in the collection *Major Pieces*.

I'm currently working on wrapping up the major plot arc of the Peltedverse, which has been in the works for over twenty-five years! I hope you'll join me for the finale. Rest assured, Reese, Hirianthial, and all the others have plenty left to do.

—M

ABOUT THE AUTHOR

Daughter of two Cuban political exiles, M.C.A. Hogarth was born a foreigner in the American melting pot and has had a fascination for the gaps in cultures and the bridges that span them ever since. She has been many things—web database architect, product manager, technical writer and massage therapist—but is currently a full-time parent, artist, writer and anthropologist to aliens, both human and otherwise. She is the author of over 50 titles in the genres of science fiction, fantasy, humor and romance.

The *Her Instruments* series is only one of the many stories set in the Paradox Pelted universe; more information is available on the author's website. You can also sign up for the author's quarterly newsletter to be notified of new releases.

If you enjoyed this book, please consider leaving a review... or telling a friend!

mcahogarth.org
www.twitter.com/mcahogarth

Made in the USA
Columbia, SC
30 November 2023

26919478R00117